The Wildes

THE
Wildes

A NOVEL IN FIVE ACTS

Louis Bayard

ALGONQUIN BOOKS OF CHAPEL HILL 2024

Published by
ALGONQUIN BOOKS OF CHAPEL HILL
Post Office Box 2225
Chapel Hill, North Carolina 27515-2225

an imprint of Workman Publishing
a division of Hachette Book Group, Inc.
1290 Avenue of the Americas,
New York, NY 10104

Printed in the United States of America.
Design by Steve Godwin.

This is a work of fiction. While, as in all fiction, the literary perceptions and
insights are based on experience, all names, characters, places, and incidents either are
products of the author's imagination or are used fictitiously.

The publisher is not responsible for websites (or their content) that are not
owned by the publisher.

Library of Congress Cataloging-in-Publication Data

Names: Bayard, Louis, author.
Title: The Wildes : a novel in five acts / Louis Bayard.
Description: First edition. | Chapel Hill, North Carolina :
Algonquin Books of Chapel Hill, 2024. |
Identifiers: LCCN 2024011061 (print) | LCCN 2024011062 (ebook) |
ISBN 9781643755304 (hardcover) | ISBN 9781643755311 (ebook)
Subjects: LCSH: Wilde, Oscar, 1854–1900—Fiction. | Wilde family—Fiction. |
LCGFT: Biographical fiction. | Historical fiction. | Novels.
Classification: LCC PS3552.A85864 W55 2024 (print) |
LCC PS3552.A85864 (ebook) | DDC 813/.54—dc23/eng/20240311
LC record available at https://lccn.loc.gov/2024011061
LC ebook record available at https://lccn.loc.gov/2024011062

10 9 8 7 6 5 4 3 2 1
First Edition

Contents

Prologue

⁘

Letter of Oscar Wilde to Constance Wilde (December 18, 1884)

Dear and Beloved,
Here I am, and you at the Antipodes. O execrable facts, that keep
our lips from kissing, though our souls are one. What can I tell
you by letter? Alas! nothing that I would tell you. The messages of
the gods to each other travel not by pen and ink and indeed your
bodily presence here would not make you more real: for I feel
your fingers in my hair, and your cheek brushing mine. The air is
full of the music of your voice, my soul and body seem no longer
mine, but mingled in some exquisite ecstasy with yours. I feel
incomplete without you.

Ever and ever yours,
Oscar.

ACT ONE

Wildes in the Country

A rented house at Grove Farm, Norfolk
August 1892

1

"TELL ME IF I've met this one," she says.

To her mind, it is no different in weight or import to anything else she might say. She is living in the before times—before scandal, gaol, exile— but how is she to know? Her eyes see only a late-summer morning and a wife and husband on holiday, engaged in a late-morning stroll. And, on every side of them, Norfolk, in the thick of its annual harvest. With an almost connoisseurial interest, she watches the wagons tottering from field to farm, the children taking shade in the hedgerows, the widows sifting through the holly and hawthorn and young oak for fallen wisps. Her own voice sounds no more substantive or pressing to her than the mechanical reapers and steam engines and, really, it is only the faintest pricking of curiosity that moves her to speak at all, and she is only half-listening for the reply.

"Tell me," she says, "if I've met this one."

"Well now," answers Oscar, "I don't know that I can unless I know which one you mean."

"Oh," she says, already inclined to leave it alone. "The chap who's coming tomorrow."

"Why, yes, my love, you met him last summer. His cousin Lionel

Johnson brought him round, and the three of us had a delightful chat, and then, just as he was leaving, I said you should come meet my wife."

"And you brought him upstairs?"

"Don't I always?"

He does, always. She tasks herself once more with sorting through that stream of acolytes, the procession of narrow-chested young men, each younger than the last, each astonished by his privilege. The vast majority she will never see again, but she greets them in the opposite spirit. *You must promise not to remain a stranger. Oscar so enjoys the company. . . .*

"How was this one dressed?" she asks.

"Cream-coloured linen suit. Straw boater."

"You have described nearly three-quarters of the male population under the age of twenty-two."

"So I have."

"Was he rather small-boned?"

"In relation to me, yes."

"And flaxen?"

"Just so."

They pass under the canopy of a chestnut. She can hear a stone curlew making rapier-like calls.

"I remember now," she says. "His father is the Marquess of Queensbury."

"Indeed."

"Oh, dear, it makes no more sense now than it did then. Isn't the Marquess this rather ferocious sportsman? Rude with animal health? Always riding about or *striding* about . . ."

"We've never met him, my dear."

"Oh, but one pictures him all the same. Barking at groomsmen, wading into mud. Dressing his own stags, right there in the field. One can't imagine the son doing any of that."

"The son does other things, that is all."

She gazes at him, a light slowly dawning.

"Another poet," she says.

"Now, my dear."

"Oh, Oscar, I don't mind them as individuals, but as a category they're—"

"What?"

"Well, pale and malnourished. I always want to send them away with a good beefsteak, only Cook would be cross. Wouldn't it be rather more practical to bring home a young banker now and again?"

"Bankers require no help. Indeed, they are the reason that poets do."

"All the same, a banker might put one on a budget and make one stick to it. See that there's money left over for the servants at the end of the month. Practical things like that."

"Well, now," he answers, sliding his arm for the first time round her waist. "Is it practical you're wanting, Mrs. Wilde? Sure, you don't know the man you married."

How curious that she still quickens to the brogue he discarded before they ever met but still puts on at will. To the feeling of his arm round her waist.

"And you can say for certain he's coming tomorrow?" she asks.

"That's what today's wire said."

"But yesterday's wire said today."

"We shall always have to go with the most recent intelligence, I fear."

"I only hope he doesn't drag too much luggage with him. It's a farmhouse. It's not even *our* farmhouse."

"I should think he grasps the distinction between a castle and a farmhouse and between owning and renting. Even two years at Oxford can't make a fellow a complete imbecile."

"No," she answers, smiling. "It takes four."

She loves the light that flickers in him when she's caught him off guard. Perhaps that is why she stops, the better to savor it. Savor him, too, so slim in his tropical-wool vest. How many pounds has he shed this summer?

"Naturally," she says, "Lord Alfred must have his own room. And, as the Cliftons don't seem disposed ever to leave, I think the best resort would be to move Cyril into my room."

"He won't object, surely."

She doesn't answer. From the dull certainty that Cyril will *not* object.

"I do worry," she allows.

"What about?"

"You've been going such great guns with the play." She reaches for the hand fastened round her waist. "Surely it's because you've been so free of distraction."

"Distraction? What do you call the Cliftons, for heaven's sake, scudding like storm fronts from room to room? What do you call golf, for that matter?"

"Golf is the opposite of distraction. You get a nice walk, admit that, and your brain is humming the whole time without your knowing, and you come back and say, 'Oh, yes, I've figured out how to get them from the terrace to the drawing room.' Why, it's practically a green sward of *Muse*, extending on every side."

"I don't know," he says. "A sympathetic ear might do the same trick."

She looks at him, then softly prises away his hand.

"Why, Mr. Wilde, I had no idea you were lacking for sympathy here."

"Now, my dear. Sometimes a fellow just wants to bore somebody who's not his wife. How do you think marriages survive, anyway?"

"You never bore me."

"Because I tactfully inflict myself on others."

It doesn't hold up even to a second's scrutiny. All these years, she has yet to find anybody bored by him.

"Very well," she says, drawing his arm round her once more and advancing down the lane. "I just don't want Mr. Beerbohm Tree to come chasing after us because some flaxen poet kept you up late with his jabbering."

"Beerbohm Tree will get his four acts in three months' time. No theatre manager can ask more."

"And he's staying only the *two* days?"

"Lord Alfred? On his word as a gentleman."

"I have read enough of books and seen enough of plays, yours included, to know just how much a gentleman's word stands for."

"Books and plays are not truth, my love. They are exercises in sensation."

So are gentlemen, she is about to say, but it sounds too like him. This is perhaps the essential difference between them. She must think out the meaning of whatever she's about to say; he finds it at his leisure, as though it were simply dangling from a bough, waiting to be plucked. In a half-pique, she turns away, watches the Michaelmas geese and Christmas turkeys foraging in the new stubble.

"You seem rather put-out," he says.

"Oh, it's nothing to do with Lord Alfred. It's just that we've been having such a lovely time. Even your mother, I think, hasn't minded so much."

"I'm not entirely sure she knows she's left."

"That's it exactly. We've transplanted her. Transplanted London, too, but only the good bits. And perhaps the Cliftons *will* leave after all, and the rest of us shall stay on and . . ."

What? The target keeps moving. The lease is done after the second week. They might find another place nearby—Cromer has houses to be hired for a song—only Oscar would run screaming into the sea if he were kept too long from London, or else he would invite all of London to come to *them*, which London would. The Wildes have abandoned their usual coordinates. Perhaps this is why the sun beats a little more hotly on her shoulder, makes the handle of her parasol damp in her hand.

"You needn't worry." Oscar rests a hand lightly on her back. "From what little I know of Lord Alfred, he'll keep to his room or else wander lonely as a cloud. If you pass him in the hall, throw him some beefsteak. Otherwise leave him be."

"I shall be glad to."

She reaches in a blind way for Oscar's arm, leans her head toward his shoulder. Bees are making a holiday of their own in the miller's garden. A bed of yellow primrose glimmers out from fruit bushes. In a propitiatory tone, she says:

"We *are* happy here, aren't we? I don't mean in an extravagant way."

"Of course not; we're English."

"May the good Lord strike you dead!" she answers. "It's Irish we are." Then adds, after a pause: "Secret agents at the very least."

His smile wells straight in her direction.

"I quite agree."

2

"MUMMY!"

The seven-year-old boy she left an hour earlier is in exactly the same place she left him, hanging off one of Grove Farm's fence stiles, peering into the foreshortened trunks of a coppice. In his three days here, Cyril Wilde has been in proximity to dogs, turkeys, chickens, ducks, geese, sheep, and cows—takes a special pleasure in overfeeding the pony that Mrs. Balls has left them—but, in a way characteristic of his linear sensibilities, has burrowed down to one animal, an otherwise unexceptional rabbit, plump from a summer's diet of grass, but otherwise so identical to the other rabbits flying through the brushwood that it isn't at all clear how he's marked this one out.

Mark it he has, however, and has made it his sole aim to have this same rabbit eating out of his hand before another week. He has smuggled out carrots and turnips from Mrs. Balls's root cellar. He has laid out trails of day-old bread chunks. This morning, the rabbit came within four yards, reared up on its hind legs, and regarded him in an agnostic fashion before bounding back to shelter. By now, in the light of midday, Cyril has emerged as a study in defeat, his cap and jacket long since sloughed off, the braces hanging loosely about his bony shoulders.

"No word from your friend?" calls Constance.

Cyril is silent.

"I say now," says Oscar, "have you come up with a name for him?"

"Blackie."

"Oh, but how marvelous. A more cripplingly conventional child might have opted for Cinnamon or Russet, owing to its colour, but *you*, my little genius, have opted for—perhaps it's a more *symbolic* interpretation. . . ."

"The eyes," says Cyril.

"Sorry?"

"He's got black eyes."

"So he does," says Oscar, and says nothing more. Constance is quiet, too, for the same reason: *All* rabbits have black eyes. Yet what does that matter to a London boy taking his full draught of Nature?

"Dear boy," says Oscar. "Do you think Blackie might spare you for an afternoon? I'm in frantic need of a caddy."

Cyril sweeps his gaze one last time across the coppice.

"All right."

"Now, you mustn't laugh when you see the old man swing and miss. *The miss never counts*, or so I've been told. In fact, you might give the silly sport a go yourself. I've seen you swing a bat."

Cyril nods.

"Splendid," says Oscar. "We shall depart within the hour."

He gives his Molucca walking stick a light twirl and executes a half-turn toward the house, then pauses and, in a voice not clearly meant for anyone, asks how to make the American heiress the voice of moral judgement without making her a prig. Constance waits to see if the question is rhetorical, then suggests chalking it up to her innocence. The heiress knows better because she knows no worse. Oscar points out that she's rich, and wasn't it Balzac who said that behind every great fortune is a great crime, and Constance says that the crime is not hers. The originating sin hasn't yet touched her. She can see the world as a child. And she turns back to her child, *their* child, still on sentry, and then to Oscar, already striding toward his desk, and feels herself, in this unique moment, a kind of guest in both their worlds.

"Darling," she says, resting a hand atop Cyril's head. "A friend of Papa's is coming tomorrow, and it appears we haven't quite enough rooms, and I was wondering if you wouldn't mind—"

"Staying in your bed."

The speed with which he meets her makes her blink.

"Oh, but only if it's no trouble. Of course, the bed is quite large, and Mummy never sleeps very well, anyway, so you may thrash about all you like, and even cough a bit, and she won't mind."

"Where will Viv stay?" he asks.

"Vyvyan's not here."

"When he comes."

There is no reproach in the voice—no hope, even, just resignation. Almost identical to the resignation in Vyvyan's eyes when she delivered the news. *Darling, I think it best if we left you here with the Wallaces, don't you?*

"Alas," she says now, in a voice not entirely natural, "your brother is still quite unwell."

"He wasn't coughing any more than I was."

"Oh, but he *was*, darling. *Just* a bit. I know because I . . ." Counted the individual coughs. "I simply felt that he looked a little ashen."

"What's ashen?"

"Pale."

"He'd be less pale if he came here."

"Well, darling, it's the same sun there as here. The truth is that Vyvyan has never been as hardy a specimen as you. That is not *his* fault. That is not *your* fault."

"So he's to stay there."

"For the time being, but we can always fetch him over."

"Tomorrow, you mean?

"Well, not tomorrow. Pappa's friend is coming, but the day after, perhaps, or the day after that."

"He's not coming, is he?"

The same note of resignation. How, she wonders, does any child acquire such perfect compliance with the state of what is? God knows she never learned it.

"Why don't we think on it, darling?"

3

⟨⟩

WHEN THEY CAME to Grove Farm a week ago, Mrs. Balls made a point of asking where the "old gentlewoman" should go. "I think," said Constance, "you might put my mother-in-law in the room with the least exposure."

"Are you quite sure, ma'am? There's no sun or moonlight to go by; she might stumble."

"She will not, I assure you. And as she keeps irregular hours, kindly leave her food just outside her door. She will claim it when she's ready."

Mrs. Balls, of course, has never attended one of Lady Jane Wilde's salons. Constance was twenty-one her first time. The address then was Park Street, and Oscar's mother kept thick curtains drawn over every window, so that visitors ushered into her double drawing room would at once have to grope their way, like heathens struck blind. On that particular afternoon, the room was so crowded and the lit pastilles so ineffectual and the mirrors so large it was impossible to see how far the room extended or where exactly you stood within it.

A program of sorts was offered. There was a Miss von Trift, who played the mandolin. A Greek gentleman named Mr. Perdicaris, who lived in Tangier and wrote on the subject of Moroccan pastimes. An American girl performed a poem with endemic bird sounds, and a spiritual intellectual relayed his most recent conversation with Queen Anne. Each act, upon its completion, plunged right back into the darkness from which it had emerged, and when Constance and her mother stumbled out again an hour later, the brightly lit June afternoon came at them like a scimitar.

"Good God," muttered Constance's mother, pressing a forearm to her eyes. "It has been like crawling into a lamp to find the genie."

Here, if nowhere else, they were in accord. In Constance's enduring memory, Lady Wilde *was* the genie, granting wishes that nobody had ever supposed they had, sitting there with such blowsy improbability in a low-cut lavender silk dress and a bright-green Roman scarf, her hair primped, her face daubed. Many in her newly adopted city of London found her ridiculous, but Constance knew that, in Dublin, of a Saturday afternoon, Lady Wilde might draw as many as a hundred esthetes into her drawing room, more than could be contained now within her entire Mayfair home. Yet, even in her new confinement, she carried on as though nothing had changed, as though darkness were her truest medium.

Since then, the genie has ventured less and less from her lamp, and when Constance and Oscar first broached the idea of her joining them on holiday in Norfolk, they braced for a refusal. Perhaps her creditors were pinching particularly hard, but with a passion that caught them both by surprise, she declared:

"Take me away. I hate London."

The logistics were complicated, for Lady Wilde can no longer walk more than a block on her own recognizance, and must be heavily bundled even at the height of summer, but once she was set in the center of that rocking railway carriage, she rode it out like a galley oarsman, eyes on the horizon. Now that she has found a second womb of darkness at Grove Farm, she has remained there without a stir, except to emerge for tea and, occasionally, dinner. As best Constance can tell, her days are spent as they always were: sitting by a single squat, guttering, fattening candle, scanning newspapers and journals and volumes of poetry and dispatching the briefest of letters to friends in every quadrant of the world: Italy, Sweden, India, America. At times, her voice can be heard rising in a conversational way—she likes to unburden herself with her late husband—but at most hours, a stranger might pass her door with no knowledge that somebody lives on the other side. Even now, at three in the afternoon, Constance pauses before she knocks, as though to reassure herself that someone will answer.

"Tea already?" calls Lady Wilde.

"No, Madre. I am only paying a call."

"You are most welcome, of course."

Constance drags open the door, takes two guarded steps. Humped shapes well from the murk, one of them her mother-in-law, sitting up in her tent bed. Even sunless, the room has gathered some warmth, on top of which Lady Wilde has pulled the blanket over her and wrapped herself in a mantua. Old slide bracelets glow on her plump wrists.

"My dear," she says. "I can't be certain, but I believe there's a chair somewhere."

"There is."

Taking hold of a ladder-back, Constance seats herself in the corner and waits patiently for her pupils to dilate.

"I hope we can expect you for dinner," she says.

"Do you know," answers Lady Wilde, "I've half a mind to speak to that young Mrs. Clifton."

"What about?"

"Her demeanor. I have always believed a bride on her honeymoon should endeavor to look the part."

"The groom is no more convincing."

"That's just it. I remember you and Oscar, fresh from Paris, bright as thrushes, perfectly engrossed with each other. Heaven knows such feelings are too febrile to last, but they do get a marriage off the ground, which is what every marriage must positively do."

"Perhaps the Cliftons would have been happier on their own somewhere."

"So they wouldn't have to compare themselves every moment to you and Oscar? I shouldn't wonder."

Never once has this occurred to her.

"She's pretty," muses Constance.

"As you were, my dear."

"Ha. I like that *were*."

"I use it because what you *are* is so much better. The soul of goodness."

In the next moment, they both falter, a little. How many times has Constance received some hasty summons from her mother-in-law and come running, by cheque or in person, and told Oscar nothing? And felt nothing like the soul of goodness because she only wanted to know there was a mother who, unlike her own, needed her.

"I'm glad you came," says Constance.

"Oh, my dear, it was a summons from the angels. How perfectly oppressive London has become. So dull, so dark, so violent. Before too long, I've no doubt, my whole house must be put in entire repair. The foundation is sinking, as I think I've told you . . ."

"You have."

". . . and Number Six, Park Street, is quite beautifully done up, with substantially larger rooms. I could have it for seventy pounds a year and move at once."

"We must look into it," says Contance, with a light sadness that they are reuniting on old terms. "Might I ask you something?"

"*Cara mia*. Of course."

"Did you ever find yourself favoring one of your children over the other?"

Lady Wilde closes her eyes and draws up the question like sap.

"Oscar over Willy, you mean."

"Or the other way. I'm only wondering if you had moments where one of them felt peculiarly dear."

"I suppose," says Lady Wilde, "I always favored the one who didn't live."

This Constance wasn't expecting. Isola, the baby girl, living out her nine years on God's Earth (*nine years*, thinks Constance with a sudden pang) in the full bloom of her family's love before being claimed by a sudden implosion on the brain. Lost forever, though, more than once, her mother has tried to retrieve her via séance, with unsatisfactory results.

"Are you asking," says Lady Wilde, "because you favor Cyril over Vyvyan?"

Constance is glad of the darkness now.

"I don't always know that I do. Or, if I do, why. I suppose Cyril, being older, is a bit easier. Sunnier as a rule, when he's not fretting over his rabbit. I suppose, too, without the nanny here, the prospect of *two* boys underfoot . . ."

"My dear, please don't exculpate yourself on my account. Vyvyan is well looked after, and his presence here would be superfluous."

"Why?"

"Because he is still a child."

"Surely that's all the more reason to—"

"No, you don't understand. He lacks as yet a soul, and until he acquires one, he has no greater claim on you than a dog or a pony. Oscar was the same way, you know. *Purely* animal until, at the age of seven, he said— and I shall never forget it, Constance—he said, *Mamma, that wallpaper is perfectly scandalous,* and I said, *Ah, there you are.* For, in that moment, there flashed out a soul, and our relations could ascend to the next level, where, I am happy to report, they have remained ever since. So it shall be with you and Vyvyan before long."

"Do you really think so?"

"Oh, I do. You know, it wouldn't surprise me at all if Vyvyan turned out to be the artist between the two of them. Solitude does that to a sensitive soul."

It is meant to comfort, she knows, but does it cast her in any better a light, to be starving a child into art? Is that really how artists are made? She herself grew up in acres of solitude, and what is she now?

"Oscar has a friend," she says. "Coming tomorrow."

Lady Wilde gives the news its due gravity.

"It was only a matter of time, I fear. My son has never been the sort to pine away for his art. Why do you think he goes to so many parties? Why do you think he writes in such an obscenely collegial form as the theatre?"

"I always thought it was so that he might be multiplied. But, you see, I don't *want* him multiplied just yet. I'm selfish enough to want him undivided for a bit."

"Oh, my dear," says Lady Wilde, extending one of her arms like a bridge and waggling her bejeweled fingers. "I gave up on that long ago."

4

"She's awfully old for the terrors," she remembers her nanny saying.

And it's true—Constance was already four years old when she woke one night with the most curious sensation. The darkness of her bedroom, rather than folding round her as it had always done, was wanting to be let in.

Until now Constance had imagined her skin a perfect barrier—it had held off water and soot and sun and wind and whatever else the universe had to throw at her—but on this night, she could feel the darkness actually tapping away at her, like a miner, finding veins—so many taps she couldn't register her opposition and didn't even know she was screaming until her brother, Otho, shook her awake.

Since then, more times than she now cares to admit, she has prevailed on somebody to share her bed with her. Georgina, her dearest companion. Cousin Lizzie. Even Oscar, when he knows she's in a state, will give her an extra good-night kiss on the brow before departing to his bedroom, and, in extreme situations, will wire her twice a day and send flowers. (Lilies, which make her feel like one already dead.) She explains herself by saying she hates the wind, though many of the nights are soundless. She's plagued by terrible dreams, though bogeymen and ghouls have never troubled her.

How tedious that, at the advanced age of thirty-four, she still lacks the words to say it is the dark itself, a more intentional body than anybody knows, only waiting until her eyes are shut to seal the whole business.

And so it is a comfort to be sharing a bed with somebody on a night in August. Even better, perhaps, to have it be Cyril, whose boy breath, all clover and licorice, disperses so warmly into the surrounding air. Yet, when he is in soundest slumber, the darkness comes for her all the same—its inroads, if anything, more local, more concentrated. Tonight it is a chain of electric sensations along her right arm, like tiny needles gavotting up and down her skin. Tiring at last of their revels, they withdraw, leaving only a numbed and blank canvas. Somewhere toward morning, she falls asleep for certain and sees the Marquess of Queensbury (or so she has to presume) riding to hounds on a Shetland pony. A creature so slight that its legs, galloping under the weight of its rider, begin to dig a trough into the earth, deepening with every stride. The Marquess raises his crop to administer some peremptory strike, but the pony has already disappeared from view, and the effect is so comical—the great man borne along as if by some submerged locomotive—that Constance must fight the urge to laugh.

She wakes not too long after. By dawn, she is so smolderingly alert she feels it a rudeness to remain in bed. Behind the corner screen, she splashes night-chilled water on her face and dresses by a single candle. She is in no great hurry, for the Cliftons have been slow to emerge these past two mornings, and Oscar as a rule doesn't rise until ten, but in the dining room, Mrs. Balls is already setting plates and cutlery on the white linen tablecloth, along with a vase of French marigolds from her own garden. It's an awkwardness that Constance has always found hard to elide, paying a woman to absent herself from her own farmhouse and then expecting her, as part of the transaction, to wait upon the usurping family, cook and clean, plump pillows, scoop ash from grates, empty chamber pots. In some compartment of her brain, Constance still classifies herself as Socialist, but she could never imagine herself a servant in her own home, watching a strange family trod her floorboards. In the case of Grove Farm, the awkwardness is enhanced by finding so many signs of its current owners. Religious prints (*The Rake's Progress*, *The Drunkard's Children*). Unsmiling photographs of ancestors in starched collars. A coloured scene from the Christmas number of the *Illustrated Police Budget*. A huge family Bible, lying in state in the corner of the little drawing room. Perhaps most poignantly, a black-and-white memorial card for Mr. Balls, who could never have imagined his widow scattering lavender petals over the family rugs for a pack of London parasites.

"Did you sleep well, ma'am?" asks Mrs. Balls.

"Yes, thank you."

"The bed suits?"

"Perfectly."

"I've breakfast on the hob, but I'll hold off if . . ."

"Would you? I'm not sure when the others will be up."

"Well, bless 'em, they're all on holiday, aren't they? Maybe you'd like some tea in the meanwhile."

"That would be lovely."

"Pekoe?"

"Thank you, Mrs. Balls."

Constance circles the room, feeling the first tendrils of morning. She can hear swallows chasing each other under the eaves and the first farm wagons trundling up the lanes and, through the window, she can see the sails of a windmill turning with judicial intent on new corn. How can anyone sleep through it all?

As if in reply, Florence Clifton wanders in, wearing a soft, clinging dress of crêpe de chine, accented by a large leaf-shaped fan that seems obscurely calculated to reveal the unblemished skin of her neck and shoulders and arms. Was it like this seeing Mrs. Langtry for the first time? Without a dram of pretense, Constance says, "How beautiful you are." And wonders, with a suddenness that shocks her, why Arthur Clifton isn't even now making violent love to her.

"You're very kind," says Florence in a sleep-darkened voice, and seems about to add something, only Mrs. Balls is hustling back in with the teapot.

"Well now! There's a pair of you. Shall I bring out breakfast?"

"Please," says Constance.

She and Florence sit on opposite sides of the table. Florence drapes the napkin across her lap. "I sometimes find the country such a terror, don't you?"

Constance is brought back at once to the Marquess, driving his pony into the ground.

"In my experience," she says, "the feeling always passes."

"I am so glad to hear it. It can feel so very foreign for a Londoner to venture out so far from . . ." Something catches behind her brown eyes. "Oh, but of course, we are so very delighted to be here, I didn't mean to suggest otherwise. When I think of all you and Oscar have done for us, words fail, they genuinely do."

"We are glad to be of service, that's all."

It was Oscar who paid for the marriage. What else could he do? His old friend Arthur, in a rash moment, had pledged himself to an artist's model barely out of her teens, with red hair and violet eyes and black eyelashes. *Well*, said Oscar, *if you can't get out of it, how much would it take for you to marry the girl? A hundred and fifty pounds*, said Arthur. *That would get me started in the law and cover a tiny flat. Done*, said Oscar, for he had just got a large sum for *Windermere* and, in the next instant, was writing out a cheque for a hundred and *sixty*, Constance standing over him the whole while, never thinking to complain, for neither of them had a frugal bone in his body. Hadn't they already run through the majority of her grandfather's trust? What was money? Where Constance balked was at Oscar inviting them to stay at Grove Farm, so soon after their wedding.

"Dearest," she pointed out, "we aren't innkeepers."

"But, my love, if a man can't afford the marriage, how is he to afford the honeymoon?"

The same way any man does, she remembers thinking, and then recalled her own honeymoon. That *luxe* suite at the Hôtel Wagram, overlooking the Tuileries. The two of them strolling through an exhibition of Whistler's paintings at the Salon and watching Bernhardt wage a full-scale war on

Lady Macbeth and being greeted by her afterward, a kiss on both cheeks, like old school chums. Oscar giving interviews over croissants to all the Parisian journals and Constance, with a temerity that only endeared her to her new husband, leaning in every so often to correct his French. *Ah,* she heard him say once, *la vie conjugale. Ça ne me décoit pas.* It does not disappoint.

"Very well," she said.

The Cliftons came the next day, coated in cinders from their train. Since then, they have been unfailingly cordial to each other, have never once raised their voices, yet they seem locked in an inscrutable argument, which periodically resolves only to be snatched up again. It is a trick, thinks Constance, that only the English could manage. She watches now as Florence bows her head over her eggs, then rather groggily reaches for the salt cellar.

"Do you know," she says, "I quite like Norfolk, all things in the balance. Oh, I'm sure many girls, having just made their vows, would rather be staying at a *pension* in the Jura Mountains. Or deep in the heart of the Black Forest. Triberg, isn't that where they make the cuckoo clocks? All those Swiss inns in all those lovely Swiss cantons. But, of course, it's such a bother getting to all those places, isn't it? Hours by sea, hours by train. That's what Arthur says."

"Well."

"Arthur says I should be more like you."

"Like me?" she says, starting a little. "Oh, I'm sure he doesn't—"

"No, it's true, he's always praising you to me. He even thinks I should dress more like you."

"Ha! Are you quite certain? My brother tells me I have the ugliest clothes in the world."

"Oh, not a bit! When I see the—the way the fabric lifts right off your skin without even a quarrel, I say to myself, *Oh, Arthur's right. Arthur's always right.*"

"But you look so very charming."

"I'm not sure that's quite the thing anymore."

Constance smiles, heaps a spoonful of sugar into her tea.

"You really mustn't get me started on the subject of dress reform. I could talk for hours."

"Yes, I've seen you do it. Not for hours, I mean."

"Where?"

"At the Albemarle, don't you remember? Arthur took me to see you."

"Of course."

"Arthur said it would do me good. Those were the very words he used. *It will do you good, Florence.* And how right he was. When you got to the part about how the corset was to the Victorian woman as the yoke to the ox, I was ready to throw mine off on the spot."

"We should all have remembered that."

"But I must tell you what really made the deepest impression was seeing Oscar there on the same platform, beaming with pride. I remember thinking here is a woman with a husband who adores her, with *children* who adore her. And, best of all, a true purpose in life, a reason to rise from bed every morning. I remember telling Arthur this is what a free woman is."

"And what did he say to that?"

"I don't recall."

Constance gives her tea three clockwise stirs.

"I am not sure that any woman is altogether free."

Florence takes up her fork again, only to set it down again.

"The eggs are so delightful here, don't you find? Fresh from the hens, so very unlike the city. I could have country eggs every morning for the rest of my life, couldn't you? *And* bacon. *And* beans."

There is a soft scuff of shoes, and Arthur Clifton enters, irreproachable in a checked Norfolk jacket and lawn shirt. His brogues are freshly polished, his mustache is freshly trimmed, and he is wearing the mask of affable ease that he has been wearing since before time. Constance knows him to be thirty but suspects him sometimes of being twice that.

"Good morning," he says.

A brief vacuum of silence, into which Constance goes running.

"Good *morning*, Arthur. I'm so sorry we didn't wait, I didn't realise you were up and about."

"How could you? It wasn't as if anybody might have told you."

Florence's eyes never leave her untouched plate.

"What a delightful sleep," he says, arranging himself in the chair next to her. "The air so deliciously cool, the landscape so painterly. I seem to recall a dog baying somewhere, but it sounded like an ancestral spirit from the Roman days."

"Yes," says Constance, faintly.

"Florence, I thought you and I might give the beach a go this morning. What say you?"

The silence stretches like a glacier.

"What a splendid idea!" cries Constance. "The ocean is no more than two miles. You might take the pony and trap and be there in ten minutes. I'm told there are whole stretches of sand that bear not a single human footprint."

"Perhaps," says Arthur, "you and Oscar would care to join us."

"Oh, how very kind of you. I fear we must bide at home on account of Oscar's friend, who is due at noon, although I have already learned to think of him in approximate terms."

"Anyone I know?" asks Arthur.

"Lord Alfred Douglas. Of the Queensburys."

"Ah."

"I fear he is one of those dreamy Oxfordian poets. A well that, in my experience, never runs dry."

"*Arthur* was a poet," says Florence. "A painter, too."

There is a short pause while her new husband, lacking any food, softly scrapes the blade of his knife against the tines of his fork.

"What my cherished bride is working round to is that I was a dabbler. A well that *always* runs dry."

"When we were courting, he sent me the most marvelous letters. I've kept all of them."

"Have you now?"

"You must be hungry," suggests Constance. "Mrs. Balls will be back in a tick, I'm sure."

"She needn't hurry," says Arthur. "I've nowhere pressing to be."

There is a pause. Then Florence's voice comes back, with the barest hint of mollification.

"We might still go to the beach, darling."

"Of course we might."

"I've my bathing costume still in the trunk."

"And I mine."

Their eyes meet for the first time—no more than a second, but long enough for some communication to pass between them.

"Perhaps we might just take our ease here," says Florence.

"I was going to suggest," says Arthur.

"A spot of lawn bowling."

"Just the thing."

"Oh, we *are* of one mind, aren't we, darling?"

With a sudden blaze of awareness, Constance realises she is the only one actually eating. She sets down her fork and gives her mouth two quick blots with her napkin

"Far be it from me to prescribe," she says, "but today's weather is sure to be glorious, and if getting down to the beach is too much trouble, you might just stop at the cliffs. That's where the poppies really blaze into view in my experience. Or, if you were to travel half a mile in the other direction, there's a lovely ruined church, all mantled in ivy. One half expects some old anchorite to come stumbling out, it's all so very picturesque. Like a dream, really. . . ."

She stops, for she can hear her own throat cinching down.

In a voice of pure neutrality, Florence says, "The bread here is so fresh, don't you find?"

"Oh, I do," says Arthur.

5

As NOON BLEEDS into afternoon, Constance is writing off Lord Alfred Douglas as a phantom when, on the brink of two o'clock, a basket chaise, led by a grey pony, emerges from a fern-shrouded upland. Pauses there, as if reckoning its odds, then trundles down.

It is Cyril who is the first to see it and who, through some mixture of boredom and authority, gallops through the house, alerting the rest. In no more than a minute, as if they'd been drilled, they compose themselves as a welcome party. All that can be seen at first is a palisade of trunks, above which rests the rigid and frowning head of the driver himself. Only when the chaise has closed the distance to thirty feet does a head peep over the luggage. A hand flutters forth.

"There he is," cries Oscar.

Six pieces of luggage, thinks Constance. *Three for each day he's staying.*

The chaise demarcates a slow curve, and, at the exact moment when he will be most visible, Lord Alfred rises, looking like the charioteer of Delphi, arm raised in victory, sack suit draped like a chiton. The carriage shudders to a halt and, with an alacrity that catches them all off guard, he jumps down and declaims in a clear tenor:

"*Salvete anglici!*"

"What's he saying?" Florence whispers.

"'Hail, Englishmen,'" Arthur whispers back.

"But isn't he English, too?"

The newest visitor is an even slighter specimen than Constance remembers, and yet larger from the claim of beauty. Was she too distracted to miss it the first time? The silken hair, the unmolested skin. Eyes the same blue as the Norfolk sky. Lips opening like the most sequestered of fruit. Were it not for his man's garb, he might be a boy-actor of the Shakespearean age: Rosalind in the Arden forest.

"Aren't you all a happy sight for a sorry traveler?" he declaims. "I thought I'd never get here. Not even Moses and his wretched Hebrews had to wander through such a desert. Why, Mrs. Wilde."

He is already stepping toward her, taking the hand she has unconsciously offered and resting it with a breath of delicacy in his.

"You are more ageless than ever. Are you quite sure you don't have a painting in the upstairs schoolroom?"

She will later marvel at how slow she is catching on.

"The schoolroom," she echoes, and then Oscar steps forward, calling out each wrinkle and pouch in his face. "*I* am her painting in the schoolroom," he cries.

Lord Alfred doesn't just laugh. He tips his head back and suffers the laugh to climb from his feet to his thighs to his hips to his chest and out his throat without a single obstruction, so that he seems to be calling up the earth itself.

"What a fool I feel," she says. "I must have read *Dorian Gray* five times."

"And I twenty," says Lord Alfred. "I have declared on more than one occasion, to the very near extremity of being tiresome, that if Oxford were ever to grant degrees in *Wilde*, I should be a don by the end of the next term. Why, Arthur Clifton," he says, rounding deftly on the solicitor. "How long has it been?"

"Not long. Not long at all. I don't believe you've met my wife, Florence."

"Such a fetching bride. How did you inveigle her to the altar, I wonder?

No, my dear girl, I see you blushing, and I shan't inquire any further, but are you quite sure you didn't step out of some artist's atelier?"

"I think she might have," says Oscar.

"How kind of you all to welcome me. I wonder if . . ."

With pure astonishment, he regards his own bags, piled on each side. It is a mystery as deep as Stonehenge. He looks from face to face. At last, turning softly round, he beholds the driver.

"Bernard, isn't it?"

"Barnaby."

"Whoever you are, you've been a perfect dear. I will be sure to mention you in my prayers tonight."

A crease bisects Barnaby's forehead.

"Oh!" cries Lord Alfred. "He appears to require some remuneration."

"Allow me," says Oscar, stepping forward.

"Dear man, would you? Normally, I should have done it myself, but I left in the usual whirl, not a shilling on me, not a book to read, how I didn't die of boredom, and only as many cigarettes I still had on my person. You do have cigs, don't you, Oscar?"

"Of course."

"A whole stinking lot of them?"

"Naturally."

The chaise driver doffs his hat and turns the cart gently round. How strangely meager the whole assemblage appears now without its ballast.

"Dear Lord Alfred," says Constance, curling a hand round her husband's arm. "How pleased we are to welcome you."

"And I to be welcomed."

"I so hope you won't grow too bored while you are here. As I'm sure Oscar has mentioned, he will be hard at work for long stretches."

"And I should be the last to stand in the way of Oscar's commitments."

"You are very kind."

"I'm nothing of the sort. Or at least nobody has ever accused me of it. Oh, but what a homely little domicile we shall all be sharing," he says. "Flint pebble and brick. Speak true, Oscar, did you find it yourself?"

"Beerbohm Tree recommended it."

"Ah! He wants to keep his playwright on the straight and narrow. In the bosom of nature, sequestered from all bad influences."

"Yet here you are."

"Dear friends," says Lord Alfred, tilting his head just a fraction to the right. "Friends old and new. Would it be wretchedly ill-mannered of me to catch a kip?"

"A kip?" asks Florence.

Oscar clears his throat. "He means a nap, I believe."

"So I do. What an invaluable translator you are already proving to be, Oscar. Where did you learn this phraseology, I wonder?"

The two men stand for a time, not exactly regarding each other.

"Cyril can show you to your room," says Constance. "He knows it well."

"Oh, little man!" cries Lord Alfred, with a swell of sympathy. "Have I gone and supplanted you? It wasn't my intention. Rotten luck."

"I suspect he is just as happy with his mamma," suggests Oscar.

"I don't doubt it! A boy must always love his mother more than anybody else in the world." He wreathes Constance with a smile so unforcedly boyish that she feels for a moment like *his* mother. And hears Oscar clear his throat again.

"Your luggage, Lord Alfred."

"Cripes, I nearly forgot. I'm sure nobody will steal it, will they? It's not that sort of place."

Yet something of the old Londoner wariness must kick in all the same, for they begin at once—the men, at least—to gather up the pieces, in the resigned way of hall porters. Arthur hoists a lacquered Chinese chest. Oscar, the circus strongman, pinions a steamer trunk beneath each arm. Young Cyril grabs a leather portmanteau travelling bag. Florence is enthused enough to gather up two hatboxes. It is Lord Alfred, unencumbered, who leads them to the door.

"How I adore you all."

6

By SHEEREST CHANCE, Constance, passing through the reception room that evening, glances out the open window and finds Lord Alfred, in the first flush of dusk, playing croquet on the tennis lawn. Until now, she has assumed he was still sleeping. Somehow, in his brief interval of consciousness, he has discovered hoops and balls and mallets she never knew to exist. Further, he has declined to dress and is dancing through the shaved grass in bare feet and loose-hanging trousers and a square-cut undershirt, chasing after the red ball as if it were life. The whiteness of his skin registers all the more persuasively in the fading light, but perhaps the greatest amazement is what a more substantial presence he is without his jacket and shirt. Framed in the window, his arms and neck complicate with sinew, and the joy he takes in his sport animates him in a way that makes her feel complicit. She is about to turn away when a familiar pair of hands reaches round her and a plummy voice murmurs, "He is a perfect child, isn't he?"

In the next instant, Oscar is barking through the open window.

"Bosie! Be a dear and put some clothes on! We're all famished."

The younger man makes no sign of hearing.

"Bosie," says Constance.

"It's what all his friends call him."

"I didn't know you were friends."

"My dear, why should I go and invite a mere acquaintance to spend a holiday with my family? That would be rather irresponsible, even for me."

She feels the full weight of his jaw resting on her shoulder.

"Don't let's go through the whole rigmarole," he says. "The one where I explain in tones of abiding patience that certain things come of being a public figure, one of which is to be claimed as a friend. Sometimes by people called Bosie. No harm ever comes of it."

She cannot argue. For as long as she has known him, he has never belonged entirely to her or to anyone. She remembers, early in their courtship, attending one of his lectures in Piccadilly and realizing with a shocking suddenness that every eye in Prince's Hall was, like hers, trained on the same tall, languid figure. So many eyes! So many designs. All she could do was remind herself that *his* eyes were, somewhere on the other side, seeking hers. Operating under that same assurance now, she rests her head against his.

"Keep your Bosie," she says. "I draw the line, however, at Bessie."

"Are you sleeping well, my love?"

"Of course not."

"Then how do you stay so handsome? If not a painting, some other dark art is at work."

"The darkest. Happiness."

She has broached the proposition twice now in the space of two days. *We* are *happy, aren't we?* Only now does it occur to her that, if something is true, it need only be said once. As though to reassure her, he takes his right thumb and brushes the region of skin just beneath her ear. Outside, Lord Alfred leans into his mallet with his right hand and gazes toward the falling sun, which is reddening and burning on the lighthouse cliff.

7

IN AN OSCAR Wilde play, she thinks, the women, after dinner, retire for coffee in the drawing room; the men take their port and cigars to the billiard room. Each sex expresses relief at being left alone, then, feeling obscurely abandoned, surges back toward the other. Someone prevails upon a guest to play violin or piano in the music room, after which they wander toward the picture gallery, where the men loll on sofas and the women think of things to say about the Watteau, the Boucher. A dowager sits sewing, while those in the mood for gossip or flirtation wander out to the terrace. At all times there will be servants: butlers to announce the newest guest, white-gloved footmen to bring cushions and shawls, maids to answer the bell or stand by in anticipation of the next demand.

At Grove Farm, Mrs. Balls, the lone caretaker, retires after dinner. Lacking any other option, the guests make for the back terrace, where they find Mrs. Balls's grandson, Patrick, in a detachable collar, with an improvised pitcher of Apollinaris mineral water and hard cider. Constance has seen this same young fellow wandering in an aggrieved way after ewes and cocks and hens and can find no change in his manner now.

"Just leave the glasses, ma'am," he tells her. "Nan'll get 'em in the morning."

Nan, in Constance's mind, has already crawled into the bed of her nearest relation, not enough strength left to say prayers.

"You are so kind," she says.

In the absence of rules, the guests circle around their wooden chairs and then, through some buried reflex, seat themselves as they would at home, men on one side, women on the other. Florence takes the seat farthest from her husband; Oscar takes the seat between Constance and Lord Alfred. Somebody improvises a toast, they drink one another's health, and then at once fall silent, as if they have never met. Around them, the hedgerows and fir trees darken against a field of pure light gold. In the distance, a pheasant rustles through the fern.

"Lord Alfred," ventures Florence at last, "are those *your* cigarettes?"

"The last of them, I fear."

"The gold tips are so charming."

"By that I assume you mean awfully expensive. I can only afford them, you know, when I'm in debt."

"In debt?" says Arthur.

"Well, of course. One must have some occupation nowadays. If I hadn't my debts, I shouldn't have anything to think about. All the chaps I know are in debt."

"But don't your creditors give you a great deal of annoyance?"

"The only annoyance is that they write me. Which obliges me not to write them back."

"One thing's for certain," says Oscar. "They'll never find you here."

"*I'd* never find me here. All these years, I've looked at Norfolk on the school map, and it's always struck me as this rather unattractive protuberance on England's eastern hip. Like a knuckle or a bubo. Yet how unspoiled it turns out to be."

"Oh, yes," says Constance, leaning in. "We've had the loveliest drives, all through the bracken and the heather. The other afternoon, Oscar said it reminded him of that line—what was it, darling? *A green Thought in a green Shade.* I couldn't agree more. I think Mr. Herrick must have had this very place in mind when he wrote it."

There is a pause that stretches past comfort.

"I'm probably mistaken," says Oscar, "but I think that might have been Marvell. Of course, it's been so long."

"Do you know," says Lord Alfred, "I was thinking the same thing. With the same proviso."

How she wishes for a green shade now to slip back in. Lacking that, she reaches for her fan and mutters something about how it serves her right, speaking of poetry to poets.

"Not at all, Mrs. Wilde. . . ."

"The sentiment remains the same, my dear. . . ."

"No matter who wrote it . . ."

"Truer words never spoke . . ."

She would like to tell them they are making it worse, only perhaps that would make it worse, too. She takes another sip of the hard cider, then closes her eyes to intensify the feeling of apple atomised into mist. The effect must be greater than she suspects for, when she opens her eyes again, Lady Jane Wilde is travelling toward them, like a tragic barge.

"Mamma," says Oscar, lurching to his feet. "What a lovely surprise."

"Good evening to you all. I am so sorry I couldn't join you for dinner, but I had a most urgent correspondence with anarchist friends in North Manchuria. Constance," she says, "at what time may we expect the post-man tomorrow?"

"Around one or two."

"Let us hope he is not remiss. Human lives may depend upon it."

A mantle of respect settles over the guests as Lady Wilde scans the terrain.

"I should wish," she says, "to pay my respects to our newest guest."

With a sedimentary slowness, she lowers herself into the chair Oscar has just vacated, rearranges her outer layers, and then, in her rich con-tralto, declares:

"Lord Alfred, you were not to know this, but to each of my son's new friends, I relay the same imperative. *Tell me about yourself.*"

"Oh . . ."

"If you require to be more pointed, I will. *What is the one thing I must know about you?*"

Constance will afterward think it amusing that, in ranging through all the facts of his being, Lord Alfred should emerge with:

"I had an uncle who fell off the Matterhorn."

There is a vexed silence, broken after some moments by Lady Wilde herself.

"That seems rather careless."

"I suppose it was. They never did find the body, though my father nearly killed himself looking. He said the only good part of the whole business was that it cured him of God."

"I should have thought it would cure him of the Alps."

"Do you mean he's an atheist?" asks Florence.

"Devoutly so. When he entered the House of Lords, he refused to swear allegiance either to God or to Queen. Said it was all Christian tomfoolery."

"Well now," returns Lady Wilde. "Anybody who snubs the Queen secures a special room in my heart. Do you have any other curious relations?"

"There's my aunt Florrie. She brought home a pet jaguar from Patagonia. It escaped from her garden one day and killed some deer in Windsor Park and had to be sent to the Zoo."

"Nature cannot be gainsaid."

"And my grandfather, he shot himself whilst hunting, though nobody knows how. And I had another uncle who stood in front of a mirror and slit his throat, from ear to ear, and hang on! Back in the last century, we had an idiot Queensbury who got out of his room one night and roasted the cook's boy over the fire."

"Why," says Lady Wilde, "this is practically a parable on the dangers of inbreeding."

"Mamma," interposes Oscar.

"Well, it's not this young man's fault he has debauched ancestry. I'm sure he poses a most appealing contrast to his cannibal forebears. Tell me, Lord Alfred. What is it you do with yourself?"

A half-smile plays on the young man's face.

"I loaf," he declares.

"That is evident. But toward what end?"

"Well, I'm now in my third year at Magdalen. I *think* it's my third year; I've been gated more than once, and I was fairly *ploughed* in mathematics. . . ."

"Oh, speak to me not of Oxford. What is your *grande passione*?"

For the first time, he thinks before speaking.

"I'm a sort of poet, I suppose."

"Ah," says Lady Wilde. "I should have recognised a kindred spirit. Mark me, though, when it comes to describing one's native calling, there can be no such expressions as *sort of* or *I suppose*. One must either be bound over to it heart and soul—as I was in my all-too-foreshortened prime—or one must find a less exalted profession. Like Mr. Clifton's."

"Oh," stammers Arthur, startled from his reverie. "I don't suppose the legal profession is for all—"

"Tell me," the old lady sweeps on. "In which forms do you traffic, Lord Alfred? The tragic? The epic?"

"Sonnets, mostly."

"Petrarchan?"

"Shakespearean."

"And what is your theme?"

"Love."

"That was my fear."

"My dear mamma," says Oscar, inserting himself lightly between them. "I have been fortunate enough to read some of Lord Alfred's verses, and I consider them extraordinarily promising."

"Promising," mutters Lady Wilde. "Everything I wrote at his age I threw in the fire, for the reason that it was mere apprenticeship. I had to hear my native Ireland's cries before I could discern my own cry within them."

"How very, very lovely," says Florence. "Do you still write verse, Lady Wilde? I should think it such a consolation, really, being a writer of some sort."

"If I thought I was consoling anybody, I should have thrown *myself* in the fire."

Constance watches the younger woman's face slacken. *It is not personal,* she would say if they were alone. She takes another sip of cider and closes her eyes once more, and is all the less equipped when Cyril, bounding from the dusk, drops his full weight into her lap.

"Oof," she says. "Who's this big fellow?"

"Mummy, I can't find Blackie."

"Well, darling," she says, folding her arm round his neck, "it's getting on to night. He's surely gone to sleep."

"Where?"

"Somewhere in the woods, I expect. With his wife and children."

Cyril makes a study of the tree line.

"It's awfully early for turning in. It's scarcely nine."

"But, darling, that's when he and his family must take the greatest care."

"From what?"

"Other creatures, of course."

"What sort?"

"Well, the tooth-and-claw sort."

She can see the muscles roiling along his jawline. *Tooth. Claw.*

"Good thing I didn't bring Alcibiades," says Lord Alfred.

"Who's that?" asks Florence.

"My fox-terrier. The most carnal savage you will ever meet. Why, from his very whelping, he has been bent on conjugation—and I don't mean verbs. If he were here right now, there wouldn't be a bitch in all of Norfolk who could call herself safe. But when this same dog so much as spots a bunny somewhere, he goes straight from Eros to Thanatos. Tooth and claw *indeed.*"

Something in the silence that ensues must reach him by degrees.

"Did I misstep?" he murmurs.

"Only by the standards of civilization," says Oscar.

"Dear me, I thought I was being rather circumspect."

"That, of course, is your charm. Now see here, Cyril, the only dog *I've* glimpsed in these parts is so busy bossing around sheep—an occupation that, as anyone can tell you, is quite extraordinarily taxing—he doesn't have a spare thought for Blackie or any other of God's creatures. I have it on personal authority that, when he goes to sleep tonight, he will be counting not sheep but *rabbits*, who are, on the whole, far less infuriating. You have my solemn vow."

And still Cyril hesitates.

"Come now, darling," says Constance. "Would you like it if Pappa went in with you? You would? Very well, take his hand and give Mamma a kiss, and don't forget Grandmamma."

This occasions another pause, for Lady Wilde is a perfect terror to both her grandchildren. Florence demands her own kiss. It is only when Lord Alfred leans forward with the same expectation that Cyril once again pauses.

"It's all right, darling," says Constance. "Lord Alfred just wants to shake your hand."

The exchange is over quickly enough. A second later, father and son have slipped back inside.

"Here now," says Lord Alfred with a frown. "Does your husband do a lot of that?"

"What?"

"Ohh, putting the boy to bed and—kissing him goodnight, that sort of thing."

"Why, yes, he *adores* it, especially if he can read them stories. Or make up his own."

"*Stories,*" says Lord Alfred, lightly scandalised. "Just how long will he be about this?"

"I fear it might be some time, depending on how sleepy Cyril is."

In fact, twenty minutes have elapsed before Oscar strolls back, inscribing circles of light with a newly lit cigarette.

"Did anybody miss me?" he drawls.

"Not a soul," answers Constance, smiling.

He resumes his seat and, with a half-stifled yawn, stretches out his legs as if he'd never left.

"D'you know, it just occurred to me—of course, I wouldn't dream of raising it with the child—this Blackie fellow, for all we know, might be female. Is anyone here conversant on the subject?"

"*I* am," interposes Lord Alfred. "Hares, too."

"Bless me," says Florence, "I always thought they were the same."

"Oh, you city dwellers in your castle keep. Hares are *longer* than rabbits, and they have longer *ears*, and they are far more *sympathique* owing to their downcast mien."

"One can't blame them for feeling downcast," says Oscar. "They are about to be devoured by your dog. Or shot by your father."

"Don't be silly, the Marquess is far more animated by foxes. What is it you always say, Oscar, about fox hunters?"

"The unspeakable in full pursuit of the uneatable."

"I must ladle that in Father's ear one night. Like Claudius with Old Hamlet. Oh, Oscar, be a dear and. . . ."

The gesture comes straight from the Sistine Chapel, thinks Constance. Lord Alfred extending his unlit cigarette toward Oscar's waiting cigarette, then, with a murmur of deep commitment, drawing down a fresh draught of smoke.

"You've another lad, don't you, Mrs. Wilde?"

"Yes, Vyvyan. Lamentably, he is still troubled by the whooping cough, so we left him with friends in Hunstanton until he regains his colour."

In one of her at-homes in Tite Street, that explanation would be accepted without another thought. Here, it seems to hang a little.

"Of course, he's a dear child," she adds. "I'm sorry you can't meet him, Lord Alfred, he so enjoys poetry."

And watches those banal and possibly untrue words sail out into the darkening air.

"Oscar," she says. "Tell Lord Alfred about your play."

A look of abstraction takes hold in Oscar's eyes—as it always does when he is about to step to the fore.

"I don't want to bore," he says, formally.

"No!" cries Florence. "We're longing to hear, aren't we, Arthur?"

"Of course."

"Well," says Oscar, "it is called *A Woman of No Importance*. The title, of course, is ironical. The woman, you see, has paid the ultimate price for—let us call it her sin. . . ."

"You're always so Calvinist about her," says Constance.

"In the eyes of the *world*, she has sinned, and the man who drew her into that sin has gone free. And is now a coveted guest at every great house in the land."

"So it is an indictment," says Lord Alfred.

"You might say."

"Melodrama?"

"No need to be vulgar."

"*Windermere* was melodrama."

"It was comedy, too. I worship the instability. As did your Shakespeare."

"And where is it set?"

"In a country house."

"A bit grander than this one," Constance points out.

"But the world outside is no different." Oscar rises and begins at once to sketch the scene with his cigarette, as though it were a crayon. "There is a yew tree just like this, forming a canopy. Beneath it are people. Like us or any other."

"But what happens?" asks Florence.

"In the first act, I am delighted to say, very little. Indeed, it has always been my dream to dramatise humans doing nothing at all."

"And how," says Arthur, "do you manage that?"

"Simply by showing them as they are. Bantering, bickering. Flirting, withdrawing. Proposing theorems, unproposing them. Getting peeved, getting bored. *Yawning*," he quickly adds, for the first faint snores are emerging from the cathedral of Lady Wilde's chest. "Not a one of them is exactly idle from moment to moment, yet nothing in particular is happening, any more than anything is happening right now."

"Something is always happening," says Constance.

Though she can't in this instant say what it is. Lady Wilde slumbers. Arthur Clifton draws down his cigar. Florence Clifton stares into her lap. Oscar and Lord Alfred recline in their chairs. She herself observes. None of them has, in any meaningful way, dislodged the molecules that, according to Science, surround them all. It would take a mind-reader to pierce the cloud of each person's thoughts. Or, on the other end of the scale, an intelligence so far removed it could rise above like a falcon and plot them all against a canvas they cannot even see, graphing them in their exact relation to each other. It would tell her, perhaps, why she feels loneliest in crowds just like this one or why Oscar can feel furthest away when he is nearest. It would confirm for her whether the sense of him floating away with each new day is grounded in anything. If it's a reason to let go or grip more tightly.

8

⤜⤛

"My love," says Oscar. "Once again, you leave me feeling perfectly abject in my gratitude."

They are parting as they do each night, just outside her bedroom door, his arms curled round her, his grey eyes gleaming down.

"Why gratitude?" she asks.

"For tolerating Bosie, of course. In all his strangeness."

"We have had stranger, surely. Robbie Ross was quite alien at first."

"And remains so."

"The point is one grows used to anything with you."

"Oh, my violet-eyed Artemis."

Something must stir in him beyond the usual endearments for, in addition to leaving the usual kiss on her brow, he leaves another, more insistent, on her mouth. How long it has been, she realises, since she felt the full press of his lips. It must stir something in her, too, for she murmurs his name and runs a hand through his hair. In reply, he catches her softly by the wrist and, with great care, draws the hand away. In that interval, something changes.

Later that night, as she undresses by the candle—careful as always not to wake Cyril—she looks down at her hand and finds it lightly tarred with a coarse and strangely gritty orange-brown substance. She touches it, smells it. Only when she is sliding under the coverlet do the questions gather. How long has her husband been dyeing his hair?

9

"Mummy." Cyril is tugging, with the urgency of a newborn, on the sleeve of her nightgown. "Are you awake?"

Through the slots of her half-open eyes, the night lies heavy across the coverlet.

"Darling, is it . . ."

The lids struggle a little farther apart.

"Are you . . ."

"I think somebody might be ill."

"Who?" she asks, dragging her palm across her forehead.

"I don't know. They woke me up."

"How?"

"They made a noise."

"Just now?"

"It was an hour ago, I think."

An hour. He has been sitting bolt upright all that time. Holding vigil.

She angles her head arduously toward the open window. "What sort of a noise?"

"Bit of a cry."

"Just the one?"

"More than one."

"Was it a man or . . ."

"I don't know."

"A woman . . ."

"I don't know."

"And you're sure it wasn't an owl or some such?"

She can hear his voice in the darkness, darkening.

"I know what an owl sounds like, Mummy. Never mind, I shouldn't have said anything."

"No, darling." With a grunt, she props herself up on her elbows. "If one of our guests is ailing, we must . . ."

What?

"*See* to him. To her. No," she adds, giving an extra press to her temples, "you did the right thing telling me."

He nods again. Then, frowning toward the open window, says:

"I'm sorry, Mummy. You were having such a lovely rest."

Was she, really? Why can't she remember? Is there some world she travels to every night that welcomes her with open arms?

Cyril, having fulfilled his mission, tumbles straight back to sleep. Constance, permanently roused, lies there another hour, but all she hears is an undifferentiated rustle. Conscious of her duties, she dresses at the first peep of sun and waits rather crossly in the dining room for the others. First to appear are Arthur and Florence.

"Good morning," says Constance. "Everything all right?"

They look back.

"I mean you are both quite well?" she presses.

"Why, yes," says Arthur.

"Oh, I'm so glad. Cyril heard a sound. He was afraid somebody might be in distress."

Florence lowers herself into her accustomed seat.

"It can't have been from Arthur's room. Arthur sleeps like a lamb, doesn't he? It's extraordinary what he can sleep through."

Her groom pours a cup of tea from Mrs. Balls's urn.

"Country air," he murmurs.

Lord Alfred arrives not too long after, in the same sack suit as yesterday. He gives the back of his neck a soft feline inquisition, nods at the others, then draws out one of the end chairs and composes himself into a slouch.

"Isn't there some sort of bell to pull?" he wonders.

"No," says Constance, "there is only a woman with food. But she never keeps us waiting long."

"That's a relief. I could eat three horses."

He fumbles through his pockets—last night's pockets—for a gold-tipped cigarette. Holds it in the nearest candle and watches with a morbid fascination as it catches fire.

"You are perfectly well?" asks Constance.

"Well enough. Mattress a bit lumpy. Bed frame creaks like a maiden aunt."

Perhaps that's all it was, she thinks. A creaking bed, a groaning floorboard.

Unless, she thinks, with a quickening of despair, *unless it was Oscar*. And envisions him in that moment stretched lifeless on his four-poster and takes two long strides in the direction of the nearest door, only to find Oscar blocking the way.

"Good morning, my love," he says.

"Good morning."

One mission instantly set aside for the other: the canvassing of his hair. Is the brown any different? Are there notes of auburn or bronze that have escaped her? Surely he can't have gone grey without her knowing. . . .

"Well now," says Lord Alfred. "You didn't ask Oscar if he was feeling perfectly well."

10

OSCAR DRAWS HER aside after breakfast.

"I say, Bosie's quite keen on playing golf this afternoon."

"How nice."

"It *will* be nice, I've no doubt, for our poor Cyril."

"How so?"

"He won't have to caddy for his pappa."

"Oh, I think he rather enjoyed it."

"If so, he gave no sign of it. Looked quite extravagantly bored, if you must know, and I don't blame him a whit. No, he'll be much happier with his mamma, I shouldn't think."

Something in her must look unpersuaded because he adds, with a wink:

"Somebody has to watch out for Blackie."

It comes back to her with such a force, the image she was too distracted to register this morning from the parlor window. Mrs. Balls's grandson Patrick, striding down the lane, a shotgun under his arm and three carcasses draped over his shoulder. One a pheasant. One a squirrel. One quite clearly a rabbit, its ears swinging disconsolately earthward. The memory drives her in the direction of absurdity. Was *that* what Cyril heard? The dying cry of Blackie?

"My love," says Oscar. "You've gone quite pale."

"It's only I forgot to write Georgina," she says.

11

⟨ೕ⟩

SHE DOES WRITE Georgina first thing.

We are in such a fascinating farm in sweet air and country. The only thing I fear is that Oscar will get bored to death, but we have asked down one of his friends, Lord Alfred Douglas, to cheer him up. You need only consult your Debretts to get LAD fixed in the firmament. He is a curious sort but appears harmless and has promised to vacate the precincts before two more suns have set. I have it on good authority.

Is there a querulous note?

When Oscar and I walk in Cromer, we generally come across some friend to have tea with. It is doing us both so much good, and I am already quite well, I recover as quickly as I get ill.

And *that* note, too preemptive? Georgina is always the first to reproach her for not taking sufficient care. (The first, too, thinks Constance, to massage her limbs when they have no feeling left.) Georgina will surely wonder why she is exhausting herself in the company of strangers. Why she brought Lady Wilde and not the nanny (scarcely conceiving that Constance fears her nanny's judgement more than God's).

Can you believe it? Oscar has been bitten by golf mania. After playing his first game on the links, he has joined for a fortnight, and I have become quite the golf-widow.

And today Lord Alfred Douglas is joining him on those links, and Cyril is banished, and the old strain of petulance returns, and she sets the letter aside and wishes in that moment she weren't sitting in some strange woman's bed like an invalid, with a repurposed breakfast tray trestled across her lap, but back in Tite Street, in the front bedroom with the white bespoke writing table.

She has brought additional projects for these moments. On this same tray is an article she has promised Oscar's old magazine: "Children's Dress in This Century." The topic is tapered down to her peculiar expertise, yet when she reads the words scrawled on the page, she doesn't recognise them.

The perils of London's rains, fogs, and treacherous winds to children are manifest and may only be opposed by wool. At present it is the Navy that is predominant, and it is a very sensible dress.

Someone else's voice, surely. A Salvation Army matron.

The woolen undervest, the blue blouse for winter, the white one for summer, and the blue serge trousers are very good dress for a boy. He is warmly clad and his limbs are free for movement.

It is a continuing mystery to her that, no matter how competent her pen, she herself remains stubbornly apart from it, while Oscar, even in his worst excesses and perhaps most particularly then, bleeds straight into the paper, in ways he doesn't always appreciate.

She lifts the tray off her lap and travels to the bedroom window. The cornfields have passed from deep green to golden yellow, but the scarlet poppies have held their colour. The ferns, where even now Blackie's family awaits his return, stand rich and green against a skyline of Eton blue. A bluebottle fly cuts past her, makes a slow, unruffled browsing of the room, passes out again. She is thinking of all the letters she might still write. The persons of substance she might invite to her next at-home. Miss Terry, perhaps, or Mr. Irving. Jimmy Whistler, if he's speaking to them. A phrenologist or, if she's feeling bold, a Theosophist. The climate will be nowhere near as eccentric as Lady Wilde's salons, and the invitation will stop shy of wheedling. *Oscar, if he is in town, should be so delighted to see you.* On those occasions where he does present himself, the guests abandon whatever theme they have taken up—Christian socialism, Utopian living—and submit to the tempered blaze of his celebrity, the humble and yet anointed way he enters every room, flower in buttonhole. He confines himself to the most cursory of greetings, then settles in the chair closest to the back wall. Afterwards, the guests, taking their farewells, reiterate some version of Florence's judgement: *How proud he is of you!* They will not be wrong. It is she who can never take pride in it. Standing now before the window, watching the windmill execute its steady churn, she has a half-fantastical idea that the cry Cyril heard this morning was hers, dredged up from the riverbed of her own sleep. A woman of scant importance.

12

⸙

SOMEWHERE IN THE vicinity of eleven that morning, a cloud sails in from the north, then assembles itself into a floating frigate, and then, toward one-thirty, bursts into an incontinent fall of rain. Watching from the parlor window, Constance finds herself gladdened by the sound, and it isn't until thunder comes rumbling from the east that she remembers Oscar and Lord Alfred on the links. She scans the skies now for lightning and hovers in the front hall, casting glances through the leaded window. Just shy of three, the pony trap appears on the rim of the hill, Oscar at the reins and Lord Alfred crouched by his side. The two men spill out in a single cataract, tumbling through the front door and dragging their clubs after them like kindling. Constance drapes them in woolens; the fire is drawn up in the reception room; and before another ten minutes are past, the golfers are stretched before the blaze in lop-eared slippers that might have once belonged to Mr. Balls.

"How suddenly it all came on," says Lord Alfred. "There we were—was it the sixth hole, Oscar?"

"Possibly."

"Admiring, in the midst of our exertions, the rather voluptuous cloud formations against the blue dome of air."

"So we were."

"There came the first drop. Not a drop at all but a hailstone, diamond-like and impermeable. Within minutes, we were pelted in every quarter with ice. If I weren't so deucedly secular, I should have called it Biblical."

"And the Lord saith," cries Oscar, *"Thou shalt no more profane my grassy links with thy iniquitous and unavailing swings."*

"I shall send forth a flood! Yea, a great icy flood upon the land, which shall wash away all memory of thy duffery."

"No more shalt thy manifold bogeys stain my creation!"

From the merriment, Lady Wilde, in her tattered lace shawl, holds herself apart.

"I am sure that Our Father has rather more important things to contemplate within His all-loving and all-seeing mind than your golf."

"Oh, Mamma, what grander consideration can there be? Golf is the ideal education in the material versus the immaterial. I take an actual club, swing it at an actual ball, only the ball denies any knowledge of what I've done. I chase it, feeling the whole while I'm chasing a shadow, for what I do has no real bearing on what it does. At last, the ball, bored by my exertions, consents to drop into the nearest available hole, and it is here, at the exact moment I wish it to be material, that it vanishes altogether and becomes purely immaterial. I root round for it, drag it aboveground, at which point the whole roundelay begins again. I say to you, ladies and gentlemen, do not play golf unless you wish to question the very foundations of your existence."

He has punctuated his remarks with such uncanny recreations of his own befuddled swings that, by the time he has done, the rest of the party has no option but to applaud.

"Leave it to the Scottish," growls Lady Wilde, forgetting perhaps that their number includes Lord Alfred. "The Irish would never have invented such a perverse pastime."

"No, they would have improved upon it, Mamma. Made the holes much wider and filled them with whisky. And stopped after the first hole."

"If the Irish are fond of drink, as your Royalist friends persist in declaring, it is because they are in a permanent state of dispossession, which I hardly need tell you. . . ."

"Oh, Madre," says Constance, rising lightly. "We are all devotees of the Auld Sod in this room. As for golf, I find it every bit as ridiculous as you, but I must say I have rarely seen Oscar look so well."

"Nor I," drawls Lord Alfred. "Why, he's a positive *sylphide*. Speak true, dear boy, is it all the walking, or is it the Promethean fire of creation? Or some other fire, perhaps?"

On the brink of answering, Oscar unaccountably pauses.

"It is hope," he says at last. "That we may all still be gathered here together—in this very house, even—for years to come. Because, you see, as the Wildes fall, so falls the nation."

"Hear, hear," says Constance.

The rain continues to drum. Some noise is made about cards, about charades, but nobody grabs the lead or even bothers to keep the reception-room fire kindled. Cyril, prostrate with boredom, lies against the south window. The Cliftons wend toward every corner. Lord Alfred takes up a small volume of Swinburne and stretches out his slender legs in a perfect hypotenuse to the right angle of chair leg and floor. Around a quarter to five, the sun, like a truant, breaks free.

"Let's take a ramble," says Oscar. "Over to the cliffs."

The unanimity is astonishing. The cliffs! Capital idea! Never was there a better.

"And it's just two fields away," says Constance, for this is what Mrs. Balls has promised from the outset, grasping in some mercantile precinct of her brain that the Wildes, prisoners of London, have but a limited sense of what a field constitutes. The expedition, then, begins in high hope, Cyril at its front, all bounding legs, Oscar and Lord Alfred following behind, then Arthur Clifton, with Constance at one side and Florence the other. The sun draws back as if in awe at their effrontery. Somewhere between the terminus of one field and the beginning of another their resolve begins to falter. Cyril's bounding stride moderates into the gait of a treadmill prisoner, and the others match it. Nobody seems more affected by the change than

Florence Clifton, who ducks her head farther down with each stride. Arthur carries on, unifocal as an arctic explorer. In some other clime, Constance might take him aside and educate him. *Here*, she imagines herself saying. *This is what a wife requires.* Only what does she know of that? Has she ever, over the course of her eight-year marriage, exerted a single feminine wile? And what would Oscar have done if she had?

So on they flow, Londoners in Norfolk, toward the ocean that has been calling them the whole while. The wind rises from the south. Behind them, the last full rays of sun bear down, and, before them, the carpet of grass and crop rolls into a stand of poppies, scarlet heads weaving. On the other side lie the cliffs, not a sheer rock face but a soft, sandy retraction, laced with paths and ravines. Constance's senses pick out thistle and sea daisy, the susurrations of green water on yellow sand.

"I'm sure you can see quite how soft the clay is," explains Oscar. "I am told that, with each new year, another acre washes away. Already the Cromer church has had to be moved a quarter of a mile landward. And now cast your thoughts, dear friends, to that which was left behind. I speak now of the old tower, of the *churchyard*. All those righteously interred souls who were sent off on clouds of witness, now waiting to be swept into this very same ocean."

Gazing east, Constance imagines the formerly penned occupants of the Cromer churchyard rearing up from the bottom of the North Sea. *Memento mori.* Lost in contemplation, she does not quite register the moment when the heel of her right boot catches in the mud. Nor does her right leg register it. A nullity is already descending—or ascending, she cannot always tell. Briefly at a loss, she weaves in place, waving her parasol in a gesture that must advertise as helplessness for, in the next second, a hand grabs her forearm.

"Are you quite all right, Mrs. Wilde?"

She gazes into the cornflower-blue eyes of Lord Alfred.

"Thank you," she mutters. "Just a passing spell."

"We don't want you tumbling into the sea, do we? It would take all the spirit out of the holiday."

Does she smile? Or does she just wait with a barely contained impatience for some feeling to return to her leg?

"You are very kind," she thinks to say.

"It is nothing at all. My dear Mrs. Wilde, would you permit me to say something that has been on my mind since first I met you?"

"Oh. If it's imperative. . . ."

"You have the most glorious hair."

Her hand flies first to her hat, then to the hair that lies pinned beneath.

"Have I overstepped?" he asks. "I do that."

"No, Lord Alfred. I am sure every woman enjoys to hear such things. In their proper context."

"I say, you'll call me Bosie sometime, won't you?"

"But we've only just met."

"Not so. We met last summer."

"But that was in passing."

"And what is this?"

"Well, there is an element of passing even now. You are to leave us tomorrow, or so I am instructed. In the meanwhile, you must tell me the provenance of your quite charming nickname."

"Oh." His rosebud mouth folds down. "You must blame my dearest mother. She was wont to hear West Country farmers call their lads *boysie*, and she found the name so delightful she made a merger of it and me."

Constance forces her own mouth into something genial. "With a name such as that," she says, "you shall remain forever a boy, it seems."

"I don't know about that, Mrs. Wilde. By the time a pretty lad has got through Winchester and Oxford, he is quite an adult, all things in the balance."

His voice, perhaps without his knowledge, dips into a lower register on the last two syllables.

"You and Oscar seem to have become boon companions," she says.

"He is the soul of kindness."

"Isn't he? Was there a particular kindness?"

"Sorry?"

"A particular kindness he paid you. I always want to be properly grateful for his good offices."

She can feel the dry bemusement of his glance.

"You mean he didn't tell you?"

"How could he when I did not ask? Our marriage has never been grounded in inquisitions."

"Manifestly not. If you must know, Mrs. Wilde, I had a bit of a run-in with a rough sort."

"I hope you were not injured."

"No, nothing like that. I left a letter in my jacket—I'm terrifically careless with all my things—and this other chap got hold of it and—well, it was all just a bit of unpleasantness. Very quickly sorted out. Arthur was a great help."

"Arthur?"

"Why, yes. That's how we met, Arthur and I."

She slides her gaze toward the barrister, hands squarely in his pockets, eyes fixed in the general direction of Germany.

"But who introduced you?" she asks.

"Why, your husband."

"So you went first to Oscar?"

"Yes, who better? And then he sent for Arthur, and Arthur sent for Mr. George Lewis, and I forget who else. It was quite the skein of jurisprudence."

"All this because somebody had your letter?"

"Well, now, Mrs. Wilde, I don't need to tell you how many blackguards there are in the world. Oh, it was all nonsense, but there was a certain potential for embarrassment."

"I am glad it was sorted out."

"So am I! One hundred pounds well spent, if you ask me."

"One hundred pounds," she says.

"Perfectly disgraceful, isn't it? What a chap is put *through*. Well, I have learned my lesson, I hardly need tell you. *Mind your pockets.*"

As if to emphasise, he tugs out the linings of his trouser pockets, then tucks them back in and leans toward the sea and laughs like a thousand handbells. So silvery a sound even the gulls seem to pause in their lonely circuits.

"Dear Lord Alfred, I hope you won't find the question impertinent, but did Oscar pay the one hundred pounds?"

"Do you know, I'm not at all sure. I mean to say that when a fellow flings himself from a burning building, he doesn't always inquire as to who is there to catch him on the way down."

"That sounds rather serious. A burning building."

"Oh, it is only self-dramatization. Another of my failings. You'll be able to catechise them all before too long."

"Well then," she says, "I have only until tomorrow to make my report."

"So you do," he says.

With that, the minutest of changes comes upon them. It has something to do, she later thinks, with the peculiar density of the air at this break between land and water. Lord Alfred, it seems to her, becomes some dissolved element of the atmosphere, only to be reconstituted by the sound of Oscar, bellowing down from the north.

"Dear Bosie! There's a perfectly voluptuous shade of heliotrope."

He makes no nod to her, no formal sign of adieu. She reaches down and gives her right leg two hard rasps, careful not to break the skin. Raising her head, she finds Arthur Clifton travelling toward her.

"I hope Florence is not too chilled," she says.

"She is quite comfortable."

"In that case, what a delightful party we have formed."

He says nothing in reply. Then, as if the words were dribbling from him:

"You're holding up splendidly. Under the circumstances."

She looks at him, then at Lord Alfred, shuffling toward the point where even now Oscar and Cyril wait.

"If you advert to our noble guest," she says, "I admit to his being exotic."

"That he is."

"Did you help him resolve some little matter in Oxford?"

The tiniest sphinctering of muscles along Arthur's right jaw.

"It was at Oscar's request," he says.

"I don't suppose you could enlarge."

"I fear not."

She has already sealed the door to her own inquiry and so is a little startled to feel Arthur's hand resting on the exact patch of forearm where Lord Alfred's hand sat not a minute ago.

"You don't deserve this, Constance."

13

⟨ℭ⟨R⟩⟩

THE ONLY REGRET that Oscar has expressed since coming to Grove Farm is the absence of champagne in Mrs. Balls's cellar. Like a ministering angel, Lord Alfred has smuggled in four bottles of Moët, not to mention three of Bordeaux, nestled as carefully as baby swallows in thatches of straw. "I nicked them out of Kinmount," he explains, as if that were an explanation, and it is left to Constance to wonder if the Marquess of Queensbury has missed them from his private cellars. The wine is suffered to breathe for a half hour before dinner. The champagne, at Mrs. Balls's suggestion, is cooled in the root cellar and brought up after dinner by her grandson, Patrick, whose solemnly handsome face cracks briefly at the sight of a cork bursting toward heaven and the feel of iced lava down his arm.

"Did I not work it right?" he asks.

"My dear fellow," says Lord Alfred, "you need only stand there, and it will be quite all right with me."

With an abashed air, Patrick leaves a second bottle, still corked, on the stone tile, reminds them of the pot of tea still on the hob, "if you've a mind to it," and bids them a hasty goodnight. Without a servant to pour for them, their own hands all too quickly take up the slack. Before she knows it, Constance can feel the Moët disseminating through her, one

capillary to the next. Something similar is happening to the others. Oscar
has tossed off his suit jacket and is leaning with undue pressure against
a post. Lord Alfred, jacketless himself, is stretched like a patient across
the stone tiles, and Florence has quit her folding chair for a cushion, on
which she rests like Lorelei on her rock. The relaxation extends even to
Lady Wilde, who abandons the embroidery tambour she has brought out
and, tugging her shawl more tightly round her, begs to ask what day it is.
Nobody has any clear sense.

"I know what day tomorrow is," says Florence, ostentatiously pouting. "It
is the day Lord Alfred shall leave us. And how very, very sorry we shall be."

Lord Alfred declines to acknowledge the compliment, and the silence
stretches to the point of awkwardness when Oscar sets down his half-
empty glass.

"My dear friends, I am happy to announce a—well, a slight change
of schedule. I have asked Lord Alfred—and, of course, he has most gra-
ciously consented—to stay on for a day or two more upon a rather urgent
and delicate mission."

There is an even longer pause, broken in a kind of inevitable way by
Lady Wilde.

"Of what mission do you speak? And how might its success hinge upon
the exertions of an undergraduate?"

"I have decided to appoint Lord Alfred the English translator for
Salomé."

The name lands in Constance's ear with a sorrowing fall, even as the
third syllable lofts up. *Sa-lo-MAY*. A larkish exercise in French composi-
tion dashed off for Oscar's Parisian friends that would have remained so if
Sarah Bernhardt hadn't demanded a role comparable to Lady Windermere.
"I have already written it," Oscar improvised. "A terrible woman who
enacts *la danse des sept voiles* so that she may see her lover's head served
up on a platter like *rosbif*." At forty-seven, Bernhardt was a touch mature
for King Herod's luscious stepdaughter, but the sound of the Earth's most
radiant voice caressing his lines was all the seduction Oscar needed. At
home, he began sounding off about heraldic frescos and perfume braziers

and pearls falling on crystal discs. Predictably he put off the prosaic task of submitting his script to the Lord Chamberlain's Examiner of Plays, a gentleman named Edward F. S. Pigott ("rhymes with bigot," said Oscar) who pointed out that prevailing censorship laws prohibited the depiction of any Biblical characters in the West End.

Thus, to the barely contained glee of Fleet Street, *Salomé* was cancelled. Oscar, scalded with embarrassment, announced he would decamp to Paris and become a naturalised Frenchman. Instead, he fled to the spa at Bad Homburg, where, according to his letters to Constance, he got up every morning at seven thirty, went to bed every night at ten thirty, and, of course, took the waters. To Constance's ear, it sounded delightfully monastic. From the ashes of *Salomé*, there rose a new play, more promising, taking as its subject a woman tarred by the world's Pigotts. And so to have *A Woman of No Importance* yield pride of place to its predecessor is equivalent in Constance's mind to hearing one's husband murmur the name of a former mistress in his sleep.

Lady Wilde, for her part, absorbs the news as if it were a nasty jolt in a railway undercarriage.

"I fail to follow. Surely the Lord Chancellor won't change his mind about your play simply because it comes clothed in another language."

"If I may . . ." Lord Alfred, still supine, raises an arm like a timid fourth-former. "Oscar believes that Mr. Pigott might take a happier view of the whole production if he could hear it in his native tongue. And thereby learn that all his presumed objections were groundless. . . ."

"Just so," says Oscar, with a faint exhalation. "I did say that."

"Then," says Lady Wilde, "in the spirit of deepest maternal devotion, I must enquire as to whether you have lost your mind. The spectacle of your Salomé ravishing John the Baptist's severed head will be quite as off-putting in any language. In fact, it put me off at least three meals."

"Mamma . . ."

"Tell me, Oscar, did you not conceive the play in English before you set down a word of it in French? Are you now so amnesiac you cannot simply reverse the process?"

"Oh, Mamma, why not ask me to turn back time? The work was fashioned for the French tongue. It needs another writer to call it home."

"Then why not you? I daresay you know English quite as well as anybody and better than most. Now if you wished it to be translated into Italian, I should call down the divine afflatus of my ancestor Dante Alighieri and create *terza rimas* that would make the very cobblestones of Firenze weep. And I should smoke a good deal fewer cigarettes in the bargain."

It is never personal. That has always been Constance's default defence of anything that emerges from Lady Wilde's mouth. Yet there can be no gainsaying that, of all the fingers bared now in the moonlight, Lord Alfred's are the only ones twined round a cigarette and that, of all the cheeks, his are the only ones reddening.

"Well now," he stammers, levering his torso upward. "I do recall—no, I have absolute recall of Oscar saying that a translator requires—a certain amount of archeological *distance* from the original relic. The better to—pry it free of its originating clay. . . ."

"Did he really say that?" asks Lady Wilde. "It sounds like one of his impostors."

"There is the small matter of Bernhardt," says Constance, softly stroking the arm of her folding chair. "She won't do it in English, you know that, Oscar."

"Oh, that's all right. I think if we were to make a rousing success of it in the West End, she'd be more than delighted to bring it to Paris in its original form."

He has forgotten perhaps what Bernhardt herself told reporters at the height of the scandal. *The role is mine. Mr. Oscar Wilde has given it to me, and nobody else can perform it. No, no, no.* But Oscar is too busy warming to the new idea.

"Yes," he declares, "*à la fin de la journée*, Madame Bernhardt will have to admit that we are doing her a positive favor."

Until this time, Arthur Clifton has sat so perfectly still with his pipe that the words seem to sail out of Night itself.

"I think Constance should translate the play."

He draws down another draught of tobacco and adds, in the same businesslike manner: "She knows French better than any of us. German, too, if you're in that market."

Oscar draws his brows back to their original position.

"What an intriguing idea. Of course, my dear wife is so awfully good at . . ."

"Translating articles," she rushes in, half-shamed.

"Such a treasure," smiles Oscar.

"But I expect this is something rather different," she suggests.

"It might just be," allows Oscar.

"Requiring, I don't know, a sort of musical vocabulary."

"That's just it!" says Lord Alfred, jumping to his feet. "I have always said, *Set a poet to catch a poet.*"

"Did you mean that literally?" asks Arthur.

His voice hasn't risen a fraction, but the younger man is nettled enough to take two strides into the night. Oscar, watching, tugs on his Windsor knot, and swallows the rest of his champagne, as if girding himself for speech, only nothing emerges.

"Mightn't Arthur do it?" interjects Florence. "Oh, darling, I'm sure you would carry it off wonderfully. You were a poet, too, you know."

The statement floats, then dies, then is gathered up again like a foundling by Oscar.

"Why, yes, I quite recall! Didn't we publish something of yours, Arthur, in *Woman's World*?"

"It was a rondel," he answers in a smaller voice.

"What's that?" asks Florence.

"A poem in three ever-enlarging stanzas," drawls Oscar. "With a recurring two-line refrain and, blessed angels, how I suck all the joy from it. Arthur, won't you favor us with your example?"

The request is tendered in all innocence, but there is no mistaking the tautening it produces in Arthur's neck.

"I couldn't possibly recall," he says.

"Don't be silly," says Oscar. "A poet remembers everything he's ever written, doesn't he, Bosie? Try to recall, won't you? You published it under a pen name, I think."

Something jars loose in the barrister's eyes.

"Arthur *Marvell*," he muses.

"Marvell," says Constance, lightly chaffed. "The poet I slighted not two days ago. But what possessed you to throw over Clifton, I wonder? "

"I suppose I didn't want to embarrass my father."

"When, in fact . . ." Lord Alfred elongates his limbs like a cat. "That should be one's primary occupation in life. Dear Arthur, won't you favor us with a rendition?"

The barrister takes another drag of his pipe.

"I don't know if it's quite the thing, really."

"Oh, for the love of dead Jesus," says Lady Wilde, suffering her lids to close. "Get it over with."

And still he hesitates, and darts a glance at Constance, and she, without knowing the exact nature of the transaction, smiles back.

"I should like to hear it, Arthur. But only if you want to."

Setting down his champagne flute, Arthur rises on a perfectly vertical axis, squints into the gathering dark and begins.

In the shadow of your eyes
Love lies dreaming,
Softly gleaming,
With a pensive sweet surmise.

"There now, do you see?" declaims Oscar. "*Shadow of your eyes . . . love lies dreaming . . .* This shall be the *burden* of the rondel, soon to reemerge. Go on, Arthur."

The barrister's eyes angle ever so slightly upward, as if scouting for deliverance. The voice grows more burdened.

Will some sterner light arise,
Where now beaming

In the shadow of your eyes
Love lies dreaming?

From Lady Wilde's sagging mouth comes the first vibration of air
against soft palate. "Go on," says Oscar, gently.

With a thousand tragedies
Life is teeming,
Tears are streaming,
While unheeding tears or sighs,
In the shadow of your eyes
Love lies dreaming.

Three stanzas, thinks Constance. *Done and done.* Yet in her relief,
she is late hearing the words, which leave her struggling to say something better than *pretty* or *touching* or—what she's really thinking in the
moment—*valorous.*

"Oh, Arthur," says Florence. "If I didn't know any better, I'd think you
were envisioning *me* the whole time, only we hadn't met, had we, darling?
All the same, it seems almost predestined that we should. The words practically call us forth, don't they?"

"What a charming supposition," says Lord Alfred. "You know, if you're
a very nice wifey-poo, your husband might yet doodle an ode to you in the
margins of his legal briefs. Though I believe he's quite the busy barrister."

"So much sordidness," agrees Arthur, relapsing into his chair. "It quite
saps a fellow."

"Why, there you are! You have met my alliteration with your own.
What more incriminating evidence can there be that your poetical
instincts endure? Mr. *Marvell.*"

Constance will later conclude that the use of the name is less offensive
than the inflection. Something at any rate prompts Oscar to look search-
ingly at the stone tiles that Lord Alfred has lately vacated and to declare,
in his most parliamentary voice: "I don't give a rap if Arthur ever writes

a line of verse again. I consider him the truest of friends, and I consider friendship the highest art of all."

Lord Alfred takes a few more steps in the direction of the moon.

"How, then, do you define friendship?" he calls back.

"As kindness."

"What else?"

"Selflessness. Loyalty."

"Such neutered virtues, Mr. Wilde. What of *eros*? Now that we are scaling the pyramid of Greek love."

"*Are* we scaling? Or are we descending? Dear Bosie, you needn't *always* pollute the air wherever you go."

She wonders at first if Lord Alfred has heard, then watches the palsy of emotion take him, first in the arms, then the head.

"I should never have come here," he hisses. "I should never have submitted to such humiliations. *Oh*," he says. "You are a brute! You are a savage!"

Spittle flying from his mouth, Bosie makes straight for Oscar—Constance already rising in defence—only to be halted by, of all things, his own champagne glass, lodging under his right shoe. In a swell of fury, he snatches the glass and flings it back down on the stone. A cloud of shards flies up as he vanishes into the night.

"Bosie," murmurs Oscar, though Lord Alfred is well beyond hearing. "Don't be like that." He stands there for a space longer, canvassing the night. Then, turning to the rest of the party, he carves a smile into his face. "Oh, my dears, a thousand pardons, but I really think I must see to him, don't you? He might get lost or . . . worse. . . ."

Tooth and claw, remembers Constance, as she watches Oscar's back jogging away. The air still hums, like a telegraph wire, with the old rancor, and the broken glass gleams so luridly in the moonlight that, with a crackle of amazement, Constance thinks: *Melodrama*, breaking into the comedy of Londoners on holiday. Can it be that they have, all of them, wandered into an Oscar Wilde play? Where, despite the author's insistence, something is always happening?

14

"IS ALL WELL?" she asks.

Oscar has turned up, punctual as ever, to bid her goodnight. The only signs of his exertion are the still-damp tufts of hair along his temples and a lingering bouquet of sweat.

"My love," he says, "I am delighted to report that Bosie has regained his senses and wishes to extend his profoundest apologies to all."

"By way of you?"

"I am sure he will be more fulsome tomorrow. He is a child, of course. A perfect child."

No, she thinks. *Cyril* is a child, and now lies slumbering in her bed.

"Did you really give Lord Alfred a hundred pounds?"

"I might have."

"You can't recall?"

"My dear, if I wrote out a cheque of some kind, he was a young man in distress, through no fault of his own."

"No fault of yours, either."

"What do you wish me to say in my defence? Largesse has ever been my weakness, you know that."

She does know it. He will smuggle all the loose change in his pockets to their children when she isn't looking. He will slip a fiver to a beggar in

Swan Walk from the sheer profligate thrill of giving, and didn't Arthur Clifton get half as much again as Lord Alfred? All to stake a wildly unsuitable marriage? If Oscar is ever to get past Saint Peter, this is his best hope.

"I don't care about the money," she says at last.

"What then?"

"I only wonder sometimes what would happen if something went wrong—I mean really desperately wrong—I wonder sometimes if you'd . . ." Something clots above her clavicle. "I wonder if you'd *tell* me or just—leave me to piece it all together—without knowing exactly what I'm piecing—and that would . . ." The clot rises. "That would be so deeply silly, dearest, because you *can* tell me, I can bear nearly anything, it's . . ." She learns now, to her surprise, that she is crying. "It's the not knowing, you see, that leaves one feeling . . ."

He tucks his hand beneath her chin, raises her face toward his.

"My love," he murmurs. "Did you not say yourself, just the other day, that we were happy?"

"I did."

"And were you sincere?"

"I was."

"Then, with the same sincerity, I concur. And if anyone is to blame for this perfectly dire state of bliss, Mrs. Wilde, it is you. No, confess your crime! If you hadn't insisted we come here, I shouldn't have made such progress with the play, I shouldn't have seen the cliffs of Norfolk, I shouldn't be the gloriously rejuvenated specimen you now behold. If I hadn't had the boon of all this fresh air and delightful company—dear friends, dear family—family dearer *still*," he quickly adds, "I should be some anemic, etiolated succubus, feeding off the carrion of last year's press notices. *Instead*, I am . . ." Here he pauses for reconnoitering. "A new man."

15

⚜

It is the best sandcastle anybody has ever attempted, and it is all Oscar's.

To be sure, Cyril is there to ferry over the pails of wet sand. Lord Alfred, no less game in his jacket and knickerbockers, sculpts as needed. Florence baptises the whole business with handfuls of seawater. But it is Oscar, from the foundry of his brain, who draws from each element the long, rambling formation of moats and tunnels and towers and battlements that now rears up in purest reproach to its surroundings. Not a castle so much as a medieval hill town, fortified grain by grain. Only after an hour's worth of corporate labor is he sufficiently sure of the architecture to draw out a handful of lead soldiers, which he tasks Cyril with stationing along the castle walls. It is a production as finished as any by Mr. Beerbohm Tree. (A good thing, too, because Oscar is forsaking Mr. Beerbohm Tree to be here.)

"Mummy!" shouts Cyril. "Can you see?"

"I see very well, and I beg you to take care. If you build any farther, you shall all have to pay Land Tax."

How she loves the comical stiffening of his little spine.

"Milady," he declares. "We shall pay no Land Tax."

"Are you quite sure, milord? Her Majesty will be most grieved to hear this."

"Land Tax?" Oscar writhes upward. "A pox on Land Tax!"

And, for the ensuing seconds, in a sequence she will rehearse until her dying day, father and son dance in the sand, beating their chests in nearly perfect unison. *"A pox on Land Tax! A pox on Land Tax!"* The chant is contagious enough to draw in first Lord Alfred and then Florence. So many disparate elements drawn together, and yet, in this exact moment, Constance finds her husband's eyes resting on hers alone, as though, between them, they have conjured up the whole symphony. Why was she so foolish as to doubt his heart?

In perfect concord, the ocean has grown pacific as a pond: flat white breakers strolling down, strolling out again. A vendor, appearing from nowhere, has supplied their party with folding chairs; a photographer calling himself Herbert Mace has offered to capture their image. ("Some other time," murmurs Constance.) No bathing machine mars the view, and the beach itself is deserted, save for a shrimp man and a calico tom, each hunting, and a pair of Royal Navy sailors, etched against the laziest of morning suns. The indolence extends even to Arthur Clifton, who has cast off his shoes and socks and rolled up his trousers and waded into the chilly morning water.

"You don't think he'll catch cold?" asks Florence, dragging her chair in Constance's direction.

"No."

"What of sunstroke?"

Constance smiles, for this is the specter she has always raised with her children.

"Arthur strikes me as an entirely sturdy specimen," she says.

"Not like Lord Alfred, though."

"Lord Alfred?"

"Why, yes, he told me just this morning he was a perfect beast in the Oxford cross-country. Won the mile handicap, whatever that is, and the two miles scratch, I'm not sure what that is, either, but it all sounds fearfully impressive."

"Doesn't it?"

"He injured his knee, or else he should probably be dashing all over Norfolk."

And perhaps he means to make good on that promise, for, after frowning down at the hill town, Lord Alfred turns at once and strikes north. Fully at ease, his boater at a slight rake, his gait so unhurried he doesn't seem to register that his path, like the dashes on a treasure map, converges on the X of the two sailors. Young men themselves, or so they seem from a distance, gazing not at sea (which has long ago lost its charms, surely) but sky. As Lord Alfred approaches them, he raises his hand in greeting and the sailors answer in kind. Soon, by some miracle, they are standing in perfect propinquity, jawing like ploughmen over lunch.

"How charming he is," says Florence. "So natural with everyone he meets."

In her more fanciful moments, Constance believes herself gifted with presentiment, but it fails her here. She sees the taller of the sailors cock an ear and lean in Lord Alfred's direction, as if asking him to repeat something. Lord Alfred obliges. In the next instant, the sailor drives a palm straight into his chest.

Constance will later recall how cleanly, how purely the son of Queensbury falls, as if he grasps, at some Newtonian level, that the more he surrenders to the laws of physics, the less harm they will wreak. Even as his assailants stroll back down the beach, he is already on his feet, reaching for his hat. The whole affair has happened so quickly and with so little consequence that Constance pauses briefly to interrogate her senses, only to hear Florence Clifton bray for all to hear:

"Help! Lord Alfred is injured!"

Oscar executes a heavy twirl in the sand and squints at his friend's oncoming figure.

"Dear boy," he calls. "Are you all right?"

"Oh, quite!"

By way of reassurance, Lord Alfred jogs the rest of the way there and stands, lightly abashed, as Oscar brushes the grit from his coat and trousers.

"Did they threaten you?" asks Constance.

He shakes his head lightly.

"Or rob you?"

"No, more's the pity."

"But I don't understand. Why would they—"

"Oh, it's probably best not to enquire," says Oscar.

"Not to enquire?" cries Florence, bunching her hands into fists. "They took the most grotesque liberties with our dear friend here! By rights, we should send for the police."

She is, of course, a creature of London, where, no matter the hour, a woman of a certain station may hope to find a policeman somewhere swinging his lantern. In Norfolk, the nearest agent of justice might be half a day's ride.

"All things considered," says Oscar, with an indulgent smile, "I'd say our friend has come out of this rather well."

"Rather *well*?" says Florence. "He might have been seriously harmed."

"And it would serve him right, too! Naughty boy."

The notes won't quite cohere for Constance. Are they to rage? Mourn? Laugh?

"Really," declares Lord Alfred, "I don't even know what happened. It was just the shock of the thing. I'm quite sure I haven't sustained anything lasting. All the same, I wonder if a little lie-down might do me good."

Florence has already scouted just the space: a cave etched deeply enough into the rock face to keep a reclining man hidden from any passing eye. "You must take care," she croons, draping a sea-dampened handkerchief across Lord Alfred's brow. "Those villains might yet come back for more mischief. It is so very very lawless here."

From his bed of sand, he reaches up with a white hand and a beatific smile. "Are you quite certain your last name isn't Nightingale?"

"Oh . . ."

"You are better than nightingale, you are winged seraph."

"She is indeed," affirms Oscar. "And now, dear Florence, having been vaulted above the cherubim, will you allow a mere mortal to watch over our patient?"

"But it's so little trouble," she protests.

"Even less for me. And, you know, with all these bad men abroad, I shouldn't want my wife to be left on her own."

Constance inspects his face for signs of irony and is rewarded with the lightest of winks.

"Come," she says, resting a hand on Florence's shoulder. "I'll need you to hold my hand when I go in the water. I become quite the old dowager whenever I leave land."

This last part is true. Even with the traction of her bathing slippers, even with the water pausing genteelly at her knees, the tide now is coming with more persuasion, and as the sea bottom dissolves round her ankles and the cold water tugs at her stockings, she can feel the sensation once more draining from her right leg. It seems only a matter of time before it gives way utterly. With a light gasp, she tightens her grip on Florence's hand, but the other woman is too busy watching her husband, pacing the shore in slow, abstracted segments.

"Arthur doesn't seem the least concerned," she says at last.

"About what?"

"Lord Alfred."

"Why, I'm sure he just assumes—as do I myself—that everything is well in hand."

"But we don't know that, do we?"

Constance squints back in the direction of the cave, but there is nothing to see. Restless, her eye follows the line of the surf south to where an oystercatcher stands jabbing its orange beak into the black crevice of a mussel. Striking again and again in lancet thrusts, until at last the shell croaks open. The bird drags out its prize, raises it briefly to the heavens, and swallows it down in a single pulse.

"Dear Florence," she says. "Perhaps we *should* go back."

She finds Cyril sitting disconsolately in his chair, his head on his knees.

"What's wrong, my dove?"

"I'm not your dove. I'm a little man."

"Of course you are. Is there something troubling your manhood this fine morning?"

When he declines to answer, she drags over her chair and waits him out.

"I'd have pushed him right back," he says.

"Pushed whom?"

"That ruddy old sailor. I'd have punched him if he'd done that to me."

"You would have done nothing of the sort. A gentleman must always . . ." She falters here. "Rise above his own bestial instincts."

And falters again. What is this code she speaks of? Surely not one the Marquess of Queensbury would approve of. From her chair, she takes an idle survey of the shoreline—what time is it, anyway?—how soon may they go back?—then, with a start, sees Oscar's sandcastle, sinking with no great protest beneath an influx of water. Moats have swollen into lakes. The barbican and portcullis sag drunkenly. This is the fate of every such castle, she knows, and she can't say why this should be any different, only she is rising from her chair (with no small difficulty) and staggering in the direction of Lord Alfred's cave, for surely Oscar will wish to say farewell to this most evanescent of his creations. The sand slows her progress enough that, by the time she has reached the cave's mouth, the younger man's voice is already sailing toward her.

". . . and I looked down, as how could I help, and there on his right forearm was a tattoo of Buffalo Bill—at least that's who I took it to be—and on his left, a quite bosomy mermaid in the form of an anchor. And coursing *through* her, Oscar, in the most divinely obscene fashion, his actual *vein*, like a cobalt river. Need I tell you I got the shivers?"

On the next freight of air comes Oscar's reply.

"I'm getting shivers now, just thinking."

She knows it's the sort of conversation that surely could be interrupted at no cost to anyone. What restrains her, then? Only, perhaps, the conviction, growing with each second, that she was not meant to hear it. At a loss, she wheels slowly round and finds Cyril grimly plucking the lead soldiers from their castle battlements, bearing each one to safety as the sea surges round.

16

CONSTANCE HAS ALWAYS been told there is nothing so invigorating as sea air—she has repeated the same bromide to her sons—yet, from the time she quits the beach that morning, she toggles between sleep and waking and watches in utter lassitude as the others bowl and play lawn tennis. She toys with a nap without having the motive force to embrace it. That evening, Mrs. Balls's dinner of Brancaster mussels drops into her stomach like lead shot, and as they adjourn once more to the back terrace, the night air, still sultry, coupled with the latest magnum of Lord Alfred's champagne, makes her that much drowsier. From her litter of seat cushions, she only half-listens to the talk on each side of her and has nearly resolved to retire when Lord Alfred, extending his legs in a perfect hypotenuse to the right angle of his chair, says:

"Dear Mrs. Wilde. Won't you tell us how you and Oscar met?"

"Oh," she says, with all the vagueness she feels. "How we met."

"Do tell!" cries Florence from her own bed of cushions.

For a few more moments she holds off, waiting for Oscar to provide a reprieve, and then hears the voice of Lady Wilde, emanating like a Ptolemaic curse from her wrapping of mufflers.

"I don't know why nobody thinks to ask me. Was I not there? Had I not eyes and ears? Oscar was visiting me in Dublin—this was May of eighty-one, as sure as I breathe—and, by way of distraction, I took him one afternoon to call on my dear friend Mrs. Atkinson in Ely Place. Unbeknownst to us both, Mrs. Atkinson had invited her enchanting granddaughter to stay with her. No further cunning was needed. Oscar and Constance took to each other like multiplication and division, and as we were leaving, he whispered in my ear. *By the by, Mamma, I think of marrying that girl.*"

"Ah," says Florence, with a trailing sigh. "How very very dear. But *you*, Constance, what did you think?"

She gives each temple a slow rub.

"I suppose I only thought . . ."

"Yes?"

"How natural he was."

"Natural."

"I mean as opposed to his public self."

"By that," interposes Oscar, "you are to infer that poor Constance had already been dragged to one or two of my lectures."

"Not at all dragged. But, yes, I was expecting *that* fellow, with the— the lily and the extravagant cadences, and this one was not *that* one. No," she corrects herself at once. "They *both* of them spoke better than any man I'd ever met."

"Can you fail to see?" cries Lady Wilde. "It was true love from the start, only it could not run smooth. Oscar had to travel to America for a lecture tour of three months, which, as cough graduates to croup . . ."

"Mamma . . ."

". . . turned into a year. Not long after, he was obliged to *return* to those precincts for the premiere of—what was that infernal play of yours, Oscar?"

"*Vera; or, The Nihilists.*"

"Yes, a comma *and* a semicolon. At least you had the good sense to write that one in English. Not that anybody understood it."

"I beg to differ," he says, rearing up from his chair. "I sent that charming granddaughter of Mrs. Atkinson a privately printed copy and received her review in the next post."

"Oof," says Constance, smiling in spite of herself.

"Dear Mr. Wilde. I like the impassioned parts, but some of the minor dialogues strike me as being slightly halting or strained."

"How like him to remember the one line of criticism and omit all the heapings of praise."

"I have also left out the true crucible of our disagreement, which has never been resolved and I hope never shall."

"And what is that?" asks Lord Alfred.

"If I may speak for us both, my wife has always held there can be no art without morality."

"Just so," she answers.

"Whereas I have always kept those two dodgy specimens in separate rooms and forbidden them to speak. To me, a work of art has no more moral value than a flower. A book is neither moral nor immoral, it is only well written or badly written."

So this is all it takes to rouse her: the memory of a fond old argument. Rearing up from her cushions, she declares, in a fuller voice:

"Need I remind you, Mr. Wilde, that *Dorian Gray* has a moral?"

"Which is its weakness, my love. A bit of rawhide thrown to the hounds of commerce. I repent of it every day of my life."

"Whereas I contend . . ." She rises with no great difficulty and advances smilingly on him. *"I* contend that, absent any moral, *Dorian Gray* would be precisely the exercise in sensation that its critics—not to mention all the friends who cut us in the wake of its publication—claimed it to be."

"Wrongly."

"Of course wrongly." Her hands rub sparks into each other. "Whether through commerce or art, you divined that, once an author enters his character into a Faustian bargain, he must let the devil come a-knocking at the eleventh hour."

"Unless the whole point is that there is no devil. Just one's self."

She is the only listener tutored enough to hear the voice, naturally so musical, flattening into the most tranquil of lines. Always the portent of some incipient sadness, and she is already thinking how to comfort him when, from behind, she hears Lord Alfred say:

"Oh, my eye, *fin de siècle*, and we still speak of devils."

With a suddenness her body can't quite contain, she rounds.

"Dear Lord Alfred, when I speak of the devil—when I speak of *morality*—I do not invoke ancient gods or demons. I mean only that the things that people do to each other—*with* each other—matter. On the page as in life. Do you disagree? If so, on what grounds?"

The hypotenuse of his legs bends into right angles.

"Dear Mrs. Wilde, I shall respectfully decline to engage further."

"How very chivalrous. Yet, not fifteen minutes ago, to avail yourself of a cigarette, you plunged your hand into my husband's trousers pocket. Was that *chivalrous*, Lord Alfred?"

"Constance . . ."

"Was that the act of a *translator*, in which case I am longing to know what was being translated. Or was it not a gesture of the most revolting intimacy? Pray enlighten me. *Do* enlighten me."

The ferocity quells even her. She turns and finds every eye trained her way, as though she has been publicly sick.

"Mrs. Wilde," says Lord Alfred. "I meant nothing by it."

"He was only saving a step," protests Oscar.

"Dearest Constance," says Florence. "Don't be cross."

The only mute parties are Arthur, standing with his usual back to the congregation, and Lady Wilde, sealing herself in her sarcophagus. How lonely it is, of a sudden. How sharply the night air prickles.

"I pray you will all pardon me," she says at last. "I must have taken a bit too much sun this morning."

"Early to bed," suggests Oscar.

"Just the thing," says Florence.

With a force that surprises every onlooker, Lady Wilde prises herself from her rattan throne.

"Come, Constance. Let us go in together."

It is the same pilgrimage they have taken every night, the pair of them, only when they pause outside the older woman's door, Lady Wilde leans in and murmurs:

"My dear, you needn't worry."

"Worry?"

"He is only infatuated, and it can't possibly last. Any more than Florrie Balcombe lasted, or that Langtry creature. Oscar is a butterfly, we all know that, and he must flap his wings, and the result is only air."

"You speak of infatuation but—"

"Just remember that you are named Constance for a reason. You will *be* here, my dear, when the other pretenders have fallen away. Now if you'll excuse me, I must go commune with Sir William's spirit. He gets *so* tetchy when I forget."

17

⁓

HER DREAMS IN the early hours of night are too jumbled for classing. A bosomy mermaid. A cartwheel Gainsborough hat. A painted stork that leaves its Japanese fan to fly back home. Picking berries with Cousin Stanhope. Watching Cousin Stanhope sink beneath the North Sea. Watching a lead soldier dance on Cousin Stanhope's head. Nothing rises clear, and she is weary enough of the clangor that the pattering on her bedroom door, which registers at first as squirrels in a great oak, begins to feel like the thread she has been seeking the whole while. Grasping it, she hauls herself toward waking and hears a man's voice, stage-whispering from the other side.

"*Constance . . .*"

Her first instinct is to cast an eye toward Cyril, but his sleep is as just as ever.

"One moment," she calls back in a strangled voice.

She slips out of bed, draws the wrapper over her nightgown, and tugs the door open a few inches. There stands Arthur Clifton, still in his lounge suit.

"What o'clock is it?" she asks, squinting into the light of his lantern.

"I can't precisely say. I heard the fourth chime, but I don't know that I heard the double chime."

"Has anything happened?"

"Florence is gone."

Grimacing, Constance takes a step into the hallway, closes the door after her.

"What do you mean gone?"

"We had a row."

"Another."

"A bit worse than the others."

"Mm."

"It got to the point—and I don't altogether blame her—where she announced that she couldn't bear to look upon me another second, and I believe I may have uttered something of the same character, and off she went, and I—I *presumed* she was stalking the hallways in a fury, which is what I should have done, but then I passed on to the next speculation, which was that she had found somewhere to retire to—the better to gain philosophical distance—but here now it has been two hours—more than that—and she is not to be found anywhere."

This is more language than she has ever heard Arthur expel in a single stream.

"She's not in any room," she ventures, palming up her eyelids.

"Not as I have discovered."

"Then she must be out of doors."

"My thoughts exactly."

"Then," she says, dragging the skin back from her temples, "you wish me to venture out into the night for the sole purpose . . ."

"The *joint* purpose . . ."

". . . the *joint* purpose of locating your absconded wife."

"I was on the verge of editing your remark further and realised there was no point. Won't you please, Constance? I daren't ask anybody else."

And, indeed, if she were to canvass the house's other occupants—Oscar, Lord Alfred, Lady Wilde—who better to answer?

"Let me get my shawl," she mutters. "And my slippers."

They confer briefly in the hall, where it is decided that Arthur will forge out from the back, Constance from the front. Whatever befalls, they will reconnoiter within fifteen minutes. "Do take care," he suggests. With no good grace, she drives her candle stump into the mouth of an empty champagne bottle. Dragging open the front door, she is met by something that looks remarkably like daylight. She is not sure she has even seen the landscape that now rolls out before her, until, with a start, she realises that the harvest moon has risen over Norfolk. How was it able to sneak up on her? To her eyes, the night is as light as day. The primroses glower. The apples spangle. From somewhere in the radiance a sound emerges. Lofting her champagne-candle, Constance follows a gravel path toward a hammock, rocking dreamily in the night breeze. In it reclines Florence Clifton, still clothed in her evening gown. At sight of Constance's candle, she sits up and, in a voice of summery brightness, calls out.

"Good evening!"

"And to you," says Constance, smiling softly. "Though I wonder if *Good morning* might be more to the point. It being closer to dawn."

"Is it? I've quite lost track. Dear me, where are my manners?" She pats the patch of canvas alongside her. "There's room for two."

"Well, I don't . . . I'm not sure . . ."

Constance cannot choose this moment to say she has always hated hammocks, precisely for the disequilibrium into which she is now inserted. Two bodies, deprived of axis, first floundering and then, before they know it, *fusing* at the shoulder, incapable of further movement. It is closer than Constance has ever been to Florence or indeed the bulk of her relations. She stares down at her slippered feet. She smiles tightly.

"Your husband is perfectly sick about you," she says.

"So he sent you, did he?"

"Well, yes, left to my own devices, I don't normally stagger about like Lady Macbeth, but it's a lovely night, and I don't blame you for getting your fill."

"I went to his room."

Constance angles her gaze back to the house.

"Whose?"

"Lord Alfred's."

"I must ask you on what earthly grounds."

"Do you know I can't even recall? It had something to do with spiting Arthur and something to do with—well, if you'd seen the way Lord Alfred looked at me on the beach this morning."

"And how was that, exactly?"

"As if he were a soul marooned in a great desperate lonely sea, requiring only a rescuer. It's funny, in childhood stories, it's always the man who rescues the woman, isn't it? But with Lord Alfred, everything seems *reversed* in a funny sort of way."

"And did you rescue him?" asks Constance.

"I can't say. I mean, he didn't appear to know why I'd come. *Oh, what a lark,* he said, *draw up a chair.* I made a point of saying my husband didn't know where I was. He said, *Not to worry, we'll just keep our voices low. Why,* he said, *it's like being back at Winchester.* As though I've ever been to Winchester."

Constance smiles. "Perhaps he didn't grasp the sacrifice you were prepared to make in behalf of his marooned soul."

"I sat there on that hard settle, and he sat there propped up in bed like a little dauphin. Oh, you mustn't think I'm boasting, Constance . . ."

"I would never."

". . . but, for most of my life, men—the garden-variety sort, I mean—when they look at me, they have but the one thing in mind, and everything else, good or ill, comes of that."

"I can imagine."

"Lord Alfred had nothing at all in mind, at least none I could make out. He just wanted to talk."

"About what?"

"Himself."

"Ah," answers Constance, with a light laugh. "So he is a man after all."

"He told me of some lady he'd met in the south of France while he was still a lad. A divorced countess. He said she was his guide into the Hymeneal mysteries, whatever that means. Only she was such a bother, and she *would* keep after him, and I kept waiting for him to explain what this countess had to do with me, and I still haven't cottoned on for he never so much as breathed at me. He even had a *cobweb*, Constance, hanging from his ear like an icicle. I tugged at it, and he looked altogether baffled, as if he didn't know where he'd come by it."

"Perhaps Mrs. Balls needs to dust more."

And feels, in the next moment, a stab of disloyalty toward the woman who has been arranging their lives these past days and nights without a note of complaint.

"At least," Constance rejoins in a brighter tone, "you have preserved your honor."

"I wish I could say as much for my pride. I sat there, listening and nodding as one does with men, you know. Then, after half an hour, I stopped listening. After another half hour, I wandered out. I don't know that I bothered to excuse myself or that he noticed I was gone. It was all so indecently decent."

She falls then into a trough of silence so deep Constance is moved to reach for her hand.

"My dear, it's just as well it ended as it did. You have a husband who loves you."

"Does he?"

"I'm sure of it."

"But for how long?"

"Long as love lasts."

"That's just it, Constance. I've seen enough of passion to know it's not the sort of thing a girl can bank her future on. She *will* grow old."

"As will we all."

"Yes, but when *you* get old—really old, I mean—you'll still have your salons and your causes and your children. What will I have? Tell me a painter who employs a female model past the age of twenty-three. And don't speak to me of Mrs. Langtry; she is famous. The point is I'm not famous, and I'm not clever, and I don't know any languages, I'm not some stinky old poetess like Lady Wilde, and, judging by tonight's shambles, I'm not even a seductress. I'm just a chain of canvases—none of which I even own—and once that's done, then what?"

"Then Arthur."

She proposes it only neutrally, provisionally, but, in reply, Florence's head bumps softly against her temple.

"Then Arthur."

The night gathers round them like a surplice. Two fields away, the sea is moaning, and the revolving lamp on the lighthouse is carving paths of gold across the moon's gold. Over their heads, a bat sketches spirals.

"You know," says Constance, "it's a funny thing. When a woman first takes a husband, she doesn't necessarily know why. She tells herself it's about love or security—solace in life's journey. She is almost always wrong. Or else Time makes her wrong. At some juncture, then, she just has to make a new calibration and hope she gets it right the second time. That's why I really quite envy you and Arthur. You're doing *all* your recalibrating now and getting it straight out of your system."

"Do you really think so?"

"I do."

For some minutes more they sit, shoulder to shoulder. Then, with a pair of grunts, Constance extricates herself from the hammock. Stares at the house, bathed in moonlight. Glances back at her companion, bathed in shadow.

"Would you like to come inside?"

"Not now," says Florence. "But I will."

18

THE AGREED-UPON FIFTEEN minutes have long since come and gone, but Arthur is still in his appointed position in the rear terrace. Indeed, there is something about his stance that suggests he has been waiting there for all time, straight as a Scots pine.

"Any news?" he asks in the flattest of voices.

"I am happy to report that no rivers need be dredged for your bride's body."

"You mean you found her?"

"Intact and unmolested and promising to return before sunrise."

"That is something."

"Yes, it is."

"I am wondering what you consider the best course under the circumstances. Shall I wait for her?"

"I don't expect she'll be ill-disposed to see you."

He inspects her rather solemnly—for signs of deceit?—then takes her hand in his and says in an even flatter voice:

"I am so eternally grateful."

"Oh, dear Arthur, it's the very least a friend can—"

Next second, he is circling his arm round her waist, his face is descending, his eyelashes are folding down, his lips parting, all of it happening so synchronously that the air is forced back down her throat. For some time after, they stand regarding each other with an air of honest speculation. Then *her* lips drive toward his. So many sensations. The hairs of his moustache—she can very nearly count them—the tang of tobacco on his lips. But then a bubble comes rising up from inside her, and, once it has cleared their conjoined mouths, it has revealed itself as laughter. Vast and incontinent, doubling her over as effectually as a punch. In her weakened state, she can only drop into the nearest chair, fingering away every last tear from her eye.

"I am so sorry, Arthur."

"No," he answers, miserably. "I am the one who should apologise. I can offer no defence."

"You needn't."

"Except that I've been longing to kiss you for as long as I've known you."

How sad mirth becomes when it is no longer mirth. Her mouth opens, then closes, then opens again.

"Long as that," she says.

"Plainly, I have repulsed you."

"To the contrary, I am merely . . ."

Surprised, she wants to say, and yet as her mind speeds back down the chain of their encounters, a thread winks into view.

Always Arthur, that's how she has always thought of him. Always smiling when he sees her. Always asking if she wants another glass. Always laughing louder than anyone at something she's said. Wishing other women had as good a head on their shoulders. Lamenting that Oscar should be the lucky one, why is Oscar always the lucky one. Plumping for her as the best possible English translator for *Salomé* when everyone knows she isn't. Yes, she thinks, he has been speaking all along in cipher, and she has only now been granted the key, and it opens in her a whole frontier of possibility.

"You must excuse me," she says at last. "It has been a span of years since somebody was foolish on my account, and yours is the sort of overture that—well, when I was a girl, it used to make me quite wretched—I never knew what to do—and now, to my astonishment, I find I quite miss the overture. I miss even the not knowing what to do. Though I don't, in this moment, know what to do."

"You might begin by reproaching me."

"Surely it's far too late in the evening for that. I've just enough strength left to question your timing."

"There is never a good moment."

"Yes, but might we agree that your honeymoon is rather spectacularly bad? As moments go? She wants you to love her, Arthur."

"As do I."

"Then why can you not find your way there? What is stopping you?"

"You."

So she was wrong, after all. A man's declaration still draws down the old wretchedness, and it is indissoluble from her present tiredness, and yet, behind it, something warms its way through. She hears him say:

"You don't even know how beautiful you are, do you?"

"Arthur, please."

"What?"

"At my age."

"Don't be absurd, you are hardly in your thirties."

"A little more than hardly. And old enough to have ceased picturing myself altogether. It is why I hate both mirrors and photographs, they are equally explicit. But, in reply to your original query, I will tell you that compliments, *gorgeous* compliments, rain down on me every day of my life. I am blessed with a husband who delights in telling me how well I look without the slightest provocation, who rejoices in picking out the most advantageous frocks, who, whenever he is called out of town, sends me flowers with the most lyrical of inscriptions for no reason at all except the joy of it. Indeed, I might say his *extraordinary* attentiveness is one of the many reasons I cherish him."

"I am not speaking of inscriptions or flowers."

"What then?"

"I am talking about what happens—what *should* happen—between a man and woman when they are alone together."

She can only bow her head over her lap and draw a pair of long breaths, and even then, it is with the sense of stepping through alien terrain that she inches her way back.

"Do you not consider that rather a private enquiry?"

"I do."

"Then, at the risk of exhibiting tact and taste, I decline to answer."

"You draw down the veil?"

"Yes."

"And yet I see you through it. I know what is in you."

"*Do* you? Perhaps it was a mistake for you to come here. It seems to me no bridegroom can oscillate between two brides without experiencing certain symptoms of vertigo."

"And what if he finds a clear head on the other side?"

"There is only one way clear. Every *other* way . . ."

She stops, or rather is stopped by her own voice.

"Every other way is muddle, you know that."

"Constance."

He kneels now. Folds out his hands in a mute entreaty.

"There is muddle on every side of us. There is horror. You feel it, don't you?"

No, she would dearly like to say, *I feel only comedy*. For what other genre could be more suited to the moment? But from the wells of her mind buds forth every unsavory image. Lord Alfred in the sand, and blue veins, and bosomy mermaids, and Blackie the rabbit, deader with each hour, and a cigarette filched from a man's pockets, and it is with the thought of driving them all away that she rises at once to her feet.

"Dear Mr. Clifton, I am no solicitor, but I believe I have fulfilled my contract with you to the letter. Your wife—*your wife*—waits for you. You cannot miss her. She is in a hammock, no more than a hundred paces off, and looking, even in her deepest distress, as pretty as a girl possibly could and only longing to hear that she is something other. Will you not go to her?"

19

꧁

SOMEWHERE JUST BEFORE the fourth strike of the hallway clock, she is back in her own bed, with the sense, unique to her, that her own child should not be lying next to her, should not have his flesh in the same neighborhood as hers, which simmers now with tobacco . . . moustache hairs . . .

But Cyril slumbers on while she crackles with sleep's opposite. Even her skin refuses to settle. Touch it, it touches back. Is she simply surrendering to the farce of the last two hours? Or is it the unexpected plot event of being desired?

You don't even know how beautiful you are. . . .

Constance can remember attending a Royal Academy exhibition years ago and overhearing some porcine esthete snarl to his companion: "Where does Rossetti even find these dream-models of his? In some Plutonian underworld? All that alabaster skin and pomegranate lips and snaking coils of chestnut hair. Ripest erotic fantasy, if you ask me." He turned round then and, at first sight of Constance, his plump face fell. "Oh, I'm terribly sorry, miss," he said. "I didn't mean anything by it, of *course.*" With every sputtering syllable, he grew redder. "I pray you'll pardon me. . . ." He began to lurch away, swerving his head back at intervals to gauge the evidence of his own senses. By the time he'd stumbled out of the gallery, she was as red as he, though strictly from confusion. It was her brother who had to explain that she, Constance Lloyd of Sussex Gardens, looked exactly like a pre-Raphaelite maiden, magically transposed from her canvas. It was the first time she made any connection between herself and a work of art and the first time she felt the helplessness of a man's desire, for it seemed to her that the haste with which he left the room was in direct ratio to his wishing to remain. Did he really not trust himself in her presence? Was her very pout, the character flaw for which her mother had chided her from earliest memory, now to be configured as power? Did other women possess it? What did they do with it?

With Oscar, those questions never needed to be answered, and what a relief she found it. He admired her in *all* her parts, and that was all she needed to know, and so she gradually tucked away thoughts of Eros into the same cupboard where she kept her other outmoded ideas. And tonight, Arthur Clifton—of all contenders!—has dragged them out again, and the disorienting thrill of being at Desire's core comes straight back, and she wonders at how long she has passed through this vale of tears without it.

Just before dawn, Cyril jabs her with his elbow and mutters crossly: "Stop giggling, Mummy."

20

By DAWN, SLEEP has utterly claimed her and, with the curtains still drawn, there is precious little morning sun to break her reverie, so she sleeps on. From time to time, an aperture of consciousness breaks open, and she wonders if she should be tending to her guests, but the mere thought overpowers her. At some interval, she thinks she hears Cyril's fretful voice. "Mummy's tired." But to whom is he speaking? Her eyelashes tremble back into stillness, and virtually every tether to earth has been loosed when a firm, gentle hand rouses her.

"Ma'am . . ."

Prying her lids apart, she beholds Mrs. Balls.

"Sorry to wake you, ma'am, but the Cliftons are wanting to say goodbye."

"Say goodbye," she mumbles. "What o'clock is it?"

"Just past noon, mum."

"So I haven't . . ."

I haven't lost the whole day. For she can feel it already sliding through her fingers.

"I don't . . . why are they saying goodbye?"

"They're leaving, ma'am."

"Leaving."

"Yes, this very minute. But they say they're happy to wait on you."

Light now extends a tongue at every angle. The doorway, the floor, the ceiling, the crevices of the blinds. Summer, demanding its reckoning. She sits up in bed, takes into account her loosened hair, resting on her forearm.

"Will you tell them I'll be down presently?"

"Yes, mum."

Reaching once more for her wrapper, she realises she is putting on the same costume she wore last night. Yet what a difference a few hours have wrought. When she opens the front door, a harvest sun greets her. Making a visor of her hand, she turns and finds a pony trap, loaded with luggage, and there, standing in the cinder track, the Cliftons. Entirely new beings, freshly toileted and clothed. How bedraggled she must look in comparison—a creature of shuttered rooms—yet Florence comes straight toward her, extending a pair of gloved hands.

"My dear Constance, how shall we ever repay you?"

"Oh, there's . . ."

The sun forces her once more to seal her eyes, then open them again by degrees.

"Dear me," she says at last. "What a lie-abed I've been."

"And who has better earned the right?"

"I didn't . . ."

"Yes?"

"I didn't quite appreciate that you were leaving today."

"Neither did we!" cries Florence. "But we woke up this morning and looked at each other, and we said, practically in the same breath, *Well now, let's get on with it.* Didn't we say that, Arthur?"

"Something to that effect."

"And do you remember what I said? I said, *Constance will be glad to see the back of us!* Ha ha! I was joking, of course, you've been the most marvelous hostess, hasn't she, Arthur? And you *will* give our best to Oscar, won't you?"

"Of course," she says, taking a step back into the shade. "He'll be so sorry to have missed you. And once you are both *settled*—I mean in your lodgings—you really must come see us in Tite Street. You are . . ." She blinks at them both. "You are both most welcome."

"Oh, you haven't got rid of *us*." Florence impulsively wraps an arm round Constance's shoulder and draws her close and whispers, "I shall never forget what you've done."

What I've . . .

Constance's eyes travel from the bride to the bridegroom, who is looking at her now as from a distant corridor of memory.

"It was no trouble," she murmurs.

The trap driver taps his whip against his boot. The pony whisks at flies with its tail, then lets out two arpeggiated whinnies.

"Well now," she says. "We can't have you missing your train. Pleasant trip."

In the next breath, Arthur is handing his wife into the carriage and climbing in after her. He glances back down at Constance, doffs his hat and says, in the pleasantest of tones:

"Goodbye."

"Goodbye," she says.

She watches them the whole way: Florence's head resting like a tulip on her husband's shoulder. *She'll be glad to see the back of us.* Twelve hours ago, that would have been true. Now? It is just as Oscar always says: When the Gods wish to punish us, they answer our prayers.

She is still watching long after the trap has slipped over the fern-covered down. In her own mind, she has herself disappeared, just a trace, and is the more startled to find Cyril, awkwardly braced in the front doorway.

"Oh, darling," she says. "Good morning. Or good afternoon as applicable. Is Pappa off to the links again?"

Cyril nods.

"With Lord Alfred, I expect."

He nods.

"And what have you been up to all morning?"

He shrugs.

"Is Lovebird a trifle bored?"

"I'm *not* bored, I was just wanting to show you something."

"Oh, darling, might it wait a bit? Mummy's had a long night, and she's still rather the worse for it. After tea, perhaps?"

Cyril nods, but it is the second's pause before the nod that stays with her.

"Is it far?" she asks in a heavier voice.

"Just to the attic."

Here he reaches for a candle, that is the first ominous sign. Another: the low door which he must drag from its jamb and which leads up a steep flight of plank-stairs, lacking any rail. She is stooped from the moment she enters the space and can't quite uncoil even when she is standing in the attic itself, breathing not just the still, close air but the concentrated heat of an entire summer's afternoons: dust and pollen and manure and horse sweat and leather. The sunlight, coursing through a single dormer window, calls up a desultory collection of old trunks and rush-baskets and chicken coops and a defunct butter churn and a chopping block and an agricultural breeder's calendar and a two-humped settee missing most of its stuffing. There is none of the cleanliness and cheerful order that Mrs. Balls has imposed in all the other rooms. It is almost as if the house comes here to escape her.

"Darling," says Constance, reaching for his candle. "What on earth possessed you to come all the way up here?"

"I thought I might be able to see Blackie."

Blackie. The name has dropped so far from her memory she must dive after it.

"It took a bit, Mummy, but my eyes got used to the dark, and it was then I noticed this rope hanging from the ceiling. Do you see it now?"

"Yes."

"I thought at first it was a noose, which gave me no end of shivers, but it's too small to fit a head in, isn't it?"

"I should say."

"So then I wondered if it was for *yanking* on so then I . . ."

She is awaiting more exposition, but, as if to demonstrate the limits of language, he flings his small frame straight at the rope. His white hands grip tight and, with a gasp, she watches the ceiling groan and yawn open.

Two seconds later, with a clatter of hinges, a sectioned ladder has unfolded itself into a magic causeway. At its base, stands Cyril, grinning.

"Do you see, Mummy?"

"Why, how extraordinarily clever of you, darling. I wonder what can possibly be up there. More attic?"

"You mean you don't want to climb up and see?"

"Certainly not."

"That's how I was, too," he says, rather complacently. "I was being quite the cowardly custard, but sometimes a chap must dare what comes."

"He certainly must."

"So I climbed right up and—why, it's just a wee room! *All* covered in dust. Not a spook to see anywhere, just the one bed."

"Bed?"

"Not even a bed, Mummy, just a mattress. Straw. No pillow, no sheet."

"How very curious. Mrs. Balls never made mention of it."

"That's just it, you see! It's a secret room. You can't even see it from outside. Pappa said it must be a priest's hole."

Priest's hole.

There could be no phrase better engineered to call her back to her schoolgirl days, bowing her head over the old lore. Persecuted Catholics sprinting toward their secret chambers, sealing themselves away with chalices and rosary beads for months or even years, it was said, prisoners of their faith, waiting to walk once more in the light of day.

"Can you imagine, Mummy? Being burned just for being Roman Catholic?"

"Well, yes, I can, I'm afraid."

"Pappa said they might even have held Masses up there. He said, if I closed my eyes, I could hear them still. Though I haven't brought it off yet."

Oscar and his spectres, she thinks. Surely, any straw mattress from the days of Queen Elizabeth or King Charles the Second would have long since been consumed by mice and mold and dust. Whatever is there now must have found more recent usages. Housing a poor relation, perhaps, or an incontinent dog. An escaped prisoner, why not? So many mysteries packed into such a small space, but, to her surprise, one crawls to the fore.

"You mean to say you showed this to Pappa?" she asks.

"Of course."

"When?"

"The day Lord Alfred came."

"But, darling, you never told me."

"Oh, Pappa said it was to be our little secret. Between us two men."

She peers up the ladder into an ambergris effusion. Waits for something to emerge.

"So you told nobody else," she says.

"No."

"And Pappa told nobody else."

"Well . . ." Cyril's mouth skews left. "I think he might have mentioned it to Lord Alfred."

"Why do you think that?"

"Because Lord Alfred spoke of it. Just yesterday."

"Where?"

"On the tennis court."

More lucidly than when it was happening, she sees their two white-jacketed figures, Cyril and Lord Alfred—lunging, sometimes simultaneously, for the same ball and then—she sees this, too—retiring, when the occasion seemed to warrant, into private conferences.

"But what did he say, darling?"

"He said, *Isn't 'priest's hole' the funniest name you've ever heard?* And I said, *Isn't it?* But I don't know what either of us meant."

Constance sets the candle on the floor, then seats herself on the nearest steamer trunk. Round her the light and dust seem to shimmer in alternating waves.

"Are you quite well, Mummy?"

"Of course I am, darling. Are there, by any chance, cobwebs up in that little room of yours?"

"Ever so many! I had to brush them all off me when I was done. Haven't been up there since."

She will struggle later with the proper metaphor. After some trial, she will settle on architectural blueprint. Not of the house they currently occupy (though that house is incorporated within it) and not assembled in the usual draughtsman's way but bleeding in no obvious sequence from a paper that has only now been tilted to the light. Room after room wells into view. In one, two gentlemen go golfing on the links. In another, a solicitor makes cryptic remarks. One room contains an unexpected translation assignment; another, a quarrel on a terrace; another, a sequence of moans in the middle of the night. Here now, winking into sight, an old straw mattress. Here now, a cobweb found on a young nobleman's person. With each new room, the larger structure stands better revealed, and the world draws more tightly round.

"Cyril," she says.

"Yes?"

"If this was all to be a secret, why are you telling me now?"

"Because you've been so unhappy."

"Oh, darling, I haven't been. Not exactly."

"But you have, Mummy. And there's nothing so jolly as a secret, is there?"

She looks at him.

"I can't think of anything," she says.

21

ᗢ

THE WONDER IS that, as the rest of the afternoon unfurls, she grows only calmer, more lucid. Come dusk, she is stationed by the west window, watching the white summer light soften into an aqueous grey, which decants like rain water into the room and puddles round her feet. She is quiet during dinner, though not conspicuously so, and excuses herself directly afterward, pleading tiredness. By nine, she is already fast asleep, and when she awakes in the thickest hour of night, there is none of the usual disorientation. She rises without prompting, reaches for her gown, takes one last glance at Cyril, then steals down the hallway.

Pausing before Oscar's room, she gives two soft raps, two louder ones, then opens the door. The bed lies untenanted, the coverlet undisturbed. Stepping inside, she closes the door after her and seats herself in the chair by the window. Should she have brought knitting? A book? It turns out that the soft ferment of her own mind is all the distraction she requires. A half hour passes, another. Then, through the cloak of silence, her ears pick out the distant Wilde tread. All spondee: *Thump. Thump.* She listens to him fiddle with the latch, then watches his burly form shuffle inside. It isn't until he has shut the door after him, kicked off his slippers and reached for the belt of his Jaeger dressing gown that he notices the rival candle. His eyes widen with interest before piecing her out from the shadows.

"My love," he says. "Have I got my rooms crossed?"

"I don't know, have you?"

His brows jab briefly together. Then, feeling easier, he sets down the candle and lowers himself onto the space of counterpane directly across from her.

"I had a devil of a time sleeping," he says. "Took a bit of a stroll."

"I had a stroll, too. Who would have guessed we'd end up in the same place?"

She leans toward him, draws a strand of cobweb from his ear.

"The spiders must be rampaging tonight," she says.

"Old farm houses . . ."

"Yes. Perhaps I should speak to Mrs. Balls about it. She's usually so thorough."

"Let's not bother the poor dear."

Rather ostentatiously, he yawns and stretches his arms toward the ceiling.

"I am a bit tuckered at last."

"I am sure you are."

Without premeditation, she lowers herself on the square of comforter next to him. Feels the mattress ripple at the news.

"Do you know," she says in a bright, crisp voice, "I've half a mind to leave tomorrow? Oh, I'm sorry," she adds. *Today.*

His head cocks lightly to the right.

"Soon as that?"

"Yes, why not?"

"But I thought we had the place for another week."

"Four days."

"Just so."

She smiles, says nothing. Feels the night's own stillness gather round.

"Do you mean you would go by yourself?" he asks.

"Oh, I think it would be a trifle sadistic to leave you with Cyril and your mother both. No, I only mention it because I thought you might care to join us."

His head cocks farther to the right.

"My love," he says. "As you were the first to point out, I've been going such great guns with the play."

"Yes, that was certainly true when I said it. The last two or three days, perhaps not so much, and it occurs to me that your inspiration might be flagging."

"Oh, I don't know about that. Still have gobs and gobs of ideas, you know. Particles of speech just floating about, waiting to be plucked down."

"Like a cobweb, you mean?"

"Something like that." His lips swell as he rests his hand on her forearm. "It's just that it's all so sudden, this declaration of yours. I had assumed you were having a grand time."

"I was."

"Then what has changed?"

Very gently, she peels away his hand. Rises and moves to the window and pauses there with her hand on the blind cord.

"I have come into the possession of certain knowledge," she says.

"Oh?"

"I'm afraid it took me a rather shocking amount of time to acquire it, but, you see, the clues were on the oblique side. No eyewitnesses. No confessions. No blackmailers with incriminating letters from somebody's coat pocket. I should add that there was somebody else blocking my view the whole while."

"Who?"

"My husband, if you can believe it. Dear fellow, he kept assuring me my suspicions were the idlest feminine fancies. Kept patting his little loyal helpmeet on her little loyal head and sending her—"

"I have never said you—"

"—on her little loyal *way*—"

"—were a helpmeet—"

"Nothing to fear *here*, he kept saying. Off you go."

He makes as if to rise himself. Then, on second thought, stretches his bulk across a bed that can barely contain it.

"All in all," he drawls, "your husband sounds like a sensible chap."

"Does he? Then why isn't his wife any more at ease?"

"Because she persists in misreading circumstances which have perfectly harmless constructions."

"Tell me, then—pray tell me—where she is in error."

"Wherever she finds herself most anxious."

"That is too general."

"Then she should be more pointed."

It is not the remark itself but the mask of genial indifference that sparks something new in her. She comes toward him now a more furrowed person.

"Imagine me, then, a court," she says. "Shall that be more suited to you?"

"It shall not be unsuited."

Over her head, she draws down an invisible powdered wig. Over her person, an invisible black robe. Folds her arms behind her back and lowers her voice by steps until it is, to her ear, some approximation of the Old Bailey, a place she has never been.

"Mr. Wilde," she declares. "Should you not now be standing in the dock?"

"It is far too late in the evening for that. Can't you just imagine me standing?"

"I must ask you then. Do you deny that Lord Alfred has, in recent months, been slipshod with his affections?"

In the ellipses of light cast by the two candles, something rises from his face.

"All affections are slipshod, my love. That is why they are affecting."

"I must ask you not to indulge in your usual wordplay."

"You might as well ask me not to breathe air."

"Do you deny, Mr. Wilde, that the letter taken from Lord Alfred's coat, somewhere in the vicinity of Oxford, would have subjected him to stern criminal penalties?"

"You must ask his solicitors."

"The court has already spoken with one of them."

Here, to her gratification, the first note of trouble gathers—not so much in his eyes, which she cannot expressly see, but in the tautening of his neck.

"Do you deny," she continues, "that Lord Alfred came here not on a whim but at your express invitation?"

"I toss out invitations as flower girls posies. There is no saying who will catch one."

"Do you deny that Lord Alfred's arrival, here in Cromer, has brought a certain change over your situation?"

"By situation, you mean . . ."

"Your family, let us begin there."

"And by change, you mean . . ."

Here she pauses, the better to retain her character.

"Do you deny," she says, "that you and Lord Alfred have stolen off together at certain hours of the night?"

"Stolen off where?"

"Toward a certain priest's hole," she says, and, as she says it, *colours*—straight up from her toes—as though she were the defendant, and the only thing that keeps her from falling out of character altogether is the uncharacteristic haughtiness that subsumes Oscar's voice.

"I hardly think it anybody's business where I steal off to."

She draws down a breath, resumes her slow circuit.

"Do you deny, Mr. Wilde, that this same Lord Alfred exerts a particular claim on you? A peculiar *hold* over you? Something that prompts you to spend many hours, unsupervised, in his company?"

"If there is anything peculiar, it is the bent of your questioning."

"I should have thought it was the manner in which you decline to answer."

Here at last he does stand. On his bare feet, folding down his rich lips and squaring his shoulders.

"May the record show," he says, "that Lord Alfred is a friend. I shall not deny it for I have many such."

"In that case, he might surely be replaced. Why, this very day, you might wire a Mister Robert Ross to join you."

"Robbie." A hollow chuckle. "What a threesome *that* should be."

"And why is that, Mr. Wilde?"

"Oh, he and Bosie don't at all get along. They'd be snapping at each other the whole while like crocodiles."

"In view of that, why not simply send Lord Alfred away?"

The chuckle, to her ear, grows hollower.

"Away," he says.

"Why, yes, back to his doting mother and his brutish father and all their suicidal relations. Why not make him *their* problem henceforth?"

"Because to do so would be intolerably rude."

"Rude! Mr. Wilde, have you not devoted many wells of ink to satirizing the etiquette of the ruling classes? Do you ask us now to believe you care for said etiquette?"

"It is about common courtesy."

"In that case, I am sure that, with your permission, the court would be uncommonly discourteous. I've no doubt the court would derive even a certain small amount of pleasure from it."

And it is the pleasure with which she says that last bit that finally drags her out of character for good. Blinking in the candlelight, she beholds them both. She cannot be sure who is more afraid.

"Heavens," he mutters. "Is that where all of this has been tending?"

"All what?"

"Your little spasm of playacting."

"I thought you liked plays."

"Good ones, yes. But your first act needs considerable work, and your fourth resorts to the kind of melodrama to which even the French would not stoop. Expelling the serpent from Eden? My dear, that was a little tired even in Milton's day."

"And yet what if we did it all the same?"

Perhaps it is the bareness of proposition that finally catches him where he lives, for something peremptory and humorless claims his voice.

"Bosie can't go. It's as simple as that."

"Oh?" She leans toward him now, mysteriously armored. "And what prevents him? Has he developed blister from all that golf? What is the debility that keeps him here?"

"The interrogation carries on."

"It does."

"You know as well as anybody he is working on the *Salomé* translation."

"And just how far has he got with that? Has a single one of your irregular French verbs found its proper English conjugation?"

"My dear, it is not a mechanical process, it is a matter of minds *meeting*, of—back-and-forth colloquies . . ."

"All of which might be conducted by post."

"This is intolerable. I demolish each objection, and you erect a new one."

"Because there is a larger objection, which has yet to be demolished."

"And what is that?"

She doesn't mean to touch him, but as soon as her hand makes contact with his sternum, he topples straight backward, and in the next moment, she watches herself—*feels* herself—climbing atop his supine form. Her unloosed night-hair spills round his face, rakes against his dyed, pomaded, cobwebbed hair, and her strangled voice hisses into the quadrant of him that will best hear.

"Understand me."

She can see his eyes now, irises swarming.

"There is no longer any court of record here, Mr. Wilde. There is only me, but the objection stands. What stops him from leaving?"

With a license she can scarcely fathom, she draws closer, her lips inclining toward his ear, her voice the more urgent for travelling so small a distance.

"I have already explained to you—I am quite certain I have explained to you—that you needn't be squeamish on my account. I am stronger than you know—stronger than even I know sometimes—and for your sake, and for the children's sake, I can be mighty as Samson, I can pull down every last temple if it comes to that, but I must know what I am pulling *down*, and so I must ask you once more—as your wife—as the mother of your children—what stops him from leaving?"

She levers her torso back up and gazes upon his stunned, whey-coloured face. Surely, she thinks, this is where he will resort to words. To *paradox*, which is always, in his telling, the straightest road to wisdom. What better sign of their changed relations than this? The answer, when at last it comes, is but the one syllable.

"Me."

In the next moment, she is pounding on him as if he were a tympanum, only he doesn't resound in the manner of percussion but recedes, retracts, with each blow, until she begins to feel she is pounding straight to his heart, a thought that would give her satisfaction if it did not make her own heart quail. Later, much later, she will reassemble what she has said.

"And *you*! And *you*! And your tales of old whores and old syphilis, and we could no longer lie together and be husband and wife, but you *may* go to your golf links, and you *may* go to your priest's hole and make someone *else* your wife, and your own son slumbering two stories below and me alongside and your mother two rooms over, and you dared! You *dared*!"

Down it rains, the rage, the bile, her spittle, bathing every promontory of his face, baptizing the whole ruin of him. It is a perfect marvel, she supposes, that the rest of her should remain so utterly dry, not a tear to be found. No, in this moment of reckoning, the tears come exclusively from her husband, and it is finally a measure of what a good helpmeet she is, has ever trained herself to be, that she ceases after a time to pound.

"Oh, my dear," she listens to herself. "Oh, my dear. Bad as all that?"

"Rather worse."

"And to think," she says. "We were on holiday."

She angles her ear toward his shaking breast. From inside comes the sound of muscle flinging itself against cage. With a trailing moan, she stretches herself alongside him.

"Tell me," she says. "Tell me what it is like."

"I can't," he stutters.

"Tell me anyway."

"It is," he says, "like feeling yourself every day dissolving. Through every crevice and pore. It is like realizing that the man you *were* has had quite enough of *you* and is vacating the premises. Not even a proper good-bye and you don't know quite what will be left once he's gone."

She reaches for his hand. "What do you *want* to be left?"

"That's the hell of it. I can't imagine life without you and the boys and Mamma—*all* the old anchors. But there are times those anchors feel like *anchors*, and there is a shoreline in view, and it is beautiful, and it is nowhere I have ever been."

"And what will happen when you reach it?"

"I wish I knew."

She rolls toward him, slides a finger down his wet cheeks, rests her head against his shoulder.

"Oh, my love. I know you appreciate this better than anyone but you—the *pair* of you—won't be suffered to stay on that shore alone. Not for long. The world will find you, it always does."

She curves a hand round the back of his neck.

"I don't give a rap about the world," he says.

She nearly laughs. For she has seen more times than she can count how he composes himself for his public. The cigarette, the green carnation. The blasé mien of his curtain speeches, the whole air of half-disdaining the attention he has with no small effort attracted. And she knows from experience it is all just a way of hiding how much he craves that attention. And, in the same pulse, fears it.

"Very well," she says. "Let the world have its way with you. But what of your anchors? Are we just to drop?"

The reply is as sudden as it is unexpected.

"Anchor each other," he says.

The words have scarcely escaped him when he rolls toward her and presses his brow against hers and whispers in a perfect fury:

"We can't let them sink."

"Who?"

"The *boys*, Constance. We can't let them sink."

22

When dawn comes for her the next morning, she is wide awake, eyes dry. She rolls over and finds Cyril, his breath a slow, pulsing stream on the pillow. *Roll on, sweet Thames,* she thinks, and then imagines his face actually widening or contracting like a river. Which direction the nose? Which the chin? In ten years' time, she might hardly recognise him, or he might loom before her just as he does now, a mass of curls, a pair of ruddy lips, a scattering of freckles. Only the eyes, she thinks, beneath their lids, will remain forever unchanged. She rests her head in the declivity between his neck and clavicle and casts her gaze toward the window. Then she gives him two soft tussles.

"Cyril," she whispers.

"Mm."

"How should it be if we left today?"

She expects him to imbibe the question into his morning mind—swat at it or ignore it altogether—but in the next instant, his eyes spring open.

"Will we see Viv?"

For a moment, she cannot speak.

"Why, of course, darling. I'll check the train schedule, but I know it isn't too far to Hunstanton."

"Tonight, then."

"Certainly. Perhaps." She glances back to the window and, in a less confident voice, says, "I am sure that Vyvyan has been having a grand time of it. As have you, haven't you, darling?"

He doesn't answer. The last shreds of night draw back over him. His breath flows once more like a river.

23

⁓

IT IS EARLIER than she has ever thought to come to Lady Wilde's room, and she cannot honestly be sure what welcome awaits her. Perhaps the old lady requires a very specific isolation at this time of day, or perhaps she is simply fast asleep, not to be roused. But, to Constance's surprise, her single rap receives an answering call.

"Come in."

The room is no brighter in the full light of morning than in the dying light of afternoon. Whatever identity it once had has been subsumed by its occupant, and any connection to the world outside is notional. Constance is glad at least to meet the same basic outlines: the humped human shape in the tent bed, the ladder-back chair waiting in the corner.

"Oh, good morning, my dear," says Lady Wilde. "It *is* morning, I suppose?"

"For another hour."

"Just as I thought."

The smell, too, is the same, only more sedimentary than ever. Not to be uprooted. *Why*, thinks Constance, *she will live here for all days.*

"Dearest Madre, something has arisen and, as a consequence, we are making preparations to leave."

Lady Wilde reaches for the fat, guttering candle. "Today?"

"That is the thought."

The older woman frowns. "Is this owing to Vyvyan? Has he not yet recovered from his whooping cough?"

"Oh, no, that's—"

"My dear, it does not speak well of a boy's virility if he cannot evacuate his lungs at the first time of asking."

"Really, he's quite—"

"Now I recognise that my maternal philosophy shades at times toward the unorthodox, but when Oscar and Willie were lads, the moment they developed so much as a sniffle I sent them straight into Nature. *Do not come back*, I told them, *until your lungs are throbbing with Irish country air like an Aeolian harp.* So instructed, they went away and returned only when they felt themselves up to snuff. Once, as I recall, they took one or two days about it but were altogether healthier specimens when they staggered home. Sadly, the air in this particular crevice of the world—"

"Madre."

"—is of a most inferior—"

"Madre."

Constance presses her hand into the old woman's mattress until she feels the mattress pressing back.

"Vyvyan is quite all right, I promise you. It is simply that I want to go home."

There are no tears, she is glad of that, but Lady Wilde studies her all the same.

"Well now," she says, "you are in luck. After ten days in the beating heart of Norfolk, I am no closer to discerning its value to civilization. If you want for company, I am happy to make a party with you."

"Dearest Madre."

"Now it is true that your timing is a touch unfortunate as I am expecting a secret communique from Vienna. It will be in a cipher impenetrable to an average intelligence, but I shouldn't like it falling into the wrong hands."

"I expect Oscar could forward it."

Lady Wilde rears back. "Do you mean to tell me he is staying on?"

"Yes."

"With that marionette?"

"Well, they are hard at work, Madre. On their divers projects."

"Their ridiculous golf, you mean. If this is what English country living does to men's faculties, give me London at its most miasmic. Oh, my dear, is it not shocking what we wives are obliged to tolerate?"

For the first time since coming to this house, Constance thinks upon the man who died before she could meet him: Sir William Wilde. The eminent eye and ear surgeon who, prior to marriage, fathered three children out of wedlock and who, in the very year of Oscar's birth, embarked on an affair with the daughter of one of his own colleagues, producing yet another child and, a decade later, a courtroom scandal, all of which Lady Wilde brazened out as only she could, staring down every Dubliner who passed her. Constance sits there a while longer, marveling. Then:

"We'll call for you in another hour, Madre."

24

THE NECESSARY ARRANGEMENTS are made with Mrs. Balls, and by noon, the luggage lies stacked in a pyramid in the gravel drive. The basket chaise is set for one-thirty, and for the first time all day, Constance feels herself at loose ends, wandering from room to room with an almost proprietorial air. At last, lacking any other prospect, she opens the front door and steps out onto the landing. The last flushes of scarlet poppy have faded from the walnut-brown corn shocks. A thrush sings in the pear tree. From the other side of the stile fence, a horse gazes at her, like an old gossip. She is still standing there, her head rested against the door, when a solitary man blurs into view on the lip of the hill. In the next second, he is trundling down, slow and inexorable, a pack on his back and a smile slowly dawning on a face so weathered she takes him for a mendicant and is already composing her excuses when he calls out in a voice of briny vigor.

"Mrs. Wilde?"

"Yes."

"Herbert Mace. Of Church Street, Cromer."

"Yes?"

"We came to a certain understanding on Cromer beach the other morning."

"Did we?" A flicker of revulsion. "I don't recall anything of that nature."

Herbert Mace of Church Street sets down his pack and, with his index finger, gives his mustache a luxuriant sweep. His smile stretches so wide now she can almost fancy it wrapping round his head.

"Bless me, Mrs. Wilde, I'm what you call a photographer. At your service."

She stares at him.

"There must be some mistake."

"I think not."

"I never engaged you."

"But your husband did. Had me write it down special. He said, *You be sure to come on ex-and-ex date at ex-and-ex time*, and here it is, ex-and-ex."

"Are you quite certain? My husband never breathed a word."

"He breathed it to me. Herbert Mace don't travel all this way without knowing he's welcome. No, he does not."

"Ah, Mr. Mace!" Oscar comes striding out the doorway in his lounge suit and Homburg. "You are a man of your covenant."

"I am that, sir. If nothing else, I am a man of my covenant."

"Oscar," she murmurs.

"My love, it shall be the work of no more than a quarter hour."

And shall exist forever, she thinks, and is poised on the brink of a scene when Cyril blows in as if on the next wind.

"Mummy, mightn't we get a picture taken together? It'd be ever so much fun."

Was he put up to it? Or did he, upon reflection, decide that the best way to keep her happy was to treat the whole business as the game that, with each passing second, unfolds before them? Lord Alfred trotting out in a double-breasted suit and boater with grosgrain hatband. Mrs. Balls, in defiance of the heat, draping herself in not one but two shawls. Mrs. Balls's grandson, corduroy trousers spattered with blood, spitting into his hand and parting his black hair straight down the middle. *Yes*, thinks Constance. *We belong to our public now.*

"Exquisite ensemble," says Mr. Mace.

After some minutes of surveying, he suggests, for purposes of lighting, the rear terrace, where they have spent so many of their evenings. Early afternoon exposes it as a smaller, meaner place than Constance would have guessed. For the first time, she sees the patching of glue on the chair legs, the water damage on the wine table. Tiny cairns of cigarette ash, strewn across the stone.

Mr. Mace takes but a single shot of Mrs. Balls and grandson, in the full knowledge he will not be compensated, and then, with a touch of the herald, declares, "Bring forth the Wildes."

Lady Wilde, of course, hasn't bothered to emerge, but Cyril, responsive to the occasion, has put on a tam-o'-shanter and changed out his shirt for the striped blouse Constance made him for his seventh birthday. It both touches and pains her to see how tightly the fabric clings to him now. Was it Oscar, she wonders, who tucked the mauve handkerchief into his shirt pocket?

The photographer groups them with some difficulty around the wine table. Constance, feeling the sensation seeping from her left thigh, asks if she might sit. There is a further adjusting of tripod, a further fussing with lenses. There is a less accountable silence, punctuated at last by Cyril's whisper.

"Mummy, you're not looking at the camera."

"Must I?"

"How now, my love," says Oscar. "Suppose we were to place a book there? You might pretend you've been captured in the act of reading."

With no further prompting, Mrs. Balls drags out the family Bible and spreads it across the table. The words rise up from the page in all their King James randomness. *And there came forth little children out of the city, and mocked him, and said unto him, Go up, thou bald head; go up, thou bald head.* At her periphery, she sees Oscar wrapping an arm round Cyril's shoulder and angling himself with that intuitive grace toward the lens, his cigarette prised as ever between his index and middle fingers.

"Smile, Mummy," whispers Cyril.

Until this moment, she has believed she was smiling. Afterward she will believe that, at his injunction, she did smile. The print of the photograph, arriving by post exactly two weeks later in Tite Street, will find her still frowning. At a book not her own. Wearing a roomy, entirely progressive dress that looks, in the context, like a flounced tent.

During this whole time, nobody suggests that Lord Alfred join the family tableau. The only thing left to resolve is how he and Oscar will pose for their own portrait. Here, to her surprise, the two men grow diffident. Sitting seems to accentuate the difference in their sizes, as does standing shoulder to shoulder. It is Mr. Mace's suggestion to enlarge slightly the space between them. "Making you and Your Lordship look the proper gentlemen you are. As *indeed* you are." Lord Alfred overcorrects by another few inches, at which Oscar draws him back. By the time Mr. Mace has disappeared beneath his photographer's mantle, the older man is once again his public self, whereas the younger man, at the last second, jams his hands into his coat pockets, producing a strange upward pouching.

This photograph, too, Constance will see again. In roughly three years' time, converted into a line drawing and splashed across the front cover of the *Morning Post*. A newsboy will be hawking it across the full length of Covent Garden, and as she escapes into the nearest hansom with her two sons, she will think back to Herbert Mace and wonder how handsomely he was paid for the negative. She will wonder, too, about that other photograph—Oscar Wilde and his family—the one with no takers.

25

MR. HERBERT MACE departs on the same stream of affability that carried him here, giving his jacket pocket one last tap to be sure of Oscar's cheque, then strolling back through the house with a smiling nod to each room. "Such an honor," he says. "Such a privilege." The rest of the guests trail after him, leaving Constance, to her great relief, alone, looking out in an absent way at the tennis court, the croquet wicks. The hedgerows, sloughing off their fringe of meadowsweet. The yew tree, dropping berries. Behind her, a door scrapes open, and a throat clears. With a nettled motion, she looks back to find Lord Alfred bearing a tray.

At sight of her, his mouth winches up into a smile.

"Mrs. Balls is rather occupied."

"So it would appear."

Several more seconds pass.

"Spot of tea," he suggests.

Years of watching servants perform this very task have apparently not equipped him to imitate it, for, with each step, the teapot lurches farther toward the edge. At last, just as it is about to tumble over the precipice, he rights the tray, then, lacking any other home port, prepares to drop it straight onto Mrs. Balls's Bible before Constance drags it out of harm's way.

"There now," he says, reaching for a chair of his own. "Isn't this perfectly cozy? I couldn't recall how you took your milk and sugar, or if you took them at all, so I've brought the whole blessed business."

"You are most kind," she says.

"Oh, cripes, it's the least a guest could do."

She takes her allotment of sugar, imparts the briefest of stirs, then returns the spoon to the tray, quite as if it has never been used.

"I haven't long to sit," she says.

He leans back in his chair and, in a mindless way, plunges his index finger into the hot tea, making two revolutions before transferring the same finger, pink and puckered, to the sanctity of his mouth.

"Dear Mrs. Wilde," he says. "I sincerely hope you are not leaving on my account."

"And what if I were?"

"Why, it would grieve me to no end."

"Then I am."

He stares down into his cup, moving his lips soundlessly before at last venturing into sound.

"Well now, I've been speaking with your Oscar . . ."

"*My* Oscar?"

"Yes, we had a lovely chat, and it's—you see, it's occurred to me that you might be entertaining certain ideas about me which—well, they might be a bit off the mark. . . ."

"Pray be more specific."

"Oh, well, I don't know if one should speak plump *out*, what with the—the *lad* about. . . ."

"Lord Alfred."

"I only wanted to say—to begin with, it was never my purpose in coming here to offend you or to *transgress* in any way."

"Then what was your purpose?"

"I . . ."

He pauses, briefly helpless.

"I wish I knew."

The smile he flashes now is the pickled grin of a boy called up before the headmaster. How much trouble it must have spared him.

"Here's the thing, Mrs. Wilde. I have always despised men who fall back on their years to excuse their lapses. Whether they be young or old, I consider it the grossest form of sentimentality. Yet I can see now that a chap—well, shall we say in his salad years . . ."

"Yes."

". . . upon receiving an invitation from a gentleman of a more autumnal age—"

"I follow."

"—cannot really—I mean hasn't it in him, really, to reckon for consequences. He can only think it will be ever such larks."

"Is that what you thought?"

"Yes."

"And has it been?"

"In bits. Oh, I needn't tell you Oscar is the jolliest company a fellow could ask for."

"On that point we agree. But tell me, Lord Alfred, what are these consequences you speak of?"

"You are one."

It is more directness than she was prepared to entertain.

"On the whole," she concludes, "I am pleased to hear it."

Frowning now, he rises and takes two strides in the direction of the yew.

"Mrs. Wilde, I confess that, prior to meeting you—in full, I mean—I imagined you simply as a type."

"The Constant Wife, you mean."

"Only that's not who you are at all. At least not merely."

"And you, Lord Alfred, what type are you?"

Something sly steals into his eyes as he turns round to face her.

"The Idle Dilettante. Isn't that what you all took me for?"

"We were wrong about the idle part."

"As for Oscar, well, I was in no way prepared for . . ."

"The Good Father," she suggests.

He nods, relieved.

"I presumed, you see, on the weight of rather scant evidence, that Oscar would be cut from the same cold cloth as all the Queensberry patriarchs. To my astonishment, he is a family man." He smiles softly and holds her gaze. "To my astonishment, that makes him dearer. Oh, Mrs. Wilde, I won't insult you by saying I shall make things right—I wouldn't know how if I tried—but I shouldn't at all mind if you were disposed to be friends going forward. You'll find that, once you've inured yourself to me, I'm not such a reprobate."

"On the weight of rather scant evidence," she says, "I cannot believe that my opinion of you matters. At least it has not so far."

Against expectations, he laughs. The same unforced, unobstructed sound that seized him on the Cromer cliffs, causing even the gulls to pause in flight. It passes through him now like a breeze and leaves him utterly still on the other end.

"I must beg to differ with you," he says. "Whether by design or no, you have chosen the best possible strategy for bringing Oscar to heel. Once you are gone, he will be so hobbled with guilt he won't be able to walk straight."

"I am confident you will guide him."

"You are mistaken. I shall myself be leaving before the day is out. You'll be quit of me altogether."

She squints at him. "Does Oscar know?"

"I'm not sure I should tell him, really. He'd only try to talk me out of it, and you know how persuasive he can be."

"I know how persuasive you can be."

He regards her rather solemnly for a few moments, then lowers his cup gently onto the table.

"I am sorry you don't care for me, Mrs. Wilde. I quite like you."

In a fluid and unruffled motion, he travels toward the door and is nearly inside when he turns back, almost as an afterthought, and says, with what she will later diagnose as compassion:

"And I don't want you to think I was his first."

26

ALL IS VERY nearly ready when the time for departure comes. The driver has piled the bags in the trap; Lady Wilde is piled there, too, looking particularly statuary in her black bombazine and lace headdress. After making a silent inventory, Constance realises that the only missing element is Cyril. She makes a pass of every room, peers through every window, stands in the gravel drive like a fishwife, calling his name. Her rewards are silence and then, a little worse than silence, Lady Wilde's own inflamed voice, descending from above.

"My dear, are you quite sure you gave him the proper time? Boys do have a way of slipping off the face of the earth. I remember, when Willie and Oscar were young, they seemed to live entirely by the faery calendar. Dropped from view by day, then rematerialised at nightfall. Always so fantastically hungry and bad-tempered—as if I'd deliberately starved them! I told them, *You should ask your faeries to feed you for they see quite a bit more of you than I ever do.*"

"Mummy!"

Constance hears the cry first, then the boy it belongs to, galloping toward her. At last, drained of air, he stops a few feet shy of her, resting his hands on his knees.

"Mummy," he gasps. "We saw Blackie. . . ."

"Dear me, how did you manage that?"

"Pappa . . ." Another draft of air. "Pappa found him. . . ."

"Darling, catch your breath."

"The peculiar . . . *blackness* . . . of the eye. . . ."

"Ah."

"And he was quite right, he . . ." He draws down one last gale of air. "What a stroke of luck."

"Wasn't it?"

Still in his Homburg, Oscar draws up before them now and impulsively assumes the character of a Hyde Park orator, thumbs in buttonholes, voice steeped in East End.

"Ladies and gentlemen, I say to you now that aforementioned Blackie, far from being the uncouth sort one sometimes encounters in the wild, was the most civilised bunny I have yet had the pleasure of addressing. Fairly *bowed* his ears to us, did he not, and just before we bid him adieu, was heard to tell Master Cyril here—for I am conversant in Lepus—*Young man, it has been an honor, and it has been a privilege.*"

"Stop it," says Cyril, only half-angry. "Bunnies don't talk."

"They do if you know how to listen. But see here, you infernal child, you've kept your mother waiting quite long enough. Up you go! Now listen here, you must promise me on your word as a gentleman that you'll look after Mamma and Grandmamma while I'm gone, will you do that? And your brother, too? Blackie assured me on oath I might depend upon you, and I shouldn't want him shown up. You'll do that? Saints rejoice, give us a kiss."

Constance has taken her own seat alongside Lady Wilde and is training her gaze wherever her husband isn't. But the world isn't large enough, he circles the cart, blowing kisses in every direction and then, in an ineluctable way, positioning himself just below her. A middle-aged Romeo, she thinks, crooning up to his Juliet.

"It seems I shall be alone after all," he says.

"There is always Mr. Mace."

Because, to her own surprise, of all the things she can't forgive him for in this moment, Herbert Mace of Cromer straddles the highest peak.

"Dear me," he laughs. "I might just as well enquire into village-hermit vacancies."

Do not smile, she instructs herself. *Forbear to enlist.* But as the cart draws away, she hears him calling after.

"I shall be home before another week is out."

And as the pony drags them over the hill, the voice comes back at higher frequency.

"The whole wretched play will be finished!"

They are very nearly to the Cromer railway station when Lady Wilde leans toward her and murmurs, in the susurrations of the confessional booth:

"Dear Constance, it just now occurs to me I haven't paid Cook in two months' time. There is as well the distinct possibility that I've been putting off Emily a bit longer. If they're both still there when we get back—I mean, if they haven't given notice—would it be too much trouble . . ."

27

Vyvyan is waiting for them on the platform in Hunstanton in a light flannel suit and knickers and a pair of stockings that somebody has turned over a pair of supporting garters. *Who?* wonders Constance, for she would never have dressed him this way. And why, in this moment, does he loom so large? Is it a property of her absence? She must draw closer to understand that he is standing atop his own steamer trunk. To gain a better view, she presumes, only, having picked her out of the crowd, he doesn't surrender his altitude but continues tracking her, waiting until she is within touching distance to dismount.

"Hallo, Mummy."

She wraps herself round him with a ferocity that surprises her, but his eyes are already wandering over her shoulder to Cyril, who arrives in his own time and who, in the act of escorting his younger brother down the platform, leans in and murmurs in a voice that Constance cannot pretend not to hear:

"You were well out of it, old man. I nearly had to cat, it was so dull."

28

THE TELEGRAPH COMES for her in Babbacombe.

> DEAREST CONSTANCE CHANGE OF PLANS BOSIE HAS FALLEN ILL
> MUST REMAIN TILL BETTER WILL WIRE YOU SOONEST RE TRAVEL
> LOVE OSCAR

She considers wiring him back, but her own vanity recoils at the urgency. Better, surely, to take every word at its surface value and respond in kind. The next morning, she leaves a letter for the postman.

> *I'm so sorry to hear about Lord Alfred and wish I was at Cromer to look after him. If you think I could be any good, do telegraph to me, because I can still get over to you.*

A week later, Oscar sends word by letter that he is to attend a garden party in Reading and catch a *Lady Windermere* production in York. There is talk of meeting up in Glasgow with Beerbohm Tree, who, by the way, has taken Grove Farm for the final week of September and has suggested that Oscar return there to put the finishing touches on Act IV. "What can a poor playwright do?" asks Oscar.

There is no mention of Lord Alfred and nothing in the itinerary to suggest anything out of the order. Oscar, she reminds herself, has been a nomad since the first years of their marriage, answering invitations from every corner of the realm, changing plans at the last moment, and always with her blessing. No sense wiring back a query of her own—he will have moved on by the time it arrives. All she can do is peer into the silence around his words.

Early in their marriage, she and Oscar attended an exhibition of American watchmaking in South Kensington. It was really just a pair of steel hands moving in synchronised orbits, manipulating screws so tiny one would have required a magnifying glass to see their threads. The whole operation, she was told, produced something like five hundred cogged wheels in a single day, but what shoved all other considerations to the side was the sheer drudging implacable monotony of those *hands*, carrying out the same instructions again and again without once imagining another way. Her awe ebbed by degrees into a dull fatalism, and it is this same feeling that seeps through her as she follows, via postcards and telegraphs and letters, Oscar's progress through the land. Can the screws rebel against the hands?

ENTR'ACTE

~~

LETTER OF MARQUESS OF QUEENSBERRY TO HIS SON,
ALFRED DOUGLAS (APRIL 1, 1894)

ALFRED,
Your intimacy with this man Wilde must either cease or I will
disown you and stop all money supplies. I am not going to try
and analyse this intimacy, and I make no charge; but to my
mind to pose as a thing is as bad as to be it. With my own eyes
I saw you in the most loathsome and disgusting relationship, as
expressed by your manner and expression. Never in my experience
have I seen such a sight as that in your horrible features. No
wonder people are talking as they are. Also I now hear on good
authority, but this may be false, that his wife is petitioning to
divorce him for sodomy and other crimes. Is this true, or do you
not know of it? If I thought the actual thing was true, and it
became public property, I should be quite justified in shooting
him on sight.

YOUR DISGUSTED, SO-CALLED FATHER,
Queensberry

⊂ʃ⊃

REPLY OF DOUGLAS TO HIS FATHER, VIA TELEGRAPH

What a funny little man you are.

⊂ʃ⊃

CARD LEFT BY THE MARQUESS OF QUEENSBERRY *with the hall porter at the Albemarle Club in London (February 18. 1895)*

For Oscar Wilde, posing as a somdomite [sic].

⊂ʃ⊃

TESTIMONY FROM RESULTING LIBEL ACTION BROUGHT BY WILDE AGAINST QUEENSBERRY (APRIL 1895)

Edward Carson, Queensbury's defence attorney: Do you know Walter Grainger?
Wilde: Yes.
C: How old is he?
W: He was about sixteen when I knew him. He was a servant at a certain house in High Street, Oxford, where Lord Alfred Douglas had rooms. I have stayed there several times. Grainger waited at table. I never dined with him. If it is one's duty to serve, it is one's duty to serve; and if it is one's pleasure to dine, it is one's pleasure to dine.
C: Did you ever kiss him?
W: Oh, dear no. He was a peculiarly plain boy. He was, unfortunately, extremely ugly. I pitied him for it.
C: Was that the reason why you did not kiss him?
W: Oh, Mr. Carson, you are pertinently insolent.
C: Did you say that in support of your statement that you never kissed him?

W: No. It is a childish question.

C: Did you ever put that forward as a reason why you never kissed the boy?

W: Not at all.

C: Why, sir, did you mention that this boy was extremely ugly?

W: For this reason. If I were asked why I did not kiss a door-mat, I should say because I do not like to kiss door-mats. I do not know why I mentioned that he was ugly, except that I was stung by the insolent question you put to me and the way you have insulted me throughout this hearing. Am I to be cross-examined because I do not like it?

C: Why did you mention his ugliness?

W: It is ridiculous to imagine that any such thing could have occurred under any circumstances.

C: Then why did you mention his ugliness, I ask you?

W: Perhaps you insulted me by an insulting question.

C: Was that a reason why you should say the boy was ugly?—[The witness began several answers almost inarticulately, and none of them he finished. Carson's repeated sharply: "Why? Why? Why did you add that?" At last the witness answered]:

W: You sting me and insult me and try to unnerve me; and at times one says things flippantly when one ought to speak more seriously. I admit it.

C: Then you said it flippantly?

W: Oh, yes, it was a flippant answer.

꿍

Note of Queensbury to Wilde after the court ruled in Queensbury's favor

If the country allows you to leave, all the better for the country; but, if you take my son with you, I will follow you wherever you go and shoot you.

⟨ഗ≀ാ⟩

Testimony from Wilde's first criminal trial (April 1895)

Prosecuting Counsel C.F. Gill: What is the "Love that dare not speak its name"?

Wilde: "The Love that dare not speak its name" in this century is such a great affection of an elder for a younger man as there was between David and Jonathan, such as Plato made the very basis of his philosophy, and such as you find in the sonnets of Michelangelo and Shakespeare. It is that deep, spiritual affection that is as pure as it is perfect. It dictates and pervades great works of art like those of Shakespeare and Michelangelo, and those two letters of mine, such as they are. It is in this century misunderstood, so much misunderstood that it may be described as the "Love that dare not speak its name," and on account of it I am placed where I am now. It is beautiful, it is fine, it is the noblest form of affection. There is nothing unnatural about it. It is intellectual, and it repeatedly exists between an elder and a younger man, when the elder man has intellect, and the younger man has all the joy, hope and glamour of life before him. That it should be so the world does not understand. The world mocks at it and sometimes puts one in the pillory for it. [Loud applause, mingled with some hisses.]

Mr. Justice Charles: If there is the slightest manifestation of feeling I shall have the Court cleared. There must be complete silence preserved.

G: Then there is no reason why it should be called "Shame"?

W: Ah, that, you will see, is the mockery of the other love, love which is jealous of friendship and says to it, "You should not interfere."

. . .

G: I wish to call your attention to the style of your correspondence with Lord Alfred Douglas?

W: I am ready. I am never ashamed of the style of my writings.

G: You are fortunate, or shall I say shameless? [Laughter.] I refer to passages in two letters in particular?

W: Kindly quote them.

G: In letter number one you use the expression "Your slim gilt soul," and you refer to Lord Alfred's "red rose-leaf lips." The second letter contains the words, "You are the divine thing I want," and describes Lord Alfred's letter as being "delightful, red and yellow wine to me." Do you think that an ordinarily constituted being would address such expressions to a younger man?

W: I am not happily, I think, an ordinarily constituted being.

༄

Sentence passed by Justice Alfred Wills on Wilde (May 26, 1895)

The crime of which you have been convicted is so bad that one has to put stern restraint upon one's self to prevent one's self from describing, in language which I would rather not use, the sentiments which must rise in the breast of every man of honor who has heard the details of these two horrible trials. That the jury has arrived at a correct verdict in this case I cannot persuade myself to entertain a shadow of a doubt; and I hope, at all events, that those who sometimes imagine that a judge is half-hearted in the cause of decency and morality because he takes care no prejudice shall enter into the case, may see that it is consistent at least with the utmost sense of indignation at the horrible charges brought home to both of you.

It is no use for me to address you. People who can do these things must be dead to all sense of shame, and one cannot hope to produce any effect upon them. It is the worst case I have ever tried. . . .That you, Wilde, have been the center of a circle of extensive corruption of the most hideous kind among young men, it is equally impossible to doubt.

I shall, under the circumstances, be expected to pass the severest sentence that the law allows. In my judgement it is totally inadequate for a case such as this. The sentence of the Court is that . . . you be imprisoned and kept to hard labor for two years.

[Cries of "Oh! Oh!" and "Shame!"]

Wilde: And I? May I say nothing, my Lord?

The court adjourned.

∽

Excerpt: Letter of Oscar Wilde to Alfred Douglas from Reading Gaol (1897)

I remember one morning . . . sitting in the yellowing woods
at Bracknell with your mother. . . . You had stayed with me at
Cromer for ten days and played golf. The conversation turned on
you, and your mother began to speak to me about your character.
She told me of your two chief faults, your vanity, and your
being as she termed it "all wrong about money." I have a distinct
recollection of how I laughed. I had no idea that the first would
bring me to prison and the second to bankruptcy.

ACT TWO

Wildes by the Sea

A rented villa in Bogliasco, Italy
September 1897

1

CRD

"IT IS A matter of geography, Signora."

Dr. Bossi raises his tisane cup until it is level with his hazel eyes.

"Your England, it sits up *here*, can you see? And now France," he says, lowering the cup an inch. "And now Germany." A lateral. "And so on, one after the other, and now *Italy* . . ." A swift but arrested plunge. "*Here* we lie, at the bottommost rim. Thus, we become the—the *drain*—no, that is not the—*setaccio*. . . ."

"Do you mean sieve?" she asks.

"That is possible."

"Basin?"

"*Basin*. Just so. Italy, by virtue of where it lies, must be a basin which will *catch* the rest of you when you fall."

Constance, having drained her own cup, sets it down on the small, lightly tessellated marble table.

"That's awfully decent of you, Doctor."

"Oh, we do not congratulate ourselves. It is merely our destiny. When I make my rounds in Hotel Nervi, Signora, I come across men and women, high-born such as yourself and hailing from across the Continent. It is my opinion that virtually all of them—and please know that I am not their judge—have transgressed in some fashion. You follow me thus far."

"I do."

"Perhaps they are escaping creditors. Or have cheated at the cards. Or at love, that is quite common. Just last week, I met an exquisite Parisienne, no more than twenty-two and of the most impeccable breeding. She did not give me her actual name—they seldom do, Signora Holland—but I know for a fact that this lady is seven months with child and has neither mother nor husband at her side. Well, you and I both understand that a lady in such a state cannot turn her face toward society. No, she must *drop* for a time and be collected. . . ." This time, his cup descends all the way to the marble table, coming to a rest by hers. "*Here*," he concludes. "In this beautiful basin."

Only now, as his hands withdraw, does she grasp how expressive they are. All the more so for the coarse black hairs that stand suddenly revealed in the mid-afternoon sun.

"This Parisienne," she says. "Did she volunteer her story?"

"Her maid told me."

"Heavens, that's what we call a sacking offense."

"Oh, if the maid did not speak, the other guests would. They are positively bursting with one another's sins at Hotel Nervi. I am merely the helpless conduit."

Just to the right of her, the setting sun begins to gild the grape leaves. Above her, the poplars rustle. Across the terrace sidles a tortoise: wrinkled neck, inquiring head. Searching for slugs, she thinks, and always a step or two late.

"Do they ever speak of *me* there?" she asks.

"Ah, Signora. So few have set eyes upon you."

"That makes no matter."

Dr. Bossi considers, then, in an accent of soft regret, says:

"There is idle talk. *En passant.*"

"And what is its theme?"

"They believe you to be a lady who has tasted of life."

"That sounds sinister."

"*Scusami*, that is my English. I mean a lady who has known sorrow. A widow, it is suggested."

"Yet I wear no black."

"To be sure. And a ring rests on your finger. Though, of course, Genova has widows who bear their rings straight to their tombs. And beyond, it might be."

"Tell your informants I would never be so tasteless."

"Bless me, Signora!" Dr. Bossi rears back in his wrought-iron chair. "That which we speak of here is kept close to my bosom. On my oath as a physician."

She can't help but smile, for he has just betrayed at least one patient's secret, and piety sets a little oddly on his amphitheatre-sized ears, the impish wrinkles round his eyes, the waxed curlicues of mustache above his beard-shrub. Yes, she thinks, he is a few years past forty and on the small side and smells rather fiercely of bay leaf, but he is made for delight, and she wonders if, without knowing it, she has been flirting with him this whole while. Is that why he has yet to leave? For some minutes more, they sit under the arbor, the Doctor feasting with some relish on Sophia's chestnut cake. Perhaps none of the guests at Hotel Nervi ever feeds him.

"Your *sons*," he says at last, with a mouth half full. "They are spoken of broadly. Ha ha! You need not fear. It is said they are high in *spiriti animali* but conduct themselves as gentlemen. And such entrepreneurs! Do you know they sell our local flowers to the English *turisti*?"

"I must reproach them, then, for despoiling your meadows. And for not sharing their revenue."

"That last is their only flaw. Tell me, please, their ages."

She pauses. As she always does now.

"The older is twelve," she answers at last. "The younger, ten."

"And they are here on school holiday?"

"For a few days more. Then back to their cloisters."

"Ah!" His jaw hinges open. "There are no more cloisters, Signora. I speak now of the nurses in my clinic, who are Sisters of Our Lady of Mercy. Before their first day is complete, they are sisters of the world. You see, each of my patients brings with her a tale, yes, and to hear this tale is to be changed by it." He gently rests his forefinger on the rim of her cup. "You yourself have a tale."

"Of interest to nobody."

"I mean the tale which, *scusami*, your body tells. I note that, in the hour we have sat here—a most pleasant hour it has been—you have not arisen from that chair. No, nor leaned in my direction. I take this to mean that you have not just now the capacity for standing. . . ."

Here, too, she pauses, but only because the question of standing remains ever open. At all times she can *picture*, say, the act of rising. This image might then generate enough impulses to be realised or might not—she has no way in advance of knowing—and there are days she misses not so much the sheer animal fact of locomotion as the way in which thought once rolled so soundlessly, so thoughtlessly, toward action. It is a gift she never stopped to savor.

"I do not know what Lady Brooke has told you," says Doctor Rossi.

"A bit."

"Then you know perhaps that I have made my life's work the—the uniquely *feminine* ailment. It is my considered opinion that the reproductive organs, so integral to the perpetuation of our species, these are the villains which break the female body down. I speak to you now of fainting spells. Fatigue. Shortness of breath. Hysteria. My experience has shown me definitively that these ailments are uterine in origin."

He tugs crisply on the lapels of his lounge jacket, as if he were addressing a jury.

"The same holds with your creeping paralysis, Signora. It is merely one more price which Woman pays for being Woman. I do not pretend to understand God's will in this matter. I wish only to be your humble intermediary before Him."

There must be something nettled in the shake she gives her head, for he at once modulates his tone.

"Forgive me if I presume too far, but for such as me, your confinement here on this terrace is a crime. A crime, yes, against Nature for a lady such as yourself and so abundant in—"

"Solitude suits me quite well."

He nods. Then, with a light sigh, rises and takes a couple of bandy-legged strides in the direction of the sea.

"Please to know, Signora, I am not one of your Harley Street doctors. I do not stand here with my pipe—how your English love their pipes—and tell you *all is shipshape* and *pip pip, old bean*. I see *you*, Signora Holland, and I see, if you will pardon me further, one who would be saved."

"Is it now that I'm to blush, Doctor?"

"There shall be no need. If you should but consent to the procedure we have already discussed . . ."

"I don't wish to speak of that just now."

"Then we shall not."

His hands drifts toward his trouser pockets. His blocky head lilts toward his blocky shoulder. So relaxed is he in outline one might almost think *he's* the one on holiday. A cloud blurs into salmon on the Ligurian Sea's horizon. Ropes of salt air scale bone-dry hills. And, from somewhere down below, comes a glittering, metallic sound, of no certain origin.

"Mandolin?" she asks.

"It has that character," he says, and in the next thought, turns to her. "Signora. When was the last time you danced?"

"I can't begin to remember."

"What if I were to say that you shall dance again one day? Would you say to me that I am a liar?"

"Not to your face."

Once more, he flashes that hairy and expressive hand. With a mounting alarm, she understands she is to clasp it.

"Do not be afraid," he says. "You shall not fall."

She might explain to him that, every time she discerns herself to be falling, she has already fallen. It has happened more times than she can count. The strangest part is not to feel the chastening impact of ground, only to see it reflected a day afterward in a chain of bruises, like calling cards left while she was out. She reaches out a hand of her own and, in the next moment, is levered up. With a sommelier's delicacy, he closes his arm round her waist.

"It begins," he says.

They move gingerly at first, his voice gradually converting the mandolin rhythm into a melody. Not one she recognises, either in its first or last beat, but the meter she discerns: a stately, pulsing five-quarter. How even to dance to it? Yet here they are, moving, and for now she is upright, and he is humming, and his arms are twined round her as if from old habit, his face angling over her shoulder, his pores breathing out Toscano tobacco and bergamot and rosemary and lemon. An entire *land*, she thinks, breathing over her. She cannot say how much time passes before a purely British contralto crosses the distance.

"What fun."

From the terrace doorway, Lady Brooke gazes at them, as if from a great height.

"Is it to be the tarantella next?" she asks.

2

FAR FROM BEING abashed, Dr. Bossi professes wonder at being surrounded by two such blooming specimens of English womanhood. Never mind that Constance is thirty-nine and Lady Brooke easily six or seven years older. (The exact date is between her and her Maker.) In his eyes, they become their most maidenly selves, and it is with multiple expressions of regret and the barest breath of a kiss on each of their hands, that he departs. For some time after, Constance can still smell him on her skin.

"I'll have a spot of tea," says Lady Brooke. "If it's all the same to you."

Perhaps she has already ordered it, for Maria is even now setting out the service in the living-room. Here in Liguria, sandwiches and scones are supplanted by focaccia and amaretti, but the tea is Lady Londonderry, imported by Lady Brooke herself from Jacksons of Piccadilly. "The paisanos are all very dear," she likes to say, "but some things are best left to the English, don't you find?" The marble floor is cool beneath their feet as she and Constance take their places, but the air is still languid with heat, and the steam from the pot makes a colloquy with the cords of sunlight.

"Well now," says Lady Brooke. "You and the Dottore seem to have got along."

"Oh, Margaret."

"I imply nothing. I merely want to know if he inspires confidence."
Constance frowns.

"He *acquires* confidences."

"That is not at all the same thing. But tell me, please, what is his diagnosis? Pray don't tell me he called you an hysteric. That is only what doctors say when they haven't the foggiest."

"He merely tucked hysteria into the whole carpetbag of haven't the foggiest. Oh," she hurries on, "I don't mean to impugn him, but he wishes me with all the force in his little Italian body to undergo a rather large procedure." She tilts her head back toward the terrace, half expecting to find him still there. "I suppose, if I were back in London, I should scout out a second opinion."

"The second opinion is Princess Salm's. The third is Baroness Wrangel's. The fourth—well, I might list a good half-dozen irreproachable ladies who speak of Doctor Bossi with the greatest assurance. In particular of his *discretion*. I will confess that, for a gynaecologist, I find him a touch ardent. I always think that men, when they descend to those precincts, should be grave as undertakers."

"For all I know, he *was*. I wasn't exactly looking back."

"And what did he find?"

"I suppose you'd call them growths. He believes they might be connected in some way to . . . all the rest. . . ." She sketches a vaguely apologetic circle along her right flank. "Best to wipe the slate clean, he says. And, of course," she speeds on, "it's quite a common surgery. Then a month of bed-rest in the clinic—attended by the most worldly of nuns, it would seem. Another month here. Naturally, I couldn't possibly schedule it until the new year. February or March, at the earliest."

"Constance."

"The boys deserve an uncomplicated Christmas."

"So you mean to wait until your left side has become quite as useless as your right?"

"Oh, it's not so bad as all that. You should see me operating my new typewriter. Letters take half the time they used to."

"Yes," muses Lady Brooke, "and become one-tenth as intimate."

What Constance has yet to tell her friend—tell anyone—is that the most deranging symptom of all has been the blind spot in her right eye, which has enlarged from a pinprick to a thumbprint and which leaves her entirely at the mercy of invaders. The latest case in point: Maria, bustling in from the kitchen, entirely invisible until there is no unseeing her, a granitic figure swooping in with shawls and blankets.

"Ah, Signora! Troppo freddo! Avvicinati al fuoco, o prenderai il raffreddore. Ecco! Il tuo scialle. . . ."

She drapes Constance in layer upon layer until the only part of her still bare to the air is her face, peeping out from vast folds of wool. Had she a better command of Italian, she would explain to Maria that the villa itself is quite warm enough and that, if she had her way, she would thrust open every window. Instead, she waits until Maria has ushered her toward the hearth—and tossed another log onto the fire and then retired to the kitchen with warnings of occult significance—before throwing off all her layers and reaching for her fan. From the opposing armchair, Lady Brooke scowls.

"It's your fault, you know. You let her baby you."

"Don't you think somebody should?"

"I do not. It weakens character. And, in this case, blurs the necessary boundary between servant and mistress. Before too long, she will be taking you out for walks in a perambulator."

Constance fingers a bead of sweat from her temple, flicks it lightly toward the floor.

"I wish I could be as fierce as you," she says.

And means it. Lady Brooke lost three sons to cholera during a single passage through the Red Sea, then promptly birthed three more. Sold off the Star of Sarawak without a twinge to fund their education. There is something of the flint about her even when she is doing nothing more than staring into a fire.

"How much time do we have?" she asks. "I mean, before that tiresome creature comes bustling in with another log? Or an entire tree?"

"Ten minutes, I'd say."

"And is she the sort to listen behind doors?"

"Even if she were, I doubt she could follow."

"One can never underestimate the Ligurians; they are as cunning and resourceful as any Sarawakian. Good heavens," she says, briefly waylaid, "I believe I have failed to limn for you the extreme horror of your red walls. They aren't your doing, of course, nor would you be my friend if they were, but you must swear to me on some holy relic—I don't altogether care which—that you will paint them yellow before spring has crossed the meridian."

"Mustard?"

"Pray do not compound the horror. Make it canary, and consider yourself well off. Now another thing you must swear. Not to overreact or be in any way womanly when I say what I have to say to you."

"I shall try."

Lady Brooke makes a canvass of her, another of the room.

"Just yesterday, I received a letter from a friend in Posillipo. She asked in a rather pointed manner if you were staying here."

"If I . . ." Constance's lips part a fraction. "Who was this friend?"

"Nobody you know."

"Did she refer to me by my old name?"

"She did."

For want of anywhere else to look, Constance stares at her hands. Her *two* hands, for she has got into the habit of thinking of them as opposed forces.

"How will you answer?" she asks.

"I shall deny it, naturally."

"Good."

"I should not even have raised the subject if it did not signify that the rumor is abroad."

Constance nods, and her gaze, without intending, shifts toward the north-facing window, where, just this morning, she watched the boys trying to corral a whip-snake in the herb garden. They were having the devil's own time of it and, as she watched, the most flippant of thoughts rose up. *Every garden must have its serpent.*

"I shall send them away tomorrow," she says.

"Don't be a booby. They'll be back in school before the week is out."

"One can't be too careful. . . ."

"Do you honestly imagine they'll be spirited away by some *journalist*? If there breathes a Fleet Street scribbler agile enough to scale these cliffs, I shall greet him with a wreath of laurel before knocking him back over. My point is not to inflame you into melodrama but to shore up your redoubt. Think carefully now. Who else knows you're here?"

Constance squints into the near distance.

"My brother, of course. My attorneys. Georgina."

A lengthening pause before she adds, with a grating edge of embarrassment:

"Him."

Lady Brooke's eyebrows compose perfect Norman arches.

"Him," she echoes tonelessly.

The arches turn Gothic.

"Him?"

"Margaret. I was going to tell you, *truly* I was, but . . ."

"Do you to mean to say that you have been in contact with that scoundrel?"

"It is not entirely incredible that I should. He remains my husband."

"I would suggest that he forfeited that title three years ago. If not in the divorce court, thanks to your forbearance, then in God's tribunal."

God, she thinks, and not for the first time. *Where does He fit?*

"Dearest Margaret, would it return me to your good graces if I told you he wrote me first?"

"And when was that?"

"Last May. He'd only lately been freed from gaol, and he was—oh, I do believe even your adamantine heart might have cracked a little. Every line was perfectly *choked* with penitence."

"Fancy that."

"It was genuine, I tell you. The first thing he asked after was my health. The second was the boys. He begged me for news of them—demanded photographs—said he couldn't rest until he'd seen them again. Oh, I might have ripped up the letter, I suppose—I'd half a mind to—but there were the boys themselves to think of, and there was—oh, God, how to explain, Margaret? For all he's done to us, there's nobody else alive who could know what Oscar and I went through except, well, Oscar and me. How could I not write him back?"

Lady Brooke gives Constance's hand the lightest of squeezes before withdrawing. For some minutes, she sits there, frowning at the popping cedar logs.

"And just where has this felon of yours dragged his infernal carcass? Paris, I suppose? *Bien sur.* The one place in the world where vice is a competitive sport. He changed his name, I've no doubt."

"To Sebastian Melmoth."

"How like him to choose an alias that advertises itself as such. And what of the Unmentionable? Where has he got to?"

"Capri, last I heard."

"Then let us pray that never the twain shall meet."

Lady Brooke pauses and, in a slightly mollified tone, adds:

"I suppose you invited your Mr. Melmoth down here."

"If his last letter was any indication, he will arrive by week's end."

"Ah, what a lovely little family sojourn it shall be. Gathering *basilico* on the hillsides. Watching longshoremen fish for squid. *Tout charmant.*"

It is only in the act of replying that Constance hears her own stubbornness.

"A father should see his sons, Margaret."

"That is a notion as baseless as it is sentimental. Rajah Charles hasn't seen my children in sixteen years and, absent any evidence to the contrary, hasn't missed them."

"Our husbands are different, you know that."

"They are the same in that they are to be avoided on principle and for as long as the world affords space."

Constance gives a single chuckle, shakes her head.

"You used to adore my husband," she says.

"I did! Until he grew weak as water. Publicly debasing himself for that popinjay, and why? To be hauled before the Old Bailey and dragged off to prison like some horse thief. I am sure he fancied himself quite splendid with his *amour fou*, but I am here to say there is nothing more unattractive in a man than martyrdom."

The memory comes back as freshly as the first time: sitting on that hard wooden chair in the visitor's room and watching Reading Gaol prisoner C.3.3 shuffle in. Her first thought was that someone had erred. The half-mute, stooped, emaciated figure in the grey chevron uniform . . . the human shell with deadened eyes and slackened lips . . . this was somebody else's husband. She was about to lodge a protest, but then the man removed his Scottish cap and stepped into the light, and there lay the ruins of that once-beautiful hair, now crudely shorn and streaked with white and grey and falling away, on further inspection, to reveal the bald spot he was no longer able to conceal. His skin smelled of the tannery, his right ear ran with pus, and when words failed him, as they often did, he subsided into weeping. Lady Brooke is right: There was nothing lovely in any of it.

"What about women?" Constance asks. "Do *we* make attractive martyrs?"

"As if men gave us any alternative. No, my dear, it is the martyr he has made of *you* that I can never forgive."

"Nor can I some days."

"Dragging you and your boys into his mire. Forcing you all into exile. Obliging you to live under assumed identities. And look at you now, Constance! Dressed like somebody's governess in a rented villa. Cringing at phantom journalists and dragging your right leg after you like a sack of turnips."

Constance laughs, she can't help herself. This is Lady Brooke's way of babying her, too.

"But I have *you*, darling Margaret. And I have my very own Kodak there on the mantel. Shall I take your portrait?"

"Not now, I'm feeling peevish."

"And I have the boys, at least till the journalists get them. And there's the sea." She angles her head south. "Which has yet to disappoint and makes me wish I were one of those painters you used to subsidise, just so I could capture all its moods. And there's this divine air, and the gardens, and I've a cook whom I pay forty-five lire a month and a maid who gets thirty-five out of me and does everything I could ask for up to the point of smothering me alive. And I've at least ten thousand lizards sunning themselves every day on my terrace. I tell you I wouldn't go back to England now if she came crawling on her knees."

"She will. I promise you that. Or she will have me to answer to. Mean*time*," says Lady Brooke, rising to her feet, "we must on all accounts stay vigilant. And if that wretched Mr. Melmoth has the effrontery to show his face round here, you are to tell everyone, including the servants, that he is your brother."

"Oh, Margaret. They have met my brother."

"Goodness me, a woman may have more than one."

"Only one resembles me."

"How irksome you are. Half-brother? Stepbrother? I have never met a person so resistant to telling a good honest lie."

"And the boys, are they to call him Uncle?"

"What else? Auntie? If they know what's good for them, they'll do exactly as you instruct."

Yes, thinks Constance, *they probably will*. Back in Bevaix, they made barely a peep when she called them into the dining room and told them they were to have a new surname.

It's Uncle Otho's new name, too, darlings. H-O-double-L-A-N-D. Just like the country. Practice writing it, won't you, until it becomes second nature. Until you can say it in your sleep.

By then, of course, Constance had already forbidden them to speak of their father or share their history with anybody, so losing their name was just one more link in the chain of divestitures. They took up their pens; they filled out their foolscap. At her urging, they even went through their clothes and possessions to expunge any traces of the old identity. How dutifully, how solemnly they carried out the whole exorcism—before at last bolting to the summer house and shutting themselves in for the rest of the day. Something of their choked silence must pass into her now, for Lady Brooke's voice softens a trace.

"My dear, I do believe that the world reclaims us. After a time."

"What if we don't wish it to?"

"It happens all the same, I fear."

Will Oscar be reclaimed? she wants to ask, and the only thing that stops her is the name itself, which has gone unspoken for so long it has the air of an ancient curse.

"Margaret," she says, drawing herself up in her chair, "How might I look less like a governess? Just for a night?"

3

⹅⹆

LADY BROOKE HAS seldom required much in the way of primping—her White Rajah never much cared how a woman looked, by day or candlelight—nor does she have a grown daughter who requires dragging to the altar. But, being a traveller and student of the world, she has acquired knowledge the way visas acquire stamps and, so laden, ranges through what's left of Constance's wardrobe—the gowns that, because they didn't fetch much in the open market, now subsist in a kind of sullen servitude, waiting to be called up.

"Well now," says Lady Brooke, fingering some weight of crepe, "this isn't unacceptable. Is that Gainsborough blue? And is the underskirt frilled? I don't suppose you have any bows. No, of course not, they're quite out of season, but have you ribbons? Yes, just the one or two—not too scarlet, we don't wish to seem fast. In that vein, don't wear any rouge, but a splash or two of rosewater wouldn't go amiss. I do think actual *roses* are a bit vestal at your time of life. . . ."

Lady Brooke has enough tact at least to wait until her departure before asking whom all the preparation is for.

"Nobody," says Constance.

"Then may you and Seigneur Nobody have a lovely evening."

She departs without a backward glance. A few minutes shy of five o'clock, Cyril and Vyvyan come tumbling through the front door. The errand they were tasked with this morning was to fetch a single loaf of bread from Nervi but, by the time they stopped in Sori to watch the fishing fleet and wandered over to Recco to see the firework factory and waited for the train back, the bread was nibbled down to small chunks, and their Anglo-Irish skin now stands blotched by the sun's own reprimand. Maria rushes in with blankets—she is every bit as fearful for their health as Constance's—and as the boys huddle by the newly banked fire, they awaken to what in their immediate world has changed.

"Your dress," murmurs Vyvyan. "It's blue."

"Do you like it?"

There is a silence, broken at last by Cyril's belligerent voice.

"Mother, what have you done?"

"I don't know what you mean."

"You never dress up for us," insists Vyvyan. "Somebody's coming."

"It's only a friend."

"An *old* friend?" demands Cyril. "Somebody we know?"

"Yes, and that is quite enough interrogation for one mother to endure."

She doesn't have the heart to truly reproach them for she grasps the question that lies behind the others: What remains of the before times? Their old lives fill them now with an almost unspeakable sentiment: toys, clothes, books, all swept away in an auction. When she had to tell them that Lady Wilde was dead (the same message she conveyed to Oscar in Reading Gaol) they burst into actual tears over a woman who, alive, was a terror to them both but who, dead, recomposed herself into a lost age. "Grandmamma," they moaned. Imagine if they knew she'd died without enough money for her own tombstone and lay now in an unmarked grave in Kensal Green.

"Listen to me," says Constance. "Maria has drawn you both a bath, and you're to give yourselves a good hard scrub, do you hear? And not come back until I can stand the smell of you."

She has scarcely enough time to recompose herself, for the knock comes but a few minutes later. Under normal conditions, she might wait for Maria to answer, but the acoustics in the villa are unreliable, and, against the prospect of the caller giving up, she shuffles toward the door and drags it open as far as it will let her, then twines her head round it to find, posed in the aperture, Arthur Clifton.

His person is only lightly altered since last she saw him (the moustache a bit fuller; the chin fuller, too). It is the mere fact of him—a familiar face in strange surroundings—that makes him in this moment unbearable. It is all she can do not to shove the door back, but he is already reaching a hand toward her, and even this is hard to bear, for she can't even feel his hand, can only *see* it floating like a meringue atop her own.

"Dear Constance," he says.

This she can feel. The imperturbable baritone, buzzing once more in her ear. Next second, she is drawing him inside and thrusting her cane from view.

"Dear Arthur," she says, carefully transferring her weight to his arm. "How thrilled I was to get your wire. But bless me, what a distance you've come! You must be all done in."

"Not a bit. The express train gets a fellow places before he even knows he's gone."

"Yes, but has it run off with your luggage, too?"

"No, I left it back at the hotel."

"You don't mean Hotel Nervi? Goodness gracious, the guests are probably already rifling through your shirts. Never mind, we'll send for your trunks, and you'll spend the night here."

"I couldn't possibly."

"Nonsense, the boys will be happy to share a bed, and if they aren't, who cares? Tell me at least you'll stay for dinner," she says.

"Well, now." He makes rather precise show of leafing through an invisible calendar. "This appears to be the one evening I'm not spoken for."

"I should warn you. The boys are wondering who it is I've put on my only pleasing gown for."

"Pleasing it is."

"So do strive to be worthy of the enormous privilege that has been granted you."

It is here that Maria at last makes an appearance, not with her usual purpose but with an air of open appraisal for the stranger in her midst. She surveys Arthur from the top of his white linen suit to the patent leather of his boots. Is this the mysterious husband, home at last from some foreign adventure?

"*Grazie*, Maria," says Constance. "Kindly take Signor Clifton's hat, won't you? *Cappello*, yes. And tell Cook to hold off dinner for another hour. *Cena, si. Un'ora.* Signor Clifton and I will be out front. *Laggiù, capisci?* And . . . *una bottiglia di chianti, per favore.*"

She doesn't drink much in the way of alcohol these days—why should she wish to feel more numb? Nor does she spend much time on the front terrace, which the boys long ago colonised, demarcating their territories with chalk and string and Private Property signs on every claimable surface. So it is agreeably transgressive to gather here late of an afternoon with a carafe and Arthur Clifton. The day is thickened now with summer haze ripening into autumn: tints of peach mingling with yellow and gold. A faint whiff of heliotrope.

"Tell me about your wife," she says.

"Florence? I am happy to report she is in good health."

"I'm so glad."

"She sends her best, of course."

"How nice."

"The boys are well?" he asks.

"Quite well. As you shall see."

Absently he takes his first sip of wine, only to recoil.

"Dear me," he says. "It does bite back, doesn't it?"

"Yes, it's that rough new vintage, straight from the hills. I don't have much stomach for it myself, but I'm happy to watch you become the master of it."

"And so I shall."

She smiles. Laces her left hand into the waiting cradle of her right hand.

"Dear Arthur," she says, "I hope you won't think me rude, but I am longing to know what mission brings you to our remote outcropping."

"Need there be one?"

"Of course not, it's just that London barristers are rather *rara avis* in these parts."

With some deliberation, he draws his pipe from his coat pocket. (*How your English love their pipes.*) Lights it by the candle flame and sucks down the first vein of fumes.

"Well," he says. "I suppose you might blame it on Robbie."

"Robbie Ross?"

"Yes, he persuaded me it might be a bit of a lark to open a gallery in Bury Street. Of course, we haven't enough capital yet for the established artists, so, while Robbie harvests the new talent in London, he suggested I make a circuit of Italy. Seek out the next Caravaggio."

"And I applaud your purpose, but I am wondering if you'll discover him here. Unless you mean the sort of artist found at the pasta factory."

"Oh," he says, rather negligently. "One never knows."

She studies him for a moment, slowly unlaces her fingers.

"It does seem a long way to come on such a general errand," she says. "Here, I mean."

"I expect it does."

"In which case I must ask—and forgive me once more for coming so quickly to the point, but exile has a way of filing one down—is there some *other* reason you're here, Arthur? I mean, other than . . ."

Other than me, she would say.

"I have just seen Oscar," he says.

At first it is the mere dumb shock of hearing the name spoken, at long last. With a slow expense of breath, she follows a chain of olive trees, climbing up into crag shadow.

"By *seen,*" she says, in a smaller voice, "I presume you have been in conversation with him."

"Yes."

"Within the last week."

"Just so."

She nods. Once, twice.

"How did he look?" she thinks to ask.

"Rather better, I should say."

"Is his colour improved?"

"Very much so, the . . . the Mediterranean sun has been a blessing to him. He has also managed to regain some weight. Which I believe is to be welcomed."

"Surely."

Without thinking, she reaches for her own glass and brings it to her lips. A single small draft, at once plumping through her, quite as if she'd downed it all.

"I know it's silly of me," she says, "but I always preferred him on the portly side. I thought it would keep him more earthbound. Clearly, I was . . ." She stares into her glass. "Is he writing?"

"A bit. No plays, of course."

"Well, no," she answers, with a little manic upswell. "There's not much farce to be dredged from *that* well. Do you remember laughter, Arthur? I do."

He winces up his lips as if to say he does.

"Poetry," he says at last.

"Sorry?"

"He has taken up poetry again."

"Ah."

"Some sort of long-form narrative. Semi- or it might be *quasi-* autobiographical. . . ."

Still too close to the real thing, she thinks. *No market for that.*

"How pleased he must be," she says, "to have unlimited paper and pen. To take up old habits, as it were."

"Here's to old habits," agrees Arthur, lifting his glass in her direction. And there she might leave it, but something complicates in his eyes, and with that the dimensions of things change, subtly at first, and then baro-metrically. She sits there, revolving the conversation through her mind, and then hears herself say, faintly:

"The Mediterranean."

"Pardon?"

"You mentioned something about Oscar being in the Mediterranean sun."

It is his turn to be silent.

"I was given to understand that he was still in Paris," she says. "Or Berneval, that was the last postmark."

Arthur takes another drag of his pipe, then expels the thickest cloud yet, as if to hide behind it. At last he declares in a flat tone:

"Oscar is in Naples."

She blinks at him.

"That is quite the shift of coordinates."

"I was surprised myself."

"And what are we to derive from *Naples*, Counselor? To be *sure* . . ." She gives her throat a guttural clearing. "Geography was never my forte in school, but if memory serves—and I do hope in this event that it doesn't—Naples is but a few miles' ferry ride from Capri."

He says nothing.

"Do you know," she says, "if I were a critic, reviewing this particular plot development, I would call Oscar's showing up in Naples a coincidence that—oh, I think the phrase is *strains credulity*."

"It is no coincidence."

Against her own expectations, she begins to laugh. A jagged, mirthless sound that leaves her, in the space of a few seconds, sagging in her chair.

"Oh, dear," she says, in a weakened voice. "Is this how it is to be? Old habits, indeed."

"I cannot defend it, Constance. I cannot explain it. . . ."

"The explaining part is almost childishly simple. Lord Alfred, having managed to put him in one gaol, now desires to put him in another. And in this he has the prisoner's own consent."

She sits there quiet. Then she leans across the table and begins hissing with such vehemence that even Arthur's phlegmatic face begins to fissure beneath it.

"I must convey this to you," she says. "I desperately need somebody to understand. For the last two years, my sons and I have been running for our lives. *Running*, Arthur, from a scandal that none of us had any part in. Running from any newspaper that might allude to it, from anybody who might have any knowledge of it. We have changed our name, our domiciles, we have cast off the vast majority of our belongings, we have done everything but dig a hole in the earth and bury ourselves inside it, and the only thing that's sustained us through this—this little private diaspora of ours—is the hope—so germinal, Arthur, we have never dared even voice it—that a husband might finally come to his senses and a family might finally be reunited. Because without that—without *that*—what has this all been for?"

She can feel the violence inside her, both flaming outward and particularizing. *Like an ulcer*, she thinks. And fearful of the sound it will make if it bursts, she casts a quick glance at the windows overhead. Closed, by order of Maria, but permeable, surely.

"And to think," she says, in a smaller voice. "I even invited him here." *Lovely family sojourn. Tout charmant.*

"You didn't tell the boys he was coming?" asks Arthur.

"Of course not."

"That's just as well."

She studies him through tight eyes.

"And why is that?" she asks.

He reaches into his jacket pocket and draws out a single envelope. Sets it on the table before her.

"You wanted to know what brought me here," he says.

The name written there is hers, but the hand is most manifestly . . . *his*. That lyrical rightward tilt of letters. The soft upper hook of the capital C, which she traces in full before retracting her hand.

"Will it put me out of temper?" she asks.

"It might."

"Then give it me in brief."

"Oscar rather thinks that next month might do better for a visit."

"Next month."

With her knuckles, she begins kneading the space just above her eyebrow.

"Let me see if I have this aright, Counselor. Your client knows full well that next *month* the boys will be in school. He knows—for I have told him—how they long to be reunited with him. He knows *all* of this but would rather fritter away his days in the company of the person least conducive to his happiness. Have I missed anything?"

"Constance . . ."

"The *real* question, perhaps the only unanswerable question, is why I continue to be astonished. Why do I expect one and a half years of hard labor at the queen's invitation to make any man stronger? It never has. And he is just any man in the end, isn't he? Nothing at all extraordinary, just a stewpot of weak, rotting flesh."

"Perhaps in a month's time . . ."

"So long as he remains conjoined to Lord Alfred, he need never come at all."

There is even, she now realises, a relaxation in uttering it.

"You are a trustee, Arthur. You know as well as anyone it is *my* family income which keeps us all above water. It is subject to *my* whim and *my* will, and I will not."

"Will not what?"

"Support him in his new life of leisure under the same old conditions. Oh, you needn't trouble to convey the message yourself, I shall write the letter myself tonight. Straight from the banker's mouth."

"He won't best be pleased."

"Then we shall be on equal ground, he and I."

Forgetting her own debility, she rises as if to stride across the terrace, only to be dragged back, humiliatingly, to her original seat. Spent suddenly, she suffers her head to drop into her hands.

"Oh, Arthur. What else did he expect? That sending you in person would incline me toward clemency? It has quite the opposite effect. Seeing you here, I am reminded of all the many times he has been rescued. By you, by Robbie, by Ada . . ."

"By you, too."

"We all closed ranks, did we not? Because the alternative was so much worse. But now the alternative has *happened*. It is an explosion that never stops exploding, and here we sit in the debris, composing yet one more rescue party for him, and why? There is nothing left to rescue. *We* are the ones who need saving." In a lower voice, she adds: "You think me pitiless."

"Only put-upon."

"That is too simpering. Give me a darker raiment. Give me Revenge."

"I would, if it suited you."

She looks at him: eyes shining, mouth half-cocked into a smile.

"If you loved me," she says, "you wouldn't make me think better of myself."

4

SOME ASPECTS OF the old times survive, she finds, at least in fragments. The sight of her sons, for instance, freshly bathed and in their Eton suits, arriving sulkily for dinner—it still catches at her throat. Is it the duress that lies behind it? The fact that they have executed these rituals to please her? Or has the reflex itself long since taken over, operating independently of choice?

"Boys," she said, "you remember Mr. Clifton, I'm sure."

In unison and with nearly the same lack of conviction, they reply: "Hallo."

"Why," says Arthur, gazing down at them, "don't you both look healthy as trout? It must be all that splashing about in the sea."

Vyvyan frowns. "Mother says we're not to go into the sea."

"Oh, well, darling," she sweeps in, "don't make me sound an ogre, it's just a precaution. One hears the most alarming local reports of quick-sands. Not to mention nasty currents that might sweep a boy under."

And nasty gypsies, she thinks. *And nasty journalists.*

"I daresay it's the sea *air*," amends Arthur, "that gives them both a lovely colour."

The boys say nothing, but there is already in their eyes the same cal-culating impulse she detected in Maria. Why is this fellow being granted pride of place? They take their seats quietly around the oaken table, which, in the combination of twilight and candlelight, takes on a riverine quality: plates and bowls not so much reflected as submerged. It is, she thinks, the one piece of furniture she would take with her if she could, though she has no idea where she's going.

"Mother," says Vyvyan, holding up three strands of spaghetti to the light. "They're green."

"Darling, it's called *pesto*."

"I don't care what it's called."

"Oh, but you should watch Cook make it some time. She throws basil leaves into an enormous mortar and pounds away at them with rage in her heart, and there is some olive oil in it, of course, and garlic and I don't know what else, but out it all comes, perfectly delicious."

"It's a tad slimy."

"Nothing of the sort. It is hearty and natural and fragrant. Arthur, have you had a moment yet to sample the Ligurian diet? I warn you, it consists almost entirely of fish and pasta, polenta and bread, day and night. Most of the locals have never eaten so much as a scrap of meat in their entire lives, but I must say they look none the worse. Almost shockingly robust. Of course, the produce here is absolutely divine." She is talking too much. "This time of year, in particular, one finds the most exquisite green figs, and the boys have become quite the expert harvesters of chestnuts. Haven't you, boys?"

"Only because we're always peckish," says Cyril.

Her mind flashes back to that demolished loaf of bread.

"Mr. Clifton," says Vyvyan. "Did you have to change your name, too?"

"Name?"

"He means your surname," explains Cyril.

"Oh! Well, no, not as yet. Of course, my wife changed hers."

"Did she?" asks Vyvyan, genuinely interested.

"When we got married."

There is a baffled pause.

"But *all* wives do that," says Vyvyan. "Even *our* mother did that."

"I only meant to say that names are ever changing, you see. It's a fact of the world. . . ."

His audience is no longer listening.

"I say," ventures Arthur. "Cyril's hair has lost a bit of its curl."

"It was never curly," insists Cyril.

"Wavy, perhaps."

"If you like."

Smiling tightly, Arthur takes up his fork again.

"And how are you liking Heidelberg, Cyril?"

"It's all right."

"And your new school?"

"Could be worse."

"Perhaps, darling," suggests Constance, "you might tell Mr. Clifton something you actually enjoy about it, as I should enjoy hearing that myself."

"Well," says Cyril, "they speak English there, that's a help. Head's wife is a decent sort. Chapel doesn't drag on too long."

"Have you made any friends?" asks Arthur.

"Fellows leave one alone. Better that way."

The words are so fatigued they barely make it out his mouth.

"Cyril has blossomed into quite the athlete," rallies Constance. "So gifted at all games. I would consider that ideal training for a military career, wouldn't you?"

"To be sure," says Arthur.

"A naval officer, perhaps."

"Why ever not?" says Arthur. "A lad needn't tread the educational path laid down by prior generations. Oh, it's true that for a—for a certain small clique of esthetes, an Oxford or Cambridge degree might confer a certain—one might call it *cachet* . . ."

"Mr. Clifton?"

"Yes, Cyril."

"You needn't beat on. I wouldn't go to university if my life depended on it."

Arthur reaches for his second glass of Chianti as if it were the world's last aquifer.

"Vyvyan," he says. "Tell us what *you* like most about school."

"I'm afraid I can't think of anything, Mr. Clifton. I've no friends to speak of, and I'm a proper stinker at cricket and Rugby football. The boys all bathe together naked, and one of the masters makes us hold our papers against the wall when we write lines so the ink always bleeds onto our hands, and then we have to spend the whole of break scrubbing it off. Oh, and there's another master who puts the littler boys in scrums and then whacks us on our prats with his cane."

"Bottoms, darling."

"And, first week of term, one of the bigger boys asked me to loan him five marks, but he never paid me back, and I asked him for it two or three times, and then he began yelling at me right there in the refectory. Mother, may I say what he said? It had *hell* in it."

"Sanitise."

"He said, *To blazes with you and your five marks!* And he aimed a kick at me, and everyone laughed, and I never saw my money again."

Cyril studies his brother with an air of clinical detachment.

"Vyvyan is quite weak," he explains.

"I disagree," says Constance. "He is simply not as suited as you to this particular regimen."

"We are saying the same thing, Mother."

If there's one vestige of the old days she still misses, it is when they called her *Mummy*.

"Well now," she presses on, "I am proud to report that Vyvyan is inordinately gifted at languages. After one summer in Heidelberg, he was practically fluent in German. Two weeks here in Bogliasco, and he is having extended conversations with Cook."

"He is only begging her for food," says Cyril.

"Will you stop? Will you just . . ."

She looks down at her left fist, clenched and white. Useless.

"Perhaps," suggests Arthur, "another school."

"I wonder if you're right," she says, suddenly brightening. "Our dear friend Princess Alice speaks in warmest terms of the Collegio della Visitazione in

Monaco. Of course, we aren't Roman Catholic, but there's something so *sympathique* about the liturgy, don't you find? And one hears such marvelous reports of Jesuit tutors. . . ."

In truth, she has never heard such reports, and when she says in the next breath that Vyvyan has always been spiritually inclined, she no longer has a clear sense of who is speaking. It is *her* mouth, surely, flapping open and shut, but everything else seems colonised. The only thing that can silence her finally is Vyvyan's treble, poking through.

"Am I to go there on my own?"

"Don't be an ass, Viv." With a grunt, Cyril leans back from his plate. "They mean to split us up."

"Oh, darling, why must you—"

"They don't want anybody finding out, and they think, if they keep us apart, we'll be less likely to blab."

The argument is well enough formed to make her think that somebody has advanced it.

"I demand to know," she says, "who is this *they* of whom you speak? Last I checked, you had but the one mother, and she makes decisions based entirely on your welfare."

Cyril's mouth crimps into a middle-aged line.

"Very well, Mother."

Nobody speaks for some duration, at which point Vyvyan's treble once more comes wobbling forth, like a bird winged by buckshot.

"Mother, I wouldn't blab."

"Darling, kindly refrain from repeating that horrible verb. My only aim in life is to find some place where you both can flourish. In peace and isolation."

"Once again," says Cyril, "we are saying the same thing."

5

"WELL NOW," MURMURS Arthur. "I'd say they're making quite the best of it."

She gazes at him, incredulous. "You don't mean the boys?"

"All things considered."

"They are *surviving*, Arthur. By no definition are they doing anything more than that."

With some degree of difficulty, he is handing her down the rickety wooden staircase from the rear terrace. She holds fast to his arm the whole way, for the steps, in her experience, seem ever on the verge of crumbling. (As does the cliff face itself, which, at regular intervals through the day, sends down slurries of stone and dirt, rattling like warnings toward the beach below.) Tonight, by some good fortune, nothing slips or slides beneath her, and after a dozen or so stairs, they are rewarded with a crudely carved bench of myrtle, facing straight to sea. For some time they sit there in the drowsy shadow of night. The ocean is a sheet of silver running toward a veil of grey mist; only closer to shore does it crimple into moaning billows. As she so often does these days, Constance imagines Oscar there. Yes, she thinks, right now he would be gazing across the breakers, a litter of cigarette butts at his feet, composing some impromptu Latin ode

to Neptune, for he would have noticed that the fishermen here all use tri-
dents to spear their fish, and it would have seemed the most natural thing
in the world to draw them into the great frieze-continuum of language.
Instead, there sits Arthur, silent as a cloud, the air sweeting and curing
round the bowl of his pipe.

"Bit of a nip in the air," he says at length. "Shall I fetch your shawl?"

Shaking her head, she grips her cane and leans forward.

"It's lovely here, isn't it?"

"Quite."

"Do you want to know the very best part of it? There isn't a newspaper
to be had for love or money. If one of them ever descended from the skies,
the paysanos would use it to plaster their roofs. Do you still read papers,
Arthur?"

"One or two, I suppose. Whatever the club keeps lying around."

The club. He *has* gone up in the world.

"For reasons of health," she says, "I have had to give them up. The only
ones I could abide for a time were the European ones—they weren't quite
so prurient—but even there I kept encountering myself on the page. The
poor little waif, the blinkered wifey. How could she fail to understand—
oh, I think the usual phrasing is *her husband's true nature.*"

"The answer is very simple. He didn't want you to."

"Yes, that is the safest answer, to be sure, but, you see, I fall into fre-
netic arguments with myself on this very subject, and I always arrive at the
same conclusion. It *wasn't* his nature, not at first."

"Oh, I know," says Arthur, sounding already half-bored. *"He was the
most ardent of lovers. . . ."*

"Well, he *was,*" she answers with a note of asperity. "Even when the
love fell away, the *lover* was there in plain view. Ready to be called back,
or so I presumed." Her voice trails away, then straggles back. "I can see
now that my failure . . ."

"Constance."

"My *failure* lay in not seeing the *other* Oscar who was about in the
world—because he had so little to do with mine. But that was the Oscar
everyone met, that was the one that . . ."

That went into Norfolk. And went out somebody else.

"It's funny," she says. "There's one exchange I keep reverting to. On my last morning at Cromer, Lord Alfred said the most curious thing. *I don't want you to think I was his first.* Well, I was still such a blinkered wifey I didn't quite grasp his direction, but then—as I imagine he wished me to do—I thought back upon that long parade of malnourished youths who used to traipse through Tite Street." She smiles. "How unfailingly Oscar brought them up to meet me. *My newest poet*, he would always say, and the lad in question, whether or not he could even *read* poetry, would extend some bony hand toward mine. *Enchanted, Mrs. Wilde. Such a pleasure.* Then sweep off on a perfect flood tide of relief. It always left me feeling so queerly maternal toward them. That's how I met Robbie," she says, "come to think on it. That's how I met you, Arthur."

There is silence. Then, with a soft grunt, Arthur rises and, turning away from her, makes a straight-backed silhouette of himself in the moonlight.

"Yes," she says, gauging him now. "You were a bit taller than the mean. Gentler, too."

He says nothing.

"I wonder, Arthur. Did it happen before or after he introduced us? Oh, I beg you, don't ask me what I mean by *it*. We are in Europe's basin, all sinners welcome."

More silence.

"In *your* case," she says, "I would wager it happened after. I think it would have put you at ease, knowing that the wife—the good old missus—was somehow on board with it all. Even if she weren't."

At last he speaks, so softly she must strain to hear.

"How should I have known any of that? I knew nothing."

"Oh, yes, you were practically a child, weren't you? Just like Lord Alfred. You'll forgive me if I no longer attach much in the way of innocence to that condition. No doubt my husband flattered you."

Another pause. Then, in a rueful voice, Arthur says:

"He said I had a delicate ear for music."

"Ahh. His esteem was always so *warming*, wasn't it? I remember thinking it was like washing up in a lovely flat in Belgravia, already furnished, with the landlord making the most generous of terms. But then the rent falls due, doesn't it, Arthur? And in the end, it's not such a hardship. One lies there and accepts one's economic *duty* . . ."

With a speed that startles her, he wheels round and kneels before and prises her face between his hands and draws her toward him until they are an inch apart and she can see the tapestry of broken capillaries along his eyelids.

"After all we have been to each other, do you dare ask me what it means to betray a man's wife? Or shall I remind you of Florence Clifton?"

It is the last name she expected to be introduced, and the one she has no answer for. With her active hand, she calmly wrests her head free of his grip without quite retracting it.

"You are right," she murmurs. "Even if I had a leg to stand on, I wouldn't."

He stands once more, surveying her. Then, hooking a finger into his buttonhole, begins to make a circuit of the terrace.

"Do you remember," he says, "that day in Goring when you and Florence got caught in that downpour? I was watching from the window as you came galloping back. Drenched to the bone, arms round each other's waists, giggling like schoolgirls. Anybody would have supposed you the best of friends."

"We are friends."

"The best?"

"I am fond of her."

"And she of you. Do you remember when we came to your last at-home? We didn't know it was the last, but we damned well should have because there was nobody else there. The scandal had done its work. There wasn't a single carriage in the drive. No Mr. Ruskin, no Miss Terry. I remember pausing at your threshold, wondering if it was quite the right thing, and Florence saying, *Constance needs us.*"

She lets her head drop back until she can see nothing but a gnarl of evening cloud, indigo at the fringes.

"If you are asking whether I am racked with guilt on her account, the answer is yes. Are you not yourself?"

"We have the same defence, Constance. The most bourgeois one of all. We had the good sense to be discreet. And isn't that the most damning part? What earthly use is a love affair if it can be carried off with such exquisite tact?"

"It was not tact, it was consideration."

"Ha!"

"It was declining to pile one scandal atop another," she says, more heatedly. "Though I confess I did wonder at times why I couldn't have a scandal of my very own. Hadn't I earned the right?" She shakes her head, lets out a small draught of air. "But I suppose the time for shocking anyone has passed."

"Has it?" he asks.

In the next second, he is kneeling at her feet, taking both her hands in his and pressing them with a kind of ravenousness to his lips.

"Dear Arthur," she murmurs. "How kind you are."

"Do not insult me," he answers, with a clouded face, "do not insult *us* by calling me kind."

"I only meant . . ."

Stymied, she can only let her forehead tip until it is resting against his.

"Arthur," she says. "My current condition does not afford much in the way of benefits, but at least it admits of no backsliding. Here." She presses his hand against her right side. "I cannot even feel your touch. Extraordinary, isn't it? My body is becoming a dead land. So when I tell you *this* time to go back to your wife," she says, "I regret to say I leave you with no obvious alternative."

And remembers that night on the rear terrace of Grove Farm, all propriety discarded, the harvest moon illuminating them with such ferocity that she thought all of England might rise up in protest.

Arthur rises now with as much stateliness as he can muster and, in a dull voice, says:

"I don't know what part I'm to play here."

"You have played it, my dear. You have stood by me and Oscar both, when not many would. And for that you have our eternal gratitude and . . ." Something rolls up inside her. "And I love you."

There is just the faintest brightening round his eyes—more perhaps than he wishes to reveal for he turns away, and together, in silence, they listen to the sea, rolling and shuddering. It amazes her now to think that an entire other world carries on below that teeming surface. *Two* worlds, invisible to each other, unless by transit of dream.

"Do you ever think Oscar knew about us?" Arthur asks.

"I've no idea. Why do you ask?"

"He spoke to me once of a play he was in the process of writing."

"A play?"

"Yes, the theme was a married couple who grow bored with each other and, by mutual consent, seek distraction elsewhere. The wife flirts with one of the house guests—nice, friendly chap—falls rather hard."

"That can't end well."

"Oh, it does for her and the lover; they run off together. The husband, though, kills himself just before the fourth-act curtain. Can't remember why."

She nods. Then allows her gaze to travel downward.

"Did this play have a working title?"

"Constance."

She says nothing at first. Then a dry chuckle forces its way up. How fitting, she thinks, that this should be the one play he never showed her. Even *Earnest* she read, in fragments, snatched from the depths of his private bonfire. But *Constance*, that was shoved in a drawer somewhere or buried under floorboards. Or never written at all.

Then again, if he had shared it, what would she have said? Change the title? Shorten the first act? Replace the melodrama with farce, for a West End audience will follow you in either direction? Or would she have just asked him to save that foolish husband? To grant him the happy ending he doesn't deserve.

"Arthur," she says.

"Yes?"

"Would you stay the night?"

6

"I THOUGHT MR. Clifton was staying the night," says Vyvyan the next morning.

How grateful she is for the cover of language. For if somebody leaves before dawn, he has not, in any technical sense, stayed the full night, has he?

"Mr. Clifton had to hurry back to his hotel," she says.

"So we're not to see him again?"

"Not anytime soon, no."

Vyvyan's eyes grow abstract, as though he were calculating the exact date.

"Mother, might I have an 1840 Penny Black stamp with a Maltese Cross cancellation for Christmas?"

"Well now," she says, blinking. "I've no idea how to procure such a rare treasure, but I shall make enquiries, how shall that be? And you, Cyril? Anything you've set your heart on?"

"A sabre."

"You mean the toy kind?"

"The real kind."

"Oh, darling."

"If it can't lop off somebody's head, why bother?"

To see him there, his fugassa half-uneaten, his heavily sugared cappuccino untouched, his once-curly hair drooping over his brow, his eyes fixed monastically on *Five Weeks in a Balloon* (a gift of Oscar's for his eighth birthday) is more of an affliction than she might have guessed. By all rights, this should be a mother's golden hour. Gathered with her two boys on the ocean terrace. School still a few days off. The sea, rippling and heaving, touched with yellow and jade. Yet, however much she would anchor here, her thoughts jangle toward compass points. West toward Hotel Nervi, from which Arthur will soon depart. South toward Capri, where Oscar is reclining, surely, on a terrace like this, in a cream linen suit, smoking his first cigarettes of the day. North toward England, where Lady Wilde lies in her pauper's grave. Eastward . . . well, that belongs for now to her.

"I'll not be long," she says.

It is one of the perquisites of close confinement to gain a more intimate knowledge of one's surroundings. So it was that, on her second morning in Bogliasco, she followed the pebbled path that crooked like a pauper's arm round the villa. Once out of view of the terrace, the path diverted through a grove of fig trees—large, hand-shaped leaves stroking her hair as she passed—then traced a lazy descent before arriving at an outcropping of ophiolite. She approached with caution, not knowing if a cliff lay on the other side, but there was only more of the same path, ambling with no urgency toward the ocean. The rock was what stopped her. Aubergine and dragon-green, high enough for her to sit on and rise *from* and offering, like a small miracle, a pure and uninterrupted prospect on sea and shingle. It is on this rock that she positions herself now all mornings, no matter the weather. Not even Maria can find her here, and there are times she wonders if she will ever go back.

This morning, she is watching a lateen sail skim across the polished shell of the water. Along the beach, white-bearded fishermen as ancient as the ocean itself are wading in as far as their rheumatic legs will allow and sending back the haul from last night's nets to a platoon of women and children bearing straw baskets. Constance's eyes funnel down to the smallest of the children, a boy not much higher than the water itself, doing his level best to stay upright in the tide until a wave of unexpected force catches him square and down he goes. Even from the depths of his immersion, he takes care to keep the basket and its precious cache above water and, two or three seconds later, rises, brine sluicing from his mouth and nostrils. In that same moment, a fisherman—tall and bent and bronzed— is wading toward him and, with an inaudible cackle, dragging him to his feet and ruffling his hair. The most fleeting, most familial of gestures, nothing more than a light tousle, and she cannot explain at first why it keeps resonating, but then she remembers: This is how Oscar used to do it.

And with that, the Ligurian ocean draws off to reveal its greyer, more frigid cousin, the North Sea, and she, or some slightly younger version of herself, is back at Cromer beach in Norfolk, watching her husband and elder son erect the largest sandcastle ever seen. *A pox on Land Tax!* they cry, and, as others of their party join in, Oscar tousles Cyril's hair, *worries* at it like an affectionate spider, but, in the same instant, his eyes find hers, and how dazzling his gaze becomes the more she stares back, for it is the look of a profoundly happy man, wishing only that others might be the same, and it is this wish that in memory rains down on everyone like democracy. On Cyril, on Lord Alfred, on the two tattooed sailors, on every diving seabird and Blackie the rabbit and Mrs. Balls and even the younger version of Vyvyan, waiting for them back in Hunstanton. In Oscar's heart there is no distinction: They are all there to be loved.

And it seems to her now that, if this exact moment could have been arrested, if the world had allowed such a presumption, Oscar's love would have carried them all to the end of their days. But the world made him choose—and she herself made him choose, for her stern letter is even now in Arthur's keeping, ready to be posted in this morning's mail—because human hearts, arranged as they are, cannot comprehend such a capacity.

"There you are."

She cranes back her head to find Cyril, face swollen with outrage.

"Were you hiding?" he demands to know.

"Of course not," she answers, recomposing herself and, in the same breath, mourning her discovery as bitterly as she has ever mourned anything.

"If you want to know," he says, "it was your cane prints that gave you away. *And* the dragging foot."

Like a detective story in the Strand *magazine*, she thinks. *The Adventure of the Dragging Foot.*

"I told you, darling, I wasn't hiding."

Baleful of eye, he consents to bridge the small distance between them. Then props himself on the small space of rock alongside her. Until now, she wouldn't have guessed a human body would fit there. For some minutes, they speak not a word. Then, in response to a query she hasn't heard, he says:

"You're quite right."

"About what?"

"There's no need to tell Viv. He isn't strong like me."

She squints at him.

"Tell him what?"

"Why Father went to gaol."

Her heart beats at her now like a fist on a door.

"What do you know of that?" she asks.

"You sent me to stay with my Dublin relations. But you didn't tell them not to leave their newspapers lying about. Oh, Mother, it was child's play. I didn't have to filch them out of bins or anything."

The Adventure of the Refuse Bins. A boy so eager to learn how the world has turned against him he will plunge into a mountain of trash.

"Listen to me," she says, leaning toward him. "What happened wasn't your father's fault."

"It was."

"No. It was the doing of a selfish young man named Lord Alfred Douglas, who was waging a war against his own father. In a just world, the two of them would have strapped on gloves and had it out in a boxing ring somewhere. Instead, they got Pappa to fight their war for them. And once it was done . . ." One libel trial and two criminal trials later. "Your father was in gaol and they were the only ones left standing. Which is what always happens with a war. The generals survive."

The bitterness in her voice is so out of keeping with her surroundings that she wonders if it's really her speaking.

"He ought to have run," says Cyril, miserably. "Before there was ever a trial at all."

"Oh, darling, we all begged him to. *Go abroad. Wait for it to blow over.* I suppose it was just his Irish stubbornness that made him want to see it out."

She glances over and finds Cyril's head bowed over his lap, his voice thickening.

"You needn't worry about me," he says.

"But that's what a mother does. . . ."

"No. *No.* What I mean is I won't end up like him."

"Like . . ."

"I don't have those sorts of leanings. Chaps are just chaps."

Her tears come like blades, and for the first time it occurs to her that she was only ever lured to this rock for the purpose of having her heart broken all over again. Only more cleanly.

"Oh, my darling," she murmurs.

"I'm not your darling. I'm not anyone's."

"No," she says, recovering herself. "You are quite right. You are a young man of quite superlative strength. I wish you to know how grateful I am for that. I believe that Vyvyan will be grateful, too, once he . . ."

Once he knows what it consists of. But then how is Vyvyan to know without becoming the hollowed specimen who sits now alongside her? She rests a hand on his knee, the most glancing of touches, then draws it away and gazes out to sea. The same young lad is wending toward land now with a fully stocked fish basket perched on his head. He keeps his gaze fixed directly ahead and his chin lightly jutted out, as if defying the wind and tides to do their worst. Only when he has reached the safety of shore does Cyril think to ask:

"Are you going to get better?"

She pauses, for it is a question she has never yet dared ask herself.

"Oh, well," she says, rousing. "I am glad to say there is a physician here with decided opinions on that very subject. Why," she speeds on, "by this time next year, I shall be chasing you and your brother all the way down to the sea, how should you like that? And not so very long after," she declares, in the same tone, "I shall be dancing at your wedding."

As soon as the words drop from her, she would call them back but, glancing his way, she finds only a sequence of slow nods. And with that, somehow, her future course shines out. She will consent to Doctor Bossi's procedure because she wants to be the one thing her son doesn't have to be strong for.

"I'll miss you," he says. "When I go back to school."

"I shall miss you, too, darling," she says, at once calling back the old endearment. "But, of course, Christmas will be here before we know it. Only you really must tell me what you want this year, other than some ferocious, death-dealing sabre."

All it takes, finally, is a single glance to get her answer, for it is right there in his face. He wants the Wildes to be the Wildes once more. In the snap of a finger. She smiles and sweeps a lank strand of hair off his forehead.

"I'll speak with St. Nicholas, shall I? He *owes* me, you know."

ENTR'ACTE

Cℛ

LETTER OF CYRIL HOLLAND TO ROBERT ROSS, OSCAR WILDE'S FRIEND AND EXECUTOR (C. 1900)

It is hard for a young mind like mine to realise why all the sorrow should have come on us, especially so young. And I am here among many happy faces among boys who have never really known an hour of sorrow and I have to keep my sorrow to myself and have no one here to sympathise with me although I am sure my many friends would do so if they knew. But when I am solemn and do not join so much in their jokes they stir me up and chide me for my gloominess.

It is of course a long time since I saw father but all I do remember was when we lived happily together in London and how he would come and build brick houses for us in the nursery.

I only hope that it will be a lesson for me and prevent me from falling into the snares and pitfalls of this world.

CRTR

LETTER OF CYRIL HOLLAND TO VYVYAN HOLLAND (JUNE 1914)

All these years my great incentive has been to wipe that stain away; to retrieve, if may be, by some action of mine, a name no longer honoured in the land. The more I thought of this, the more convinced I became that, first and foremost, I must be a *man*. There was to be no cry of decadent artist, of effeminate aesthete, of weak-kneed degenerate. That is the first step. For that I have toiled. As I roughed it month after month last year in the terrible plateau of Tibet, as I trekked hour after hour, day after day, but lately, over difficult country in dangerous times, when I was weary and ill with dysentery and alone in a strange and barbarous land, it was this Purpose which whispered in my ear: "It is the cause, my soul, it is the cause.". . . .

This has been my purpose for sixteen years. It is so still. I have often fallen away. I have despaired. I have cursed my fate and mocked at the false gods. It is my purpose still. I am no wild, passionate, irresponsible hero. I live by thought, not by emotion. I ask nothing better than to end in honourable battle for my King and Country.

ACT THREE

Wildes at War

British Infantry trenches, Neuve-Chapelle, France
May 1915

1

⚶

Now kindly observe, if you would, Captain Holland.

It is Cyril's most closely guarded secret that he copes with the isolation of his post by imagining he is being watched. In his mind, the King has sent an inspection party to build competency and morale across the fighting corps and has liberally supplied them with binoculars and periscopes, through which they monitor Cyril's every action and broadcast their admiration. The voice they speak in belongs to old Hargreaves, the Royal Military Academy instructor who first put an Enfield in Cyril's hands and said, "Meet your new best friend."

Observe, won't you, how quietly and unobtrusively young Holland lies there in his blind. To the naked eye, he might appear dead, but his head, you will note, is not sunken but poised. The eyes peer continually through the gunsight. The hand curls round the trigger. He has abolished all distraction. He is a creature welded of flesh and metal toward a single end.

On this particular morning, the spring air has a particular tooth to it, and, as the dampness from the ground presses through his buttoned tunic, he can feel the blood quitting his fingers joint by joint. With a soft grunt, he releases the rifle and plunges his hands into his coat pocket, rubbing them against the wool lining. It is then that his eyes pick out a hunched figure some eighteen yards off. No soldier but the comically abbreviated figure of a French lop rabbit, ears dragging nearly to the ground. With an air of skepticism, the rabbit ventures across the great slough of mud, leaping softly from mound to mound and turning by instinct toward the farmhouse covert where Cyril lies hidden, staring down his rifle stock.

Captain Holland knows better than to fire upon local fauna. That will unnecessarily alert the enemy as to his position. Let it also be noted that the rabbit has black eyes.

And just like that the inspection party slides off, and with a speed almost dizzying, he is dragged back to the seven-year-old boy in Norfolk who, lacking children his own age for company, befriended a local bunny and named him Blackie. With a curious serenity now, his grown-up version follows the lop rabbit's mournful progress.

Captain Holland knows better than to waste a bullet.

The rabbit disappears behind the stump of an old chimney. Cyril's rifle is still in ready position when, twelve or thirteen minutes later, something stirs above the enemy's eastern parapet. He takes it at first for a stone, then realises with a kind of slaked thirst that it is a head. So hatless, so very bald that it seems, on this clear and windless morning, to be an apparition.

Captain Holland finds his mark.

How could a Bosch be so carelessly exposing himself? Why have none of his comrades thought to warn him?

Captain Holland fires within a second of sighting.

Only he doesn't. His finger pauses just long enough for the head to sketch an almost scornful retreat. Fury subsumes him. Days without a target and now this one, presenting itself like a training-camp dummy. Then, by some miracle, the same head thrusts itself once more above the parapet. This time, without knowing it, Cyril is ready: his finger contracting— *holding*—even as the trigger breaks. The air parts into a furrow. Through his sights, he sees at first a grey indeterminacy. In the next second, a single pair of field glasses tumbles off the parapet.

Captain Holland has struck true. However, a sniper knows he cannot afford complacency, for the inevitable sequel to any successful strike is . . .

A hail of enemy bullets, sweeping from east to west and back again. Blindly, of course, for, as Cyril well knows, in those first stunned moments, it is impossible to know where a sniper's bullet has come from. The only remaining satisfaction is to rain down death on every quarter. From the British side, rifles answer in kind, and as the staccato pattering carries on over his head, Cyril shelters behind the old farmhouse hearth, feeling oddly secure. It is almost, he thinks, like hearing an argument in a neighboring flat: the clatter of dishes, screamed imprecations. He waits a full hour before snake-crawling back to the sap. No bullets follow him, and he is all the way inside when he casts a look through the loophole and spots an inert figure in a nest of decaying tree roots. Too steeped in shadow to be identified at first, so he has to squint to disentangle the two comically long ears, wrapped like a shroud round a head.

Captain Holland knows there is no use mourning what is lost. Mourning is the rankest form of distraction to a sniper and indeed to any soldier in the King's Army.

2

⁓

QUIET. SO MUCH quiet for such long stretches. The minutes between stand-to and breakfast can become like a year in a sanatorium and, absent any shells or rifle grenades, the year might extend past the lunch hour. Soldiers who aren't snatching another hour of sleep are smoking or playing cards or checking their shirts for lice or, if they're feeling homesick, composing the letters that the quartermaster-sergeant will gather after bringing up evening rations. Some few of them reach for a book—invariably, a retrenchment into childhood. *Through the Looking Glass. The Wind in the Willows. Black Beauty.* In that spirit, Cyril, after reporting the results of this morning's shoot, retreats to the officers' dugout and takes up, like an old piece of knitting, *Five Weeks in a Balloon.*

"Merciful Heaven!" exclaimed Dick, "the lunatic! the madman! Cross Africa in a balloon! Nothing but that was wanted to cap the climax! That's what he's been bothering his wits about these two years past!"

The book was a gift for his eighth birthday. He has long since torn out the inscription but not the memory of the man who inscribed it. For a moment, he can imagine him strolling in, wearing the old sack suit and summer boater.

"Darling boy, do you think I might borrow your book back from you? It's so dreary up there, you've no idea. The clouds are excruciatingly uniform, and don't even speak to me of the angels and their monotonal twanging—they quite refuse to learn the new hymns because they never learned the old. It's enough to make one strike a bargain with Satan, only he's such a bore, too, don't you think? Fire and brimstone and gnashing of teeth and not a new idea in two thousand years. Where is all the magic? Oh, I know Verne was atrocious in style—even translation can't make him sing—but needs must, darling boy. Would it trouble you too much?"

Last night, Cyril actually dreamed he was flying, though not in a hydrogen balloon like Verne's nor in one of the Vickers monoplanes that rumbles overhead on reconnaissance. It was just a matter of stretching out his arms, and he was drafted upward. He sailed across the Channel, straight to London, where the door to No. 16 Tite Street opened without his having to lift the knocker. Still airborne, he browsed through the dining room with its built-in sideboard and Morris carpet, then journeyed up a flight of stairs to the two drawing rooms, then up another flight to the back bedroom that he and Viv once shared. He was travelling through time, too, for the bedroom was again a nursery, and a smiling giant had introduced into it a toy milk cart, purchased that morning from Gamages and drawn by a miniature horse with actual horse hair. Once the giant realised the cart had miniature churns, he filled each one with milk and commanded the horse to gallop in ever-speedier circles.

"Mr. Wilde," remonstrated the nurse. "There is milk everywhere."

"So there *is*," he answered. "I fear I fell under the spell of a Very Selfish Giant. My darling boys, have I ever spoken to you of that rogue?"

Of course he had, a dozen times.

"Captain Holland."

Cyril stares up at a private of two and twenty years, with a prematurely veined face and a heaving chest, crouched in the dugout doorway.

"Message from the Colonel, sir. Will you come at once?"

Cyril closes the book with a spasm of regret, but somewhere in the quarter-mile walk back to battalion headquarters, he wonders if he is about to be commended. Too much to expect a Military Cross, but a bronze star might be all right. *Really, sir,* he imagines himself saying. *I was only doing my job.*

Five minutes is all the journey takes, through subterranean corridors squelching with mud, but when he reaches the other side, there are wonders. Polished silver. Wall-paper with rosettes. An Art Nouveau table lamp. Chinaware, still bearing the aromatic remains of bacon and eggs and marmalade and coffee. A gramophone. And there, in the center of it all, the Colonel himself, small, slight, with a soft, conventional haze of mustache that reminds Cyril of his mother's old friend, Arthur Clifton. It is said the Colonel came up as a regular and has at least three wounds to his record, one from the siege of Ladysmith, but he has so internalised the cadences and posture of the ruling class that they seem now native to him. The only dissonant notes come from his head, which sags from time to time with no clear warning, and his handsome blue eyes, which have a way of closing for some seconds altogether, as though stealing a nap from the rest of him.

"Whisky, Holland?" offers the Colonel. "Cigarette?"

"No, thank you, sir."

For a moment, the Colonel appears at a loss.

"Have a seat then."

Here is the surest sign that Cyril is no longer on the front line: the oaken easy chair with rush seat onto which he now lowers himself.

"All well, Holland?"

"Yes, sir."

"No complaints, I hope, about the general running of things."

"No, sir."

The Colonel rests his finger atop a mantel clock, so unmolested it seems to have been transported straight from Bloomsbury.

"When you were recommended to this battalion, Holland, I was told you were a first-class shot."

"I am pleased to hear that, sir."

"You were stationed in India, weren't you, Holland?"

"Yes, sir."

"I expect you fired on a great many game animals. Elephants, I've no doubt."

"One or two, sir."

"Rather large targets," says the Colonel, abstractly. "What sound do they make when they die?"

Cyril pauses before answering, not simply because the question is unexpected but because, in his experience, the sound couldn't be heard, for the other elephants were already gathering round, wailing like a thousand trombones.

"They make a dying sound, sir."

"And tigers and leopards?"

"The same sound, sir, only different."

"Ah, yes," returns the Colonel. "The only trouble . . ." He pauses to stroke the clock's domed glass casing. "The *only* trouble—and do correct me if I'm wrong—is that, when one fires upon a tiger or a leopard—an elephant, too, I shouldn't wonder—the poor beast can't fire back, can he, Holland?"

"No, sir."

"Whereas the Bosch can and do fire back, don't they?"

"Yes, sir."

"Indeed, I have cause to question if the conjoined efforts of you and your fellow—specialists—have succeeded only in further enraging them, like children swatting at a hive of bees."

Captain Holland knows that a sniper must on all account be truthful.

"Respectfully, sir, from the war's very onset, the Huns have delighted in making targets of *us*, and would derive that same delight whether or not we were shooting back. Indeed, sir, it is my fondest wish that, by shooting back at them often enough, they might derive a little less delight from shooting at us."

The Colonel takes a single paper from his desk.

"I fear the numbers do not bear out your confidence. Four of our men have been shot in the last week alone. And today, an officer."

"Today, sir."

"Not half an hour ago. You mean you didn't hear the bullet whistling through the air?"

"I was in the dugout, sir."

"Ah, yes. Safe and sound. It was Second Lieutenant Mandeville caught it."

The name gyres through Cyril's brain, finds no attachment.

"Was he killed, sir?"

"Only nicked. He declined the offer of a stretcher and walked his way to the aid station with just a pad on him."

"That is good news, sir."

"Is it? Forgive me, Holland, but, despite what you declare to be your best intentions—and I've no reason to doubt you—Fritz's snipers continue to declare open season on our boys. Fire away day after day with a nearly perfect impunity. I should jolly like to know why."

His voice has not risen or become any more emphatic.

"If I may, sir?" says Cyril. "Every German sniper's rifle comes equipped with a telescopic sight. Each of those sights magnifies its target by a factor of anywhere between three and four, making it three or four times more likely to find its way home. We have no such sights on our side."

"Anything else?"

"Yes, sir. Our trenches contain but the one loophole for concealing our snipers. The Germans have at least half a dozen, which makes it a great deal harder to determine, at any given moment, where their gunfire is issuing from. There is also the matter of the parapet, sir."

"The parapet," muses the Colonel.

"Yes, sir. Ours, by decree, is absolutely flat and even. The tiniest mouse couldn't move across it without being spotted. The German parapet is, by design, uneven and multiply coloured, confusing the eye and allowing their men to move about with comparative liberty. Then, too, there is the matter of the German trenches."

"Trenches."

"Yes, sir, they are dug deeper than ours, perhaps by two or three feet, depending on . . ."

The Colonel's hand flicks upward. A motion as delicate as it is conclusive. The head begins its sorrowing declension, the eyes their sorrowing close.

"Holland," he says, "do you know the man I sent for you just now?"

"Private Holloway."

"I expect he has not apprised you of his history."

"No, sir."

"He hails from Derbyshire, second eldest of twelve. At the age of nine, he began working the coal face in the local mine to support his family. From personal experience, I can report that he can scarcely write his own name. If anyone should be vulnerable to—to credulity—to *mythography*—it should be Private Holloway, do you not think? Yet never once— and I beg you to correct me if I am in error—never once have I heard him speak of the Bosch as a superior race."

"I don't know that I have heard him speak of anything, sir."

"Have you ever seen him cower before the notion of German supremacy?"

"I don't believe so, sir."

"Or suggest that our enemy, for all its newfangled machinery, has some innate advantage over the valor, pluck and wherewithal of the British soldier?"

"No, sir."

"Then I would suggest that we both of us draw courage from Private Holloway's example and work with what we have. If the *least* of us can rise without fear to the present challenge, then the only recourse for gentlemen is to do likewise. Do I make my meaning plain, Holland?"

A sniper should not be excitable.

"Is that all, sir?"

"No."

In a single motion, the Colonel opens his eyes, rises from his seat and turns toward the wall.

"You are to report at once to the regimental aid post. You are to introduce yourself to Second Lieutenant Mandeville . . ."

"Who, sir?"

"The fellow who got winged this morning. You are to stay with him until such time as his situation is resolved."

"Stay with him . . ."

"Yes, I am quite certain that his father, Lord *Arbuthnot*, would appreciate knowing that the Royal Infantry was taking every precaution in his son's behalf."

Christ. Lord Arbuthnot.

"If I may ask, sir, why me?"

"Because you are off duty and may be spared. I should warn you," the Colonel sails on, "you might be there some time. A shell fell last night on Verdon Alley, and until our sappers can dig it out, I fear there will be no way to evacuate anyone to hospital. Let us hope that, for *your* sake, Mandeville is in good enough shape to be sent straight back to his company."

"Sir, I hope you will forgive me, but I am no nursemaid."

"Nor would you have need to be if you had managed to take down the sniper who winged Lord Arbuthnot's son. Perhaps you might make amends to the boy in person. Or even gain from the encounter fresh resolution and purpose for the days ahead. Stranger things have happened. That will be all, Holland."

A sniper never forgets his training.

Rising, Cyril executes a smart turn and takes three measured strides to the doorway before the Colonel calls after him.

"Oh, Holland? You will put up a good show, won't you?"

3

⌒⌒⌒

THE REGIMENTAL AID post is no more than a converted dugout two hundred yards behind the front lines, with a few rough steps leading down from a low doorway and, for beds, three wooden frames covered with wire netting. Only one of them is now occupied, by a snoring figure with a head so wrapped in bandages it might have been dragged from Rameses's tomb. Cyril's heart sinks until he recalls that Second Lieutenant Mandeville, when last seen, was one of the walking wounded. Widening his gaze, he finds with some relief a heavily built figure, sitting upright on a bench.

"Mandeville," he proposes.

The figure who turns to him now is both man and hardly more than boy. Straw-coloured hair rising in tousled hummocks. Baby fat tucked like a squirrel's hoard into his cheeks. A square head and a forward-thrust jaw whose bellicosity is at once softened by the rosy, slack expanse of skin and the most domesticated of milky-blue eyes.

"Why, hullo, Captain," says Mandeville, lurching up on his feet. "Don't tell me you've been hit, too."

"Oh, not at all. I was only travelling past and thought I might sit for a spell."

"Sit?" Mandeville's face draws in on itself. "With me, you mean?"

"Whom else?"

"I say, that's jolly decent of you, sir."

"Not a bit. You weren't to know, but when one of our boys gets tagged by one of theirs, both the King and I take personal umbrage. And, as His Majesty is rather tied up this afternoon, he has asked me to come in his stead."

It is not entirely clear from Mandeville's wide and unclouded brow that he understands a joke has occurred.

"Do take a seat, sir," he says.

"Come now. You need only call me *sir* in front of the men."

"What shall I call you instead?"

"How about Holland? Say it now, for practice."

"Holland."

"There you are."

As if to underscore their new intimacy, Cyril drops his pack and helmet on the ground and eases himself onto an empty ammunition box.

"How are we holding up, Mandeville? I trust the pain isn't too . . ."

"No! Just . . ."

He joints a thumb toward the bandage on his neck.

"Little sting is all."

"Which you probably didn't even *feel*, bruising chap like you. But tell me how it happened, old boy. Were you on guard duty?"

Mandeville nods.

"Lost track of where you were, perhaps. Got a tad disoriented."

He shrugs.

"Oh, no shame in that," says Cyril, "it *happens*. Especially to—sorry, how long have you been here?"

"Five weeks and four days."

"How exact you are. It makes no matter; a certain negligence takes hold even with the veterans. And, now that I look at you, you do loom as one of the *taller* chaps," says Cyril, who is six foot two and has never been shot over a parapet, has crawled out at dawn and lain for hours and never once taken a bullet.

"I expect I still have learning to do," suggests Mandeville.

His plump lips part before a placating show of teeth. It is the same smile he has been flashing at the world since he was born, inviting every bully and protector to race each other in his direction. With an unexpected ferocity, he says:

"You'll have to pick off one of theirs tomorrow."

Cyril blinks, just once.

"Happy to."

"Only, whoever it is, you must get him square in the head."

Mandeville's eyes have lost not a quantum of their mildness.

"To be sure," answers Cyril. "And believe me, sonny, that bullet will have your name on it. But don't keep us hanging any longer, give us a peek."

"A peek?"

"The *wound*, Mandeville."

"Oh." The younger man instinctively hooks a forearm round his neck. "It's nothing."

"Well, we can't know until we've seen it, can we?"

And when Mandeville continues to balk, Cyril, calling up his last tiny reservoir of charm, says,

"We've only just become friends. Don't make me pull rank."

Lightly, Cyril undoes the tape and draws away the bandage, gazes with an epicure's interest at the gouged furrow stretching from the underside of the jaw toward the clavicle. It looks as if a giant raptor has dipped in its talon and come away with the merest appetiser of flesh and capillary.

"Well now, Mandeville, I hereby declare you the luckiest of dogs. But tell me, what happened to the bullet?"

"Oh! It kept right on going. Made a bit of a divot, I think, in one of the sandbags."

"That's all right, you can fish it out later and keep it for the grandchildren, why not? You know, we once had an NCO named Gardner who took a bullet right in the throat. Lay there for weeks, talking in whispers, and today—well, I'm not sure where he's got to—my point is you are most positively *not* Gardner, and all we require is somebody to stipulate to that effect. Sorry, where has the medical officer got to?"

Mandeville swings his head woozily from side to side and mutters, "I dunno," and, to Cyril's surprise, it's all he can do not to take a palm to the fellow's slackened inbred mouth and drive it straight through his skull. There is nothing personal—nothing *yet* personal. Cyril has been sent on a mission that is, by its originating design, absurd. He is to make amends to a blighter who can't fathom that amends need to be made and who, by the evidence, lacks even the intelligence to lace up his own boots (which stand gaping now like abandoned tenements). Yet, in philosophical terms, the mission is no more absurd than any other. This very morning, he was sent crawling out toward the remains of a farmhouse for the lone purpose of finding the one unlucky bugger who forgot to duck. The resulting death will in no way alter war's grim lottery; it will only worry a little, like a midge, at war's throat. War will soldier on. Here as confirmation, the distant crack-and-smudge of a rifle grenade, passing down as if by gossip from the front line. So faint it scarcely registers in Cyril's ear yet seems to scatter through Mandeville like a colony of hedgehogs.

"Just a bit jumpy," he mutters.

"Small wonder."

"Oh, it's not the wound, it's the *sound*, isn't it? No, it's the quiet that comes *after* the sound, don't you think? *And* before? Don't you find the quiet worse than anything? Some nights, I stand up there on guard duty, and I think the whole thing must be a dream and the world's no longer there, only it's creeping nearer every second, maybe it's got its hand round my throat and it's already squeezing and I shall be the last to know."

Cyril studies him for some time in silence.

"Thing is, Mandeville, we're *all* just waiting for something to happen, aren't we? Then it happens, and we start waiting all over again. A chap gets used to it, that's all. How old are you?"

"Eighteen last November. You?"

"Not quite thirty."

"Thirty."

A look of incredulity washes across Mandeville's face. Is the number too high or too low?

"Tell me," he says, leaning forward with unfeigned curiosity. "Does a chap *ever* get used to the rats? Back home, you see, I used to keep mice as pets."

"I felt certain you did."

"But they were so docile, weren't they, and they sat so peaceably in one's hand, and one gave them names, and they didn't make these perfectly murderous *sounds*. Just the other day, one of them snatched the sandwich straight out of my hand. Bared its *teeth* at me."

Cyril gives his moustache a light rub.

"It's quite true, the French rats are shockingly boorish. Their only real value, as far as I can see, is as target practice."

By way of demonstration, he points his index finger straight at the hairy specimen making a circuit of the osier hamper. Fixes it in his sights and makes the quietest of plosives as he sends it to his maker.

"I wish you could kill them all," says the younger man, with unusual feeling. "Every single one."

Cyril studies him once more.

"Were you alone, Mandeville? When you got hit?"

"I think so, yes."

"Nobody else saw?"

"Not that I know of."

"Pity."

Here, for the first time, the younger man seems to waken to the fact of being observed.

"Why do you ask?"

"Oh, it's just that having a witness makes the reporting less of a bother. What did the medical officer say?"

"Not much."

"Mm."

"He dressed the wound, of course. All that ouchie carbolic."

"Cripes, yes."

"Anti-tetanus serum."

"Good."

"He gave me a biscuit."

"A biscuit?"

"Yes, there's a whole tin in the hamper."

No wonder that rat is paying its respects.

"Well, bless me," says Cyril, "I don't believe Galen and Hippocrates *combined* could have done more. One way or another, I'd say you're all but discharged, aren't you?"

There is a long silence. Then, with an abject expression, Mandeville murmurs:

"The doctor did tell me to hang on."

"Did he?" Cyril's grimace minces into a smile. "I wonder what he meant by that."

"Dunno, really."

"Did he say how long you were to hang on for?"

"No."

"I wonder if he meant the words as a spirit of encouragement to you going forward. Going *back*, if you will, into the welcoming arms of Company B, where you are so sorely missed."

He can hear the falsity in his own voice, but Mandeville answers in his dullest tone yet.

"I shouldn't want to go against orders."

"And who would wish you to? Not this little infantryman. It only occurs to me that there are different *orders* of orders. By that criterion, a medical officer's dictates might carry less weight than, let us say, a Colonel's."

Now it is Mandeville's turn to study *him*—and Cyril, thinking back on this moment, will discern, through the close air and thickening shadows of the aid post, a ghostly procession of Arbuthnots, crawling up Mandeville's spine and stiffening him with the memory of crusades and heretics and Gainsborough oils in drafty halls, adding the first accent of starch to his still-liminal voice. Before Cyril's very eyes, he ages ten centuries.

"Dear me, Holland, you seem in a bit of a rush. Are you saying that our Colonel wishes me to go back this very second?"

"No."

"So then you are saying he does *not* wish me to go back."

Cyril's ancestors come and find him, too. Old Irish tenant farmers, forcing smiles through their gapped teeth.

"Well now," he says, "I would imagine that our Colonel desires only what is best for our officers and for our men."

Then he waits. And watches with a subtle fascination, as the starch leeches, grain by grain, from Mandeville's spine, leaving only the pure, hard residue of caste.

"Thing is, Holland, I can't in good conscience go back without the proper clearance. To begin with, there are additional symptoms. Headache, for starters."

"Ah."

"Touch of nausea, too."

"It's quite the puzzle, isn't it, Mandeville?"

The younger man grants him his tenderest smile yet. "How grateful I am to you, Holland, for recognizing the complexity of the situation. So many in your station would not."

A smile hovers on Cyril's lips, for his grandfather was an eye surgeon knighted by the Queen herself.

"I know! Why don't you and I stay here until the Doctor gets back, and then, once he's given you the heave-ho, we stroll back together?"

"Surely, that would depend upon what he says."

"No question."

"You still seem in a rush, Holland."

"Not at all, I've brought a book with me."

And draws Verne from his sack, as well as a cigarette, which he lights by a candle wedged in an old wine bottle. With the air of a man with nowhere to be, he drags down two streams of tobacco (never presuming to offer a cig to Mandeville) and submerges himself, like a bathing Turk, in the adventures of Dr. Ferguson and Dick Kennedy. So familiar to him now they might almost be a liturgy.

"I say," says Mandeville. "Did you bring any whisky?"

"'Fraid not."

"Clever me! I just remembered. There's brandy right next to the biscuits."

He flaps his hand in the general direction of the basket. There is no question in his mind as to who is to retrieve it. No objection from Cyril, either, for waiting has a way of parching him. He aims a single kick at the still-loitering rat and, wrenching up the lid, gazes down into what seems at first only a pudding of blankets and bandages and field dressings and cotton wool. It takes a little spelunking to discover, first, the tin of biscuits, and then—his nose did not lie—a tin of F. Allen & Sons cocoa, looking as if it had just tumbled off the Debenhams shelf. Deeper down, like some old family quarrel, a bottle of Martell's Three Star Cognac and, flanking it on either side, a pair of pewter cups, which Cyril fills and carries back to the bench.

"Cheero," says Mandeville, taking his cup.

"Cheero."

They drink in silence as the afternoon draws on. Outside, the earthen wall of the trench glows with a salmon light, and there can be heard, even from this distance, a gradual crescendo of gunfire. In reply, the second lieutenant reaches for the bottle. Tries and fails to pour himself another cup.

"Allow me," says Cyril.

"Awfully kind of you."

"Not at all."

"Still a bit jittery."

"Of course."

Cradling his cup with both palms, Mandeville gazes across the dug-out's full length.

"I hope you won't be offended, Holland."

"I can't yet know until you've made a proper go of it."

"It's only that I'm a bit taken aback at your being here."

"Why?"

"Well, I never thought you much cared for me."

A sniper never reveals his emotions.

"We've only just met, Mandeville."

"No, that's not true. We've met at least three or four times. Just yesterday morning I sat next to you at breakfast. Couldn't get a word out of you. Not even a nod."

"That was you?"

"You probably just thought of me as one more irritant. And who could blame you?"

Cyril lowers his face toward his brandy.

"See here, Mandeville, you mustn't take exception to my antisocial ways. I care for you quite as much as the next fellow. Or quite as little, if that will make it more explicable."

"Yes, everybody says you're quite the lone wolf."

"For once everybody is correct."

"I expect in your sinister line of work that's an asset of sorts."

Cyril looks at him.

"I expect so," he says.

"Oh, don't mistake me. Our boys need you more than ever, Holland. I mean, we've *all* heard the rumors."

"Which ones?"

"Why, the Jerries are just a day or two away from a full-bore invasion."

Cyril stretches out his legs, lets his head drift back an inch.

"At the risk of calming you, Mandeville, those rumors have been abroad since I got here nine months ago. If the Jerries had invaded as often as they were expected to, we should all be eating schnitzel and wearing ugly clogs in edelweiss blue."

"Oh, but come now, you've been to the same briefings as I. Every hour, the other side is bringing up *more* transport, *more* trains. I can't even sleep some nights thinking."

"If you ask me," says Cyril, "that's a waste of a good night's insomnia."

There is some silence before Mandeville, in a tone of light disgruntlement, says, "I wouldn't have pegged you for an optimist."

And Cyril thinks: *It is quite the reverse of optimism. It is seeing things as they are.*

"Captain Holland."

Through the dugout doorway strides Dr. Gwynne with a lowered head. The medical officer is an object of some fascination in the battalion: a Welshman with a swarm of black whiskers and glaring eyes under an excitably hairy brow, the kind of seadog exterior that promises more violence than ever emerges. Cyril has seen him coated in blood from head to toe and still crooning like a juvenile lead in the West End. More than one soldier, in the face of the Doctor's ironclad jauntiness, has been moved to wonder if he knows there's a war going on.

"Soames!" he calls to the bandaged figure on the cot. "Feeling any more shipshape, are we? That's all right, once the way is clear, we'll stretcher you straight up to the dressing station and from there—well, honestly, I've no idea, but I'm told it's deeply erotic and involves French girls. . . ."

Soames makes not a titter in reply, but Dr. Gwynne pulls up an ammunition box of his own and funnels his chatter straight into his patient's unhearing ear.

"I don't know if you heard them, Soames, but two rifle grenades came over just now. Think they pitched just over the front line on the left. . . . Looks like they're attacking down south. Might be getting pretty hot before long, don't you think?. . .What a day for my orderly to come down with something. Rude, that's what I call it."

There is something so strangely intimate about the soliloquy that a note of apology steals into Cyril's gait as he makes his way over.

"Doctor," he says. "I wonder if I might have a word with you."

"By all means."

"Privately."

The Doctor tenders him a look of exaggerated amusement.

"Well now, Captain, if you can find somewhere private in this hell-hole, take me there at once. Failing that, why don't we just retire to the hallway?"

4

⟨ formatting ornament ⟩

RETIRE TO THE HALLWAY. The words are a reminder of the Doctor's earlier career in a Welbeck Street surgery, where he removed tonsils for six pounds a patient and where, by his own report, there really was a hallway to retire to, a gaslit wainscoted corridor with a noise-dampening jade rug and tasteful oil portraits of Ceres and Minerva. By contrast, the Doctor's present waiting area is one more tiny canyon carved from French red clay and laid in with sandbags. No nurses, no medical assistants, just signalers and runners and Angus Gwynne himself, rather casually clapping on his helmet and gazing up at the latest cloud formations.

"Smoke?" he offers, reaching into his jacket pocket.

"No thanks."

To Cyril's surprise, the Doctor draws out a crocodile-skin cigar case—the only dandyish thing on him—from which emerges the stub of a cheroot.

"Been working it down all week," he explains. "Half an inch at a time. Leaves a chap something to look forward to." He strikes the match against the sole of his boot. The drag lasts four or five seconds. "Now then," he says. "What's on your mind, Captain?"

"I would respectfully request that Second Lieutenant Mandeville be released."

"On what grounds?"

"Dereliction of duty."

"Ah," answers the Doctor, kneading the fleshy lobe of his ear. "That sounds rather serious."

"It *will* be if he's not returned to his company. I shall report him to headquarters and recommend that he receive the highest criminal penalty."

The medical officer fixes his wild eyes on Cyril before finding a pocket of space just beyond him.

"That seems rather extreme, old boy."

"Do you see any other recourse? In this very moment, a bestially stupid namby-pamby is passing himself off as a sniper victim when he is his own bloody sniper. Strip him of his pedigree, and Second Lieutenant Mandeville is just another funk trying to give himself a blighty wound so he can get shipped back home to Mummy. It isn't the first time it's happened, and we know it won't be the last."

The smoke forms a shivering mane round the Doctor's head as he takes another drag.

"It is all rather speculative," he suggests.

"Inferential, you mean. Derived from facts."

"And they are . . ."

"Mandeville has been here weeks now, and he's still jumping every time something goes boom. When I suggest he rejoin his company like a man, he uses all his aristocratic hauteur and his low animal cunning to stay put. Invents new symptoms by the seconds. Headache, my maiden aunt."

The doctor dabs a bit of ash to the ground.

"You and I both know what hell this business plays with a man's nerves. Not ten minutes ago, I had the dubious privilege of sedating Grigsby."

"Nothing dubious about it."

"Well, he certainly had it coming, didn't he? D'you know I think he rather took to it. But see here, Captain, if we were to clap irons round everyone who got a bit gnawed round the edges, there'd be nobody left but the earwigs."

"It's not just the nerves. Did you look at the wound?"

"No, I dressed it with my eyes closed."

"Then surely you remarked on the deeply *fortunate* trajectory of that sniper's bullet. How it managed to strike his neck without meeting any bone or artery or trachea or larynx—anything, in sum, that would cause him a speck of inconvenience venturing through life. Oh, I know the Bosch are crack shots, but I never fathomed how charitable they were."

"It is not outside the realm of—"

"Consider, too, that no bullet was found, at least none he has claimed, nor was anybody present when he was shot. Which means either that he found the one vanishingly small section of trench where no soldier can be observed *except* by an enemy sniper . . ."

"Or . . ."

"Or he ducked into his quarters and, with the aid of—who can say?—his own revolver—his own shaving mirror—gave himself the itty-bittiest of flesh wounds."

"It was neither itty nor—"

"Then staggered out again, howling like Oedipus."

A spark in the Doctor's lion eyes.

"Well now, Captain, even if I were to support your conclusion, there is the small bugaboo of evidence. I don't see how, absent any witnesses—"

"We're not King's Counsel, Doctor. We need only present our findings and let others make their conclusions. Pursuant to Section 18 of the Army Act . . ."

"Oh, dear."

". . . a soldier who deliberately harms himself in order to be excused from combat . . ."

"Yes."

". . . is subject to imprisonment. An advance, if you like, over the firing squad he would once have faced."

"And still might."

"You know as well as I, Doctor, they only shoot the ones nobody will ask after. At the very least," he persists, "Mandeville should no longer be classified as a casualty of war."

"May I suggest that he is a different sort of casualty?"

"Not the sort I respect."

"In my experience, once a fellow tries this sort of thing—if that is what he's done—he gets better at it with each new attempt. The trajectory grows less fortunate."

"Then let the bullet follow its natural course. We need men here, Doctor, not weak-kneed, effeminate degenerates."

The words are out of him so quickly they seem chained to each other, tumbling down the same flume. The medical officer pauses and then, surprisingly, begins to laugh.

"Dear me, Captain, you are hard."

And it says something about Cyril that he takes it at first for a compliment. What else could it be when, for more years than he can say, an obsidian hardness is all he has ever aspired to? Life in its most collapsed and concentrated form—that is the destiny of a boy whose father acted like a woman, turned other men into women. That same boy must scourge all that is female from his soul and, coming himself into manhood, embrace the most masculine of careers. Only to learn that, far from relaxing, he must grow ever more vigilant, for he is now entirely in the company of other men, with their own untellable needs. Which means withdrawing even further because, lapping at his heels always, is the memory of shame, of exile, of what happens when a fellow makes himself tender. *Chaps are just chaps*, that's what he told his mother, and the only way to keep them there is to keep the wall up, to be a sinner of one.

"I am hard," he says at last, "because I have had to be."

By unspoken agreement, both men plunge their hands into their pockets and angle away from each other.

"See here," says the Doctor, "I've no rank or standing to ask this of you but, speaking strictly as a physician, I shouldn't mind somebody staying at Mandeville's side . . ."

"No."

". . . for the next hour or so . . ."

"Absolutely not."

". . . with no object but to keep him *settled*. Once he realises he is not about to be sent to hospital—not even nerve hospital—he might set into panicking all over again, and I want to be sure somebody is standing by when it happens. Somebody with . . ." A new note of whimsy. "Well, now, I've never had occasion to measure your head, Captain, but from this angle, it impresses me as *level*."

Cyril gives that same head a single vigorous shake.

"Keeping men *alive* is nowhere in my list of orders."

"Although, curiously," the Doctor answers, "it is rather high in mine." He takes a slow draw and then puffs out the smoke in articulated segments. "I have always believed that God has a rather diabolical sense of humor. Why else would He make you the Good Samaritan to a fellow you despise?"

"Perhaps because he has, in his usual way, made a proper botch of things."

"Yet here we are."

Scratching lightly under his helmet, the Doctor lets his gaze wander down to his boots.

"I'll strike a bargain with you, Captain. If you can find a way to stick it just a while longer, I shall tell the Colonel what a mainstay you have been to Lord Arbuthnot's son in his hour of peril. It will be the most Horatian ode I have ever delivered."

"With all due respect to our commander, I suspect Latin is not his—"

"Nor is it mine. Just don't force me to deliver a *funeral* ode, Captain, we've had quite enough of that for today."

And will have quite enough going forward, thinks Cyril. He recalls the evening not three weeks ago when the officer corps found itself suddenly diminished by half. For days afterward, he would find traces of them: Saunders's toothbrush, Trotter's compass case, Hardy's box of fruit drops.

The Doctor's cheroot is down now to the barest stub, but he still makes a point of mashing it out against his boot before returning it to his cigar case. Then he beats a leisurely path back to the dugout, pausing only at the entrance to say:

"Have another brandy or two. Doctor's orders."

5

IF CYRIL WERE to enumerate what he most dislikes about army life, it would not be the threat of dying but the obligation of living—living, to be more clear, with men whom in a normal world he would run miles to avoid. By some curious feature, these same men in his experience crave his company in direct proportion to his reviling theirs. So it is with Mandeville, who, being dim, believes that Cyril has returned to his ammunition-box vigil of his own accord and who fails to register the sudden and decided cooling of his new friend's affections. And who, confronted by the spectacle of *Five Weeks in a Balloon* raised like a barricade, begins fretting away at it.

"Good book, Holland?"

"Tolerably."

"D'you like that sort of thing? Adventure?"

"Well enough."

"I say, did you read *Tarzan of the Apes*?"

"No."

"It's jolly good. It's got apes in it."

"So I presumed."

There is just the briefest of pauses.

"You must be quite the reader, eh, Holland?"

"It passes the time."

"Never was one for books myself."

"Ah."

"Nor the maths,"

"You astonish me."

"Though I sometimes think I should have been an artist. Oh, I can't draw worth a farthing, but I think I might have enjoyed working in clay. Only because it's a bit like gardening, isn't it? Only not? Yes, I think if I'd really applied myself, I might have made a middling sort of sculptor."

"Might have?" echoes Cyril. "You have many years in which to be middling at whatever vocation you choose."

"Oh, you're kind, Holland, but I sometimes think I should have been a cartographer. Don't you find maps positively diverting? The pretty sort, I mean. You know, when I was three, Nurse said I had the finest sense of direction of any child still in a nappy. . . ."

In his relatively brief time on earth, Cyril has been confronted by many a bore—his father once called it the gentleman's birthright. The solution, he has learned, is to bide one's time until dialogue becomes monologue. So it happens with Mandeville, who begins to spew out an uninterrupted stream of memoir, beginning at birth and crawling, still bearing its nappy, through the first two ages of man. Now and then an individual word penetrates—*windmill, tennis, pony, Framlingham*—but there is no sense in reaching for it because it is only waiting to be swept away. Cyril, absorbed in his reading, cannot say exactly how many minutes have passed when Mandeville's flow, out of nowhere, stops, and silence floods in. With a slow-dawning horror, he realises he has been asked a question.

"Sorry?" he mumbles.

"I only asked you where you were from."

Cyril lifts one shoulder, lets it drop.

"Bit of everywhere."

"London, I'd wager, from the accent."

Cyril reaches for the brandy, pours himself another cup. *Doctor's orders.*

"See here, Mandeville, are you quite sure you should be talking so much? I shouldn't wish to impede your recovery."

"Oh, but it helps, you see. I'm having a hard time gathering just now."

"The shock, no doubt."

"I'm sure that's it."

Cyril returns his gaze to his book and wills the dome of silence once more to descend, only Mandeville is already pressing himself against it.

"My family's from Norfolk," he declares in a voice shagged with desperation. "Have you ever been to Norfolk, Holland?"

Looking back, Cyril will see that it is the most tedious shoot Mandeville could have thrust up, yet how many tendrils it sprouts. A whole vine, curling round Cyril's ankle and tugging him back to ill-matched honeymooners. To the North Sea. Ruffian sailors. Golf. Priest's holes. Mothers melting down like snow on a furnace. *Yes*, thinks Cyril, passing a hand over his eyes, *that's where it all started going to hell.*

"I once had a Norfolk jacket," he allows.

"Isn't that funny, I never had one. Never knew anybody who did."

"That is the height of comedy, Mandeville."

"Think I might have a bit of a lie-down."

"You already are."

"Oh."

Without his own knowledge, it seems, Mandeville has taken possession of the entire bench. His gumboots hang off one end, and his arms form a rectilinear frame for his head.

"Think I might grab a little shut-eye," he says.

His lids shudder down and keep shuddering even as the first snoring tangles spill from his chest. With some tact, Cyril reaches for the pack that lies just under the bench. Opens it to find first an eiderdown sleeping-bag in an oiled-silk cover, then a folding canvas arm-chair, a Bible in India ink, a paybook, letters from home, a box of fruit drops, a cedar pencil, a stick of chocolate. Rummaging farther, he locates a single postcard that he assumes at first is pornographic before recognizing it as the portrait of a poppy. Rummaging still farther, a revolver, which, without another thought, he tosses into his own pack, along with a pocket knife.

You won't do it on my watch, he thinks.

Reaching now into Mandeville's tunic pocket, he draws out another kind of watch: large and gold-plated, still attached to its chain. For want of better entertainment, he winds it until it begins to emit its own quiet pulse, not too different, he thinks, from the low rumble of guns outside, growing steadily more personal. Lastly, he has a good look at Mandeville's boots, which, without too much trouble, might be prised free. Would they fit Cyril's own rather large feet? If he were to pinch them now, would anybody know?

Drawing himself back now to Verne, he wades in a few more yards, but the words, for all their familiarity, grow stranger, and before he knows it, he is dozing himself and travelling back to Hyderabad. A monitor lizard is forging along a brick wall, flicking its tail like a housemaid's broom, and the dirt is flying straight at Cyril, peppering his eyes, crawling down his lungs, and he's coughing it all back up—he can't help it—and he awakens to find Mandeville tipping his head in the direction of the floor and spilling out the contents of his stomach.

The smell is more disturbing for being so familiar. This morning's bacon fat and porridge and gravy . . . this afternoon's bully beef and sardine and liver . . . the tea that always tastes of onion soup. It is the vomit of a soldier.

"Pardon," murmurs Mandeville.

"Oh, that's all right," says the Doctor, coming forward at once with a pair of threadbare towels, one of which he hands to Cyril. It takes them just under a minute to mop up the whole spill, Mandeville staring down at them the whole while with a strand of vomit dangling from his fat lip.

"Feeling better?" asks the Doctor.

But the question is more than Mandeville can apply himself to just now.

"Must have been something you ate," suggests Cyril.

"Might have been *anything* you ate," suggests the Doctor.

Mandeville closes his eyes.

To dispel the lingering smell, Cyril lights another cigarette and waves it in widening circles. At the other side of the room, he watches the Doctor

slowly unravel the bandages from Soames's face. A tract of charred flesh
and two staring eyes and, like incense, the smell of liniment and, like bells,
the medical officer's Welsh croon.

"Just a little more, old bean, and we'll wrap you up again. Why, before
we're done, you'll look so much the mummy they'll send you straight to
the British Museum. Worse places to wait out a war, eh?"

Cyril feels a tug on his sleeve. Mandeville is sitting up now. Squinting,
as through a glass darkly.

"What do you make the time?" he asks.

"Six thirty."

"Morning?"

Cyril stares at him.

"Evening, Mandeville."

"Dinner, you mean?"

"Would you like some dinner? I could ask."

"No," he answers with a shudder. Then levers himself slowly backward,
as though some great hand were pressing politely against his chest.

"Why don't you clean up your face?" says Cyril, and hands him a
handkerchief. But the younger man only stares at it.

"Did you know Reggie?" he suddenly asks.

"Reggie?"

"My older brother."

"I don't believe I've had the pleasure."

"Nor will you."

"No?"

"You see, he was killed last November. In Ypres."

Cyril gives the news its full due of silence.

"Bad luck, Mandeville."

"Bad luck for *everybody*. He was far and away the better soldier."

He would have had to be, thinks Cyril, and then, rallying, says:

"Well, then, in his honor, you'll just have to . . ."

Win the war for the both of you. Stick a finger in the Kaiser's eye.

"Do him proud," he says, hating that only slightly less.

"I've got the beastliest headache," says Mandeville.

"Still? Thought the stomach might have flushed it out of you."

"Made it a bit worse."

Smiling, Cyril rises and fetches some aspirin and a water-jug. For extra measure, he brings Mandeville another blanket from the hamper, for the late-afternoon cold is biting hard enough that he has to rub it out of his own arms. He has just settled back on his ammunition box when he hears:

"Have *you* any family, Holland?"

A sniper reveals nothing of himself.

"I've a brother," he says at length.

"Older or . . ."

"Younger."

"Is he in service, too?"

Another pause.

"He's a second lieutenant in the Interpreters Corps."

"Fancy that."

"Yes, they call him in for interrogations. *Was ist sein Regiment* and all that noise. The Germans have no more defence against his hangdog countenance than I ever did."

And feels an unexpected twinge as he says it, thinking on Vyvyan. Stationed scarcely three miles away, but it might as well be a thousand because nobody's going anywhere. When was the last time Cyril wrote him? Or asked after his shiny new wife? *She so longs to meet you, Cyril.* She wouldn't, he thinks, if she knew what she was meeting.

"Mother," says Mandeville.

"Sorry?"

"Your mother. Is she with us?"

He weighs the question for a few moments.

"No."

"How long . . ."

"How long what?"

"How long gone?"

Funny, he used to be able to summon the interval at will. It says something about grief's offices that, after a time, arithmetic calculation enters the picture.

"Eighteen years," he says.

"How did she go?"

"I say, Mandeville, these are rather pointed enquiries."

But then, looking into the vacancy of the younger man's eyes, he realises that the enquirer won't recall the answer, let alone the question, that the person to whom he is speaking is not Mandeville but Not Mandeville. The sieve through which all things may freely pour.

"She underwent an operation," says Cyril. "In a Genoese clinic. Run by some sort of hack *medico* who smelt of basil. She went in and never came out."

And, prompts Not Mandeville.

"The only person to share her dying hours was her maid Maria, still piling layers of wool atop her."

And.

"Lady Brooke hustled in the next day, Uncle Otho two days after, both of them too late. The Doctor had long fled the scene."

And.

"The wires went out the following morning to the two sons, one in Heidelberg, one in Monaco. *Mother dead. Stay put.*"

"Oh," murmurs Real Mandeville. "That's rotten luck."

Cyril starts a little. Gazes into an actual face with actual irises.

"Rotten doctoring," Cyril suggests.

"Father?"

"What of him?"

"Gone, too?"

"Not long after."

"Grief?"

"Ha! He wasn't the type. Bit of a bounder, you must know."

Though, prompts Not Mandeville.

"He visited her grave. Which was more than I ever got to do."

And.

"Wept. Or so I was told."

And you.

"Never saw him again. When he died, it was just another wire."

Back comes Real Mandeville, in a voice of hushed wonder.

"You've had a rum go of it, Holland."

In spite of himself he laughs, for he has never heard it put quite so baldly.

"It's for the best, really. I'm not much of a family man."

"Gets lonely," suggests Mandeville in a breathier voice.

"What?"

"Holidays."

"Blimey, Mandeville, we're not even to May Day."

"Only saying."

"If you must know, it's a bit of a relief. No dashing into shops on December the twenty-fourth. No out-of-tune carolers polluting one's street corner. It may not be peace on Earth, but it's peace."

"I would wager . . ."

"What?"

"You had lovely . . ."

Cyril waits with a thickening suspense.

"Christmases," says Mandeville.

Where are they, then? He travels down the old corridors, and he lands, somewhat contrary to mission, in Babbacombe, a little slice of North Sea where the Wildes spent their last Christmas together—a mere three months after their Norfolk holiday. Pappa, having brought them armloads of tin soldiers from Paris, retired at once to bed with a severe cold and lingered there for days, too weak even to join them for tea, and Mamma, far from tending to him, seemed to be edging farther away. One morning, Cyril watched her drag herself to the cliff's edge and wondered if she would simply toss herself over the side just to be spared the bother of returning. It was then he sent up a prayer to St. Nicholas to make them all whole in time for Christmas.

And did it work? asks Not Mandeville.

"It never works," he says, and glances at Real Mandeville, who is no longer even listening. His breathing is labored, his face as sallow and waxy as the candle by which Cyril observes it.

"Can you hear me, Mandeville?"

Ponds of sweat bloom from the younger man's armpits. The fingers of his ploughman's hands twitch as though they were plucking at a loom's shuttles.

"You don't look altogether well," says Cyril.

Hearing no answer, he calls for the Doctor, who waves his own candle over the young man's face, waiting for the eyes to follow.

"Mandeville," he croons. "Can you hear me?"

"Yes."

"Can you tell us what else happened to you when you were shot? Something you forgot to tell us about, perhaps."

The young man's mouth opens wide enough to form a straight channel to his brain.

"Got a bit of a clout," he says.

"There's a good lad. On the head, you mean?"

"Yes."

"When you fell?"

"Yes."

"What sort of clout?"

"Dunno."

"Big? Small?"

"Dunno."

The Doctor feels round the back of the patient's head until he gets an answering wince. Smiling, he draws a speck closer.

"I say, Mandeville, did the lights go out for a bit when you fell?"

"Might've."

"Might've or . . ."

"I did get a good cracking."

"Mm."

"Can't be sure."

"Never mind. I'm just going to call Captain Holland away for a quick conference, and we'll be back in two shakes."

This time around, they have no need to retire into the hall, only to the far side of the dugout.

"Concussion?" asks Cyril.

"We've gone past that, I fear. Symptoms suggest subdural hematoma."

"What's that?"

"Just a little impingement of blood."

"Impingement." Cyril gives him a closer look. "In the brain, you mean?"

"Why, where else? Blood's like water, you know, wants to go where it may. Crack open a skull, it cries, *Huzzah!* Kicks up its feet like some dipsomaniac at the Old Stag and Bull."

"Surgery, then?"

"In here?" The Doctor gives a lyrical laugh. "Dear Captain, I wouldn't operate on a cockroach in these conditions. I wouldn't darn my own socks."

With a deepening sense of impotence, Cyril takes a full canvass of the aid station. The damp, close air, thick with candle-grease. The overturned boxes and thrice-used cotton wool. The Primus stove, shiny with black ooze.

"Morphia," he suggests. "Opium. You must have something."

"Nothing that would keep him *awake*, Captain, and that is what we must do at all costs. So long as he's conscious, we may hold out hope that the blood is being kept at bay."

Cyril's hands clench by his side.

"The damn fool," he mutters.

"The young man, you mean."

"He is no man at all, not a *real* man. And now we must pay the price for his cowardice."

"Strikes me that he's the one paying it."

Cyril closes his eyes, tamps down his last reserves of resistance. Then, with a smile the more sinister for lacking any conviction, strolls back to his ammunition-box and resumes his vigil.

"Quite comfortable, Mandeville?"

"Yes."

"Are you sure? You look to be on the snoozy side. Shall I fetch you some tea?"

"No."

"Water, perhaps. Though it might have things swimming in it."

Mandeville ponders.

"Brandy," he proposes.

"No more of *that*, we're to keep you awake, old thing. Doctor's orders."

"Awake."

"Yes, don't resist, the only remaining mystery is how we are to arrange it. Oh, I know! Let's pretend there are rats everywhere."

"Rats."

"Dear me, there's no containing them. They're swarming all *over* us, Mandeville, with their hideous chattering teeth. I can feel them gnawing at my buttons, can't you? Oh, but they're only providing cover for the *Jerries*, who, as we speak—and I hesitate even to tell you this—are breaking straight through the lines and swimming across the Channel and bearing straight for *Norfolk*."

It abets the fantasy that the shelling outside is mounting. In his nine months here, Cyril has developed a nearly barometric sense of trouble, can pick out the distinctions between a rifle grenade, a shell, or a Minenwerfer, can discern just where each is landing and by what degrees it is drawing nearer. Sitting here just now, he knows by the very hairs of his arms that, within a half-hour, the first cries will go up for stretcher-bearers. Bodies, quick and dead alike, will be borne here on clouds of alarum. More of them than the aid station can properly hold, so they will be stacked like cords of wood on available cots and boxes or simply propped against the wall. The medical officer will make a note of who can be saved; the rest will sink into Time itself.

And what of Soames? wonders Cyril, glancing once more at that bandaged nullity. Will he slumber through the whole business? Who's to say he won't outlive them all?

"Star," says Mandeville, out of nowhere.

"Star?"

Mandeville winces. "*Story . . .*"

"What of it?"

"Tell us one."

"Are you sure you wouldn't rather play cards?"

"Story."

"What sort are you after?"

Mandeville considers.

"Bedtime."

"Dear me, that sounds awfully narcotic."

"No. Helps me. . . ." A swallow travels up the column of his neck. "Helps me gather."

Cyril scowls at his boots. What excuse would old Hargreaves have? *The sniper must keep to himself at all times. The sniper must . . .*

"There was once," he begins.

And stops.

"There was once a rabbit. Named Blackie."

And stops again.

"He was named Blackie on the assumption he was the *only* rabbit in the world with black eyes. And perhaps he was. He lived in a world of tooth and nail and had to protect his wife and children from all manner of brutes, but he was, so they say, the most civilised of bunnies. Fairly bowed his ears to you. Said things like *Young man, it has been an honor and it has been a privilege.* Yes, all things considered, Blackie was getting along quite well—in *Norfolk*—until one morning . . ."

The image comes straight back: two comically long ears, utterly still in a wasteland of mud. With a show of yawning, Cyril reaches into his jacket pocket for a cigarette, lights it with no great urgency.

"Sorry, Mandeville, that one has a rubbish ending. Oh, but you're in luck! Same fellow who told me about Blackie once had a run-in with a *very* selfish Giant."

Something like curiosity flickers in Mandeville's eyes.

"Selfish?"

"Yes, you see, he wouldn't let any of the children play in his garden. Built a high wall all round and put up a notice-board. *Trespassers will be prosecuted.* Now I surely don't need to add that, with the children gone, the birds no longer cared to sing, and the trees forgot to blossom, and Winter lived there year round."

"Like here."

"Yes," says Cyril. "Just like here. Well now, these meddlesome children made a little hole in the wall and crept in and sat in the branches of the trees. And the trees began to blossom, and the birds came back."

"Ah."

"Only there was one corner that was still Winter. Where stood a little boy so small he couldn't reach up to the branches of his tree. And the Giant's heart . . . well, I am reliably informed that it *melted* at the sight. He . . ."

He trotted round the nursery, says Not Mandeville, *laughing and dragging a toy milk cart after him.*

"No," he says, rather sternly. "He stole up behind the little boy and took him gently in his hand . . . and put him up into the tree. And the tree . . ."

Broke.

". . . broke at once into *blossom*. And the birds came and sang on it, and the little boy stretched out his two arms and flung them round the Giant's neck, and kissed him, and the Giant . . ."

Was not?

". . . was not wicked any longer."

Or was never?

Cyril can't answer. Indeed, he can no longer trust himself to say anything. He ducks his head away and gives his eyes the barest dusting with the sleeve of his tunic and hears at his back the thinning voice of Mandeville.

"That was lovely."

The night now is drawing down its full raiment, and the air is sharpening round them, but Mandeville turns down the offer of another blanket and, far from shivering, grows stiller, more fixed. His eyes fasten so greedily on the dugout doorway that Cyril looks back to see what's there. He will later think it prescience on Mandeville's part for, seconds later, the sky bursts open to reveal a warm emerald gash, turning night briefly to day.

It is only one of the Germans' flare lights. To Cyril, it sometimes seems like the world's most expensive theatrical effect, illuminating for a few seconds the thousands of characters lurking in the wings. By gradients, the light dies away, but the sound, as if in compensation, scales up. Normally, he would take comfort in knowing how far back they are from the front lines. Yet the sound grows more searching—wants to be known—and from the fury, one particular thread draws clear. A whine, then a groan, then a shriek, climbing to such a frequency that the hairs on Cyril's arms stand at attention and he understands, too late to do anything about it, that it is coming for them.

First a concussive sound on the roof. Then a seismic current passing through the beams and sandbags and dislodging the very earth with a force that knocks Cyril to his hands and knees. His initial thought is that he has lost consciousness, but that is only because the candles have all been extinguished. From out of the darkness, he hears the timber props of the door frame wheeze and groan—an elderly, arthritic sound—then, after a meditative pause, give way altogether as their freight of sandbags clatters down atop them.

The silence that descends now is more silent for what came before. Cyril staggers to his feet, straining his eyes for shapes, outlines. Panting, he gropes toward his rucksack and draws out his electric torch. Fumbles with the switch.

"Bugger," he hears.

He swings the torch light toward the southwest corner, where Doctor Gwynne sits pinned beneath one of the timbers.

"Give us a hand," he says.

Cyril crawls over, squats over the beam and, with a heaving grunt, drags it clear. His reward is the Doctor's answering roar.

"Broken?" asks Cyril.

The Doctor must swallow down several gallons of air before he can trust himself to reply.

"Tibia, I shouldn't wonder. Fetch me a blanket, would you?"

It is not for the cold or the shock, as Cyril first imagines, but for the splint, which the Doctor sets himself in under a minute, cinching the blanket with the lace from his own boot, grimacing at each revolution.

"Never thought the bastards could lob it this far. They must have mistaken us for somebody important."

Cyril swings the torch toward the sunken doorway. Through the still-smoking heap of wood and mortar, he can see the tiniest patch of evening sky, no more than two feet across. Nearer to, he can hear scrabbling hands and a single strangled voice.

"We're digging you out! Stay put!"

"Stay put," mutters the Doctor. "As if we had any bloody choice." Then calls back in his most lilting of cadences: "Cheero! We'll wait on you."

It is part of the curious intimacy of war that, in this moment, Cyril can smell the cheroot fumes on the Doctor's breath, can map the trail of freckles across the bridge of his nose, can chart the tranquil rise and fall of Soames's chest. Why, if he just reached out his hand, he might even now touch that chest, feel the lungs and heart laboring away beneath. An entire *man* somewhere down there, stirring . . .

"Holland."

It is Mandeville's voice, worming out of the darkness.

"Go to him," says the Doctor.

"Are you sure?"

"Of course."

Bleeding out of the torchlight, Mandeville's face seems almost to belong to someone else.

"They've come," he whispers.

"Who?"

"The rats."

Briefly at a loss, Cyril cocks his ear.

"Why, Mandeville, that's just our boys, digging us out." He leans in, the better to study the Second Lieutenant's dilated eyes. "Yes," he speeds on, "it's only a matter of minutes before they've sprung us, and then it's off to hospital for you, old thing. Won't that be spiffing? You'll have *nurses* on every side, beseeching you to get better."

"Holland . . ."

Mandeville motions him still closer, his lips already rehearsing the words that dribble out.

"It wasn't true."

"What?"

"Sniper." ·

Two hours ago, Cyril would have dived upon that confession like a dog on gristle. Now he is stunned by his absence of appetite.

"I know," he says.

"You won't tell."

"On my word as a gentleman."

Then, in a voice that seems to call up all his remaining strength, the younger man says, "I miss my mother."

A single greasy tear wells from his half-seeing eye. Cyril, watching, thinks of Constance. Wonders: Was this how she spent her final hours? Weaving in and out of life's dark spell? Listening to some private music?

"I miss my mother, too," he says.

The news seems to fill Mandeville with such an obscure satisfaction that Cyril is on the brink of naming all the other departed spirits whom, in a certain frame of mind, he misses. Uncle Willie. Uncle Willie's unsuitable wife. Aunt Georgina. Even Lady Wilde, who filled his childhood with terrors that he is still disassembling.

"You mustn't," says Mandeville, tugging on his tunic sleeve.

"Mustn't what?"

"Be sorry."

"For *you*? Oh, dear boy, I hate to disappoint, but when you leave here, you will carry the full weight of my envy. Your surgeons won't even know how to *excise* it, that's how heavy it will be."

With a prideful show of strength, Mandeville reaches out his heavy ploughman's hand and suspends it there until the other man, equally prideful, consents to take it. *Chaps are just chaps*, he reminds himself, as he feels the soft and unfamiliar rasp of another man's skin. The ebbing pulse just beneath it.

"I'm so glad," whispers Mandeville. "I'm so glad it was you here."

The pronoun registers first: *you*. Then the tense: *was*. Some ancient knowledge has been translated to the sole surviving son of Lord Arbuthnot, and the air grows richer with it until there is no longer any breathing it.

"You know," says Mandeville. "From the first I saw you . . ."

"Hang on. Hang on, old boy."

More than once over the ensuing minutes, Cyril allows his fingers to drift toward the younger man's wrist, where he waits, with suspended breath, for a pulse to rise up. Once or twice he reaches with his free hand to pat the younger man's cheeks—just to assure himself of a reaction. But as Mandeville slides in and out of awareness, Cyril's fancy drifts, too. Not so very far. He sees the moment, perhaps half an hour from now, when the sappers break through (for already he can spy the first pale wash of moon-light). He sees the long line of wounded men waiting to gain admittance, only to be confronted with a maimed physician. He sees himself returning under quiet skies to his own quarters, where, as usual, he will ignore and be ignored by his fellow officers. Tomorrow morning, stoked with onion tea, he will creep out to that resilient stone farm-hearth and wait with a greater thirst than usual for a head to flash above the German parapet. ("You'll get one of theirs, won't you, Holland?") Tomorrow afternoon, he will be summoned back to the Colonel's office.

"Doctor Gwynne has told me what an aid and comfort you were to Mandeville in his final hours."

"I was happy to do it, sir."

"Dispiriting business. Nobody's fault. Young man wounded in combat. Happens all the time, doesn't it?"

Yes, Cyril will think, *it happens all the time.*

"Please know, Holland, that I shall be mentioning your name to the brigadier when next I speak with him."

"Thank you, sir."

"Before you go, I was wondering if you'd be so good as to write Mandeville's parents on behalf of the regiment. Seeing as how you were there in his final moments."

"Of course, sir."

"You *will* put up a good show, won't you?"

Back in his quarters, Cyril will compose the letter in five minutes, for he has written some version of it enough times that it scarcely matters now who the recipients are.

Dear Lord and Lady Arbuthnot,
I very much regret to have to write and tell you your son has died of
wounds. He was

Here Cyril will balk, but not for long. At least it won't seem that long.

He was very gallant, and was doing so well and is a great loss. He
was hit by a sniper's bullet and was very badly wounded. He was not
in bad pain, and our doctor managed to attend him.
    We have had a very hard time, and our casualties have been
large. Believe me you have all our sympathy for your loss, and we
ourselves have lost a very gallant soldier.

Yours sincerely,
Captain Cyril Holland

All this scrolls before him. What he fails to anticipate is that, when the salvage crew at last breaks through, the lead sapper will swing his electric torch toward the pocket where nobody is cheering.

"Who's there?" he will ask.

And Cyril, looking up from the lifeless hand he has become quite used to stroking, will say, "Nobody of any importance."

ENTR'ACTE

Letter of Alfred Douglas to Vyvyan Holland

I feel very sorry that you should persist in carrying on a feud against me. I was your father's greatest friend and I was also a great friend of your mother's. I knew you as a child. The legend you have imbibed about me in relation to your father is almost entirely false. It is true that I attacked him in my book *Oscar Wilde and Myself*, but I did it under frightful provocation, and I have now repudiated the book.

Could you not manage to get out of your mind the ill-feeling which you appear to cherish? I have only good feelings toward you.

ACT FOUR

Wildes in the City

Soho, London
May 1925

1

⟨ formatting ornament ⟩

"I don't like the looks of that one," says Lady Brooke.

A male ingenue with a pencil mustache has just strolled onto the stage of the Royalty Theatre in a double-breasted navy suit with a necktie and pocket square. He is grinning sociably at his fellow actors, in expectation of delivering the line that will explain why he is there in the first place, only to be greeted by Lady Brooke's voice ringing out from the balcony stalls.

"And what sort of godforgotten name is *Bunty*?"

It is, thinks Vyvyan, the one thing that makes Lady Brooke seem as old as she is (which is what?). She talks as if nobody can hear, as if she is not even talking. So it goes through Acts One and Two of *The Vortex*, the play that she herself has professed a desire to see and that, in the actual act of seeing it, seems to affront her at every turn.

"Don't tell me *he's* playing the father, he looks like a great uncle."

"I wish to God somebody would stop that gramophone."

No amount of shushing from her fellow theatregoers will persuade her that hers is a public instrument. Roughly a quarter of the way through Act Three, an usher materialises in the nearest aisle, pressing a bony finger to his lips. Whatever peripheral vision Lady Brooke still enjoys never expands to include him, and when, at the curtain call, two of the onstage actors make a point of ironically gesturing in her direction, her thoughts keep spilling out in the same clear cataract.

"I don't think they ought to raise the lights, not until that one's got her face cleaned. I have always felt that running mascara makes a woman look feral. Like a tufted grey langur, which, in my experience, was the most hated pest in all of Sarawak . . . ."

Vyvyan by now has had two intervals worth of champagne to fortify himself, but he is not sure he is prepared for the ordeal of walking her out of the theatre. His relief is exorbitant when, in the moment of offering his arm, she gives her head a tight shake.

"If it's all the same to you, I'd rather not leave just yet."

"Are you quite sure? There's but the one set of stairs . . ."

"Oh, it's the whole menagerie. Men hustling for taxis, whistles shrieking. I have always thought it more civilised to sit and allow a theatrical experience to—to wash *over* one."

With a certain foreboding, Vyvyan studies her.

"And has it washed?"

"Yes, and with great assurance I can report that this play could not expire quickly enough. The Earth could not whirl fast enough upon its axis. An alpinist could not claw his way more greedily to the summit of Everest than I to the last line."

Vyvyan smiles. "Is that all?"

"Let me now be more particular. The lead actress seemed bent on persuading us she was squalid, and the lead actor seemed squalid without having to persuade us."

"Mr. Coward is the playwright as well."

"Then he has more to answer for. The third act was nothing but Hamlet and Gertrude stretched to an interminable length, and the second act was—well, what?—a cocaine extravaganza, underscored by the most revolting piano playing I have heard outside a private nightmare. If one is going to marry music and sensationalism, the music had best be Verdi or Puccini and somebody had best die before the evening is out, or what has it all been for?"

In the silence that follows, Vyvyan is able for the first time to hear the noises that he assumes have been emanating from Lady Brooke all evening. Belches, wheezes, the gurgling of gastric juice, the creaking of bone upon bone. An entire foundry, he thinks, boiling away.

"I believe," he ventures, "that Mr. Coward is considered a leading voice of his generation."

"When he is only the most cynical of opportunists. I have no doubt he is even now being conveyed to some salon in Belgravia, where ladies of an age nearly as advanced as mine will assure him that his play was perfectly shocking and he will smile like a Rhinemaiden. I'll say this for him," she adds, gripping her walking stick and bending toward the balcony rail. "I vastly prefer but the one curtain call at the very end. It leaves the intervals free and liberates us from the overweening *neediness* of the performing artist. It is why I no longer patronise the opera or the ballet, and it is why I used to instruct my attendants in Sarawak never even to smile in my direction. I flatter myself in thinking that, owing to my ministrations, not one of them has smiled since."

She gives the handle of her stick a couple of turns, as if she were turning some great and inscrutable screw.

"Would it surprise you," she says, "to learn that I still approach a night of theatre with a certain degree of terror?"

"Why is that?"

Her body disgorges a few more sounds. Then she bestows on him the nearest thing to a smile he has seen from her.

"You must blame it on your pappa," she says.

"Oh?"

"Yes, it all dates back to the opening night of *Earnest*. I know, the most purely joyful thing Oscar ever wrote, and there was not a shred of joy in the birthing of it. A few hours prior to curtain, you see, your mother sent me a note saying the Marquess of Queensbury was in a perfect fury about what your father and Bosie were up to and he'd bought a ticket to opening night and was threatening to—I no longer recall what—hurl turnips?— there was a prizefighter in it somewhere. The point is we were all steeling ourselves for the most grotesque of spectacles."

And I was home in bed with my brother, thinks Vyvyan. *Not knowing our days were numbered.*

"Naturally," says Lady Brooke, "your father left specific instructions that the Marquess was not to be admitted, but aristocracy always has a way *round* the normal ramparts. I remember sitting there clenched the whole evening—Constance not three seats away—wondering what I should do if turnips started flying. The more the audience laughed, the more my dread deepened."

Vyvyan tenders her a sympathetic frown.

"That would be a difficult play to endure under such conditions."

"It is why I have not attended a comedy since."

"And did anything happen?"

"Nothing whatever. Which was nearly as bad as something. But, you know, the memory I shall always cherish of that evening was your mother. She'd heard all the wicked speculation about whether she would show up and bestow the—the *absolution* of her presence on her quite disgraceful husband. But when she and Oscar got out of the carriage, she took his arm and smiled with the most extraordinary placidity toward every photographer."

Lady Brooke pauses.

"Yes," she says, "it was the first time I have appreciated quite how dazzling martyrdom can be. The medieval painters got it quite right."

At the edge of their vision, the same usher who appeared during the third act reemerges with a face of naked supplication. Vyvyan at once grasps that he is to prise Lady Brooke from her seat and deliver her into a waiting world. But even as he composes the necessary words, she turns and surveys the emptiness on every side and, in a tone of genuine surprise, says:

"Can we really be the last ones? We must leave at once or they'll mistake us for people who liked the play."

2

CRD

CONFRONTED WITH A lobby emptied of everybody but ushers, Lady Brooke labors forward as if she were beating her way through the Sarawak jungle. But from the moment her surprisingly fashionable cocoon coat is returned to her, she is charging out the door of the Royalty Theatre, declining any offers of a taxi and storming up Dean Street. Her oaken walking staff seems to be oaring her onward, and Vyvyan, just this side of forty, is hard pressed to stay within sporting distance. Hoving at last within a couple of yards, he calls:

"I say . . . Lady Brooke. . . ."

Whatever she replies vanishes into the air above her. He gallops a little closer.

"Sorry, would you mind repeating . . ."

It is then she whips her head round.

"You might as well call me Margaret," she roars.

Call me Margaret. It is as if Yahweh turned back somewhere in the midst of the Old Testament and told all his huddled faithful they might just as well call him God. *Shorter and all that.* By some divine congruence, the bells of St. Patrick's begin at once to ring the eleventh hour. Lady Brooke comes to a summary halt and drops onto a park bench. Jabs her

Mosaic staff straight into the ground and angles her face toward a clouded evening sky.

Panting, Vyvyan looks round—at the plane trees, the walks, the greens—and realises, with a slight shock, that he is standing in Soho Square. How did it sneak up on him?

"Come," declares Lady Wilde. "Sit."

He squeezes himself into the space on her right and reaches into the inner pocket of his dinner jacket for his cigarette case.

"You were frightfully kind to ask me out," he says at last.

"You needn't thank me. As a mother of sons, I have learned through hard experience that a young man must at regular intervals be dragged out of doors and beaten like a rug."

"I wouldn't consider myself *beaten* exactly. . . ."

"That is only how my sons describe the experience. They are not unlike their late father in that way."

From down the street, a young couple comes tottering toward them in evening clothes. Only when they draw nearer does Vyvyan perceive that they are both drenched to the bone. He pauses to wonder if some thunderstorm has passed through without his knowledge. By now, the pair has spotted them, and for reasons unaccountable, are lurching closer. The young woman, in particular, seems lambent with delight as she unhooks her arm from her companion and, pale and slender, staggers toward Lady Brooke.

"Awfully sorry," she says, grinning liquidly through mascara-smudged eyes. "Do you happen to have a corset on you?"

Lady Brooke draws back her head by slow fractions.

"A corset?" she says.

"Yes, you see, we're . . ." She waves vaguely at her companion. "We're on a scavenger hunt, and we've got to come back with a corset, and we were thinking since you're a bit on the . . ."

"Distinguished side," her companion suggests.

"Distinguished side, exactly. We were thinking you might . . ."

The words trail away, and the young woman stands swaying in her own breeze.

"Might what?" asks Lady Brooke.

"Well, here's how it is," says the young man, dragging a child's kite after him. "We've already got the tiara and the policeman's whistle and the front page of tomorrow's *Times* and the . . ." He frowns at the string dangling from his right hand. ". . . the *kite*, and the corset's next to last on our list—just ahead of the live piranha—and if we get back in time, we might edge out Percy Rounceville."

"And who would that be?"

"Oh, the chap who won last week," answers the young woman. "He's been blathering on about it ever since. Crashing bore."

Lady Brooke makes two screwlike turns of her staff.

"I am at a loss to decide which is the more grievous insult you have paid me. That you presume me to be wearing an article of clothing that went out with the War. Or that you expect me to shuck it off in public view."

"There's a—no, I think there's a *shrub*—over by—"

"The only charitable explanation I can find for your behavior is that you are both on dope. I must also inform you that neither of you is wearing shoes."

"Oh, gosh." The young man gazes down. "We must have left them on the diving board. Next to the . . ."

"Cow's tongue."

"Yes, the cow's tongue."

Lady Brooke's eyelids scroll down like blinds which may never again rise.

"That you consider any of what you have just said to be remotely intelligible speaks more volumes than I can begin to number. I send you on your way with the suggestion that you plunder the grave of some Victorian matron in the hope she was buried with her whalebone corset. As to the piranha, you might explore some of the more exotic backwaters of the Thames. Seeing as how you are already wet."

The young people stare down at her, not quite comprehending. It is left to Lady Brooke to make two declarative thumps with her staff.

"Off you go."

Long after she has dismissed them, the two of them are peregrinating across the square, waving at the statue of Charles II quite as if he were waving back. When at last they recede into the night's shadows, Lady Brooke, in a tone almost regretful, observes:

"I can't help thinking your mother would have approved of how that girl was dressed. Limbs bared, bosom flapping. Female figure freed from its bondage. Yes, that was Constance's meat and potatoes, wasn't it? Though I confess I did stop listening after a few lectures. One can husband only so much outrage before apathy floods in. Tell me," she says, with a touch of impatience. "Do you still think of her?"

"My mother?" says Vyvyan. "Of course."

Though in this moment he is thinking of the girl.

"I think of her, too," says Lady Brooke, resting her free hand on his arm. "And not merely because I adored her but because there exists the scant possibility that I killed her." She broods over that last line. "Heavens, how appallingly theatrical."

"Mr. Coward is taking notes."

"The point I am trying to make is that I was the one who put her in the way of that egregious charlatan."

"Dr. Bossi."

"Oh, I wasn't alone, he came highly recommended and no doubt seduced by redoubtable ladies, God help their souls. Do you know he was murdered just a few years back? Yes, I read it in the *Daily Mail*."

"Who killed him?"

"A patient's husband. For having grossly unethical relations with the husband's wife. Could there have been any other end for Dr. Bossi? From his sordid obituary I have tucked away one detail. He died with his pen still clutched in his hand. Waiting to prescribe some new horror on a blameless world, which, in retrospect, imparts a certain messianic glow to his assassin."

She knits her hands rather awkwardly in her lap.

"I am only being a beast about him because I feel a beast myself. I never should have let your mother go into that clinic."

"You didn't force her," says Vyvyan. "She wanted to get better."

He is not saying that to be kind. He can remember the lines of frustration etching themselves across her face—her very body, it seemed—as she dragged herself from room to room in that rented villa in Bogliasco. There were mornings she would disappear for an hour or two altogether without any explanation. He never discovered where, and he can only assume that the public spectacle of her struggle was its own kind of affliction. Every night, in the cell of his Jesuit school in Monte Carlo, he used to kneel and pray for her release, little dreaming that the answer would be no.

"I should have understood how fragile she was," says Lady Brooke. "Someone like *me*, you see, might have come right out of that clinic the next day, nothing the worse. I can't be killed, you see, though my late husband used to hope I might be *felled* by something. An elm, I think, or a meteorite. But your mother, she was coming apart at every sinew, and I thought she might—oh, be *barked* back into place like one of my own sons. It has always been a principle of mine that what a woman desires has nothing to do with what she *needs*, but I think in your mother's case, they were one and the same."

"And that was . . ."

"Care."

The word is out of her before she has granted it permission, and for a few seconds, she inspects it for the truant it is.

"Yes, care," she affirms. "Such a simple thing that only a very clever woman like me could have missed it."

Vyvyan watches a policeman make a slow periphery of the square. A gentleman in a bowler walks two Cairn terriers.

"I don't think she would blame you," he says.

"That is all well and good, but I house within me an entire tribunal, and it is unyielding in its judgement. Would you be so kind as to turn your face to me?"

He obeys and, to his surprise, she tucks her hand lightly under his chin.

"I wish she could see you now. So kind and considerate."

"If a bit benign," he adds.

To his further surprise, she smiles—just a little—before her teeth, startled from their cavern, scurry back.

"That is only your camouflage," she suggests.

"You may be right."

"Your brother went the other way."

"You may be right."

Lady Brooke's fingers now twine round an invisible champagne flute. She raises it toward the Soho night sky and, in a mock-Valkyrie tone, cries:

"To brothers."

The glass descends, dissolves. A single horse trundles past, bearing the wagon of a junk-dealer. Ten years ago, thinks Vyvyan, there would have been nothing but horses in Soho Square, bearing busmen and lovers. How quickly they all vanished: the horses, the carriages, the arc-lights, sputtering and hissing.

"Listen to me now," says Lady Brooke in a more urgent tone. "Do you recall the gentleman with whom I spoke during the second interval?"

"Just his back."

"Yes, that was by design. You may remember that, upon seeing you, I immediately turned away. You presumably found me rude."

"A bit."

"That is entirely supportable. I was once called the rudest woman in all of Italy, and I hadn't it in me to contradict. The point is I was trying to create a screen between you and the gentleman in question."

"What an awful lot of trouble," says Vyvyan, smiling. "Who was he?"

"Bosie Douglas."

His response, he will later realise, is that of a child. He folds his arms across his chest, bracing for the next impact.

"I didn't think it right to introduce you," says Lady Brooke.

"There was no need," he says, with a rasping laugh. "We have already met."

"It is not the same. You were a child then. *Avant le déluge.* He got down on the floor and played games with you because he was himself a boy."

"Father got down on the floor, too."

"He was the same boy."

Something is rolling through Vyvyan, rolling him in the gentlest possible way to his feet. He slips his hands into his pockets and gazes into the orbed diffusion of a gaslight.

"Was that why you wanted to loiter after the play was over?" he asks. "To make sure he had gone?"

"My own father had a very wise proverb. Give the fox enough time to leave before you release the chickens."

What a curious saying, that is Vyvyan's first thought. And where does he fit within it? Is he, with his chest of war medals, one of the chickens? He takes a single stride forward and in a voice whose calmness strikes even him as ominous, says,

"Lady Brooke."

"Margaret, please."

"I hope you won't take offence, but it seems to me that, if you had wanted to protect me from foxes, you would have stepped in some years back—a quarter-century ago, even—when Cyril and I were being pitched like bags of rubbish to the nearest relations."

"Constance's family assured us you were—"

"I have lost a mother. A father, a brother, a *wife*. My very best friend in the world, Robbie Ross. I have seen unconscionable numbers of men die. I subsist on the gradually intensifying trickle of royalties from my father's literary estate and from what I can scrape together from translating eighteenth-century French romances. From day to day, I am no longer even sure why I was the one, out of all of us, who was spared. And I will freely admit that I fear many things—mediocrity perhaps chief among them— but not Lord Alfred Douglas. He has done all he can conceivably do."

Spent, he has only enough breath to conclude:

"Margaret."

It suddenly occurs to him that he has been speaking so evenly she has had no way of hearing. But she is studying him now with an attention far more undivided than she granted to *The Vortex*.

"I am sorry," he says, reflexively. "That was more than you—"

"More than I *desired*, perhaps. Not more than I needed."

Without a word, he resumes his seat. Gives his earlobe a slow and pensive scratch.

"Was he charming?" he wonders.

"I regret to inform you that he was. I found myself growing agreeable in a really disagreeable way."

"Yes, I saw."

"If it's any satisfaction, his life has gone all to blazes. His wife has abandoned him and taken the son with her. And, of course, he has just finished a six-month term in a cell of His Majesty's choosing."

"Yes," says Vyvyan.

"The irony of it happening on account of losing a defamation lawsuit is lost on nobody. It is one thing to slap back at the Marquess of Queensbury, as your father did—as anybody who knew the Marquess wished they could do—but only a blithering fool would go after Mr. Churchill. In Bosie's defence, I suppose—and I can bend only so far backward before snapping quite in two—he has made such a career of calumny that I think it must have grown upon him like a second skin. Then, too, his family have always been so gruesomely litigious or, to use another parlance, insane."

She falls silent. Then, in a more chastened voice, says:

"I didn't want you to see him because I didn't want you called back there."

"Oh," says Vyvyan, "no fear of that. I'm called back all the time, at any moment. Why, here we are in Soho Square, and I'm suddenly remembering when Cyril and I visited Father. It was a rehearsal of—oh, it must have been *Woman of No Importance*. I expect he was having an argument with Mr. Beerbohm Tree, but all he said to us was *Why don't we all go for a walk?* Well, naturally, we trundled right after him—there was nothing we liked better—and I remember we turned this very corner, and he pointed at that very statue, and he said, *Dear boys, Charles the Second has turned quite to stone because nobody speaks to him anymore. Do you think we might cheer him up?*"

"Your father wanted cheering up, too."

"No doubt. Well, Cyril and I spent I don't know how long talking to this—this *monolith*—telling it jokes and stories, singing it songs. Nothing we did seemed to have any effect, but just as we were turning to go, Father dipped a finger in King Charles's eye, and lo and behold, it was wet with tears. *Look*, said Father. *You have broken the spell*. I think it is still the most successful I have ever felt."

He stops now, in some confusion, for he feels, as he always does in such moments, that he has tested the patience of the surrounding world.

"I'm sorry," he murmurs. "I have been told that maudlinness is the most incriminating sign of advancing middle age."

"You may be right," says Lady Brooke. "However, when one is as ancient as I, one sees that some people have a good deal to be maudlin about. You might be one of them."

She glares out into Soho Square, as if daring the gaslights and nightingales to contradict her. In the next beat, she is standing.

"Dear Vyvyan, would you be so good as to call me a taxi? If I'm not back at Lady Cunard's by midnight, she'll send dogs after me."

Even at this late hour, the work of hailing a cab is but a minute. The work of handing in Lady Brooke—bestowing the staff of Moses across her lap, where it seems to lose most of its old terror—is not too much longer.

"Well now," she says. "I am catching the first train out Monday morning, but perhaps I might treat for dinner the next time I'm through. Or a new dinner *jacket*, perhaps, owing to the decrepitude of yours."

He smiles down at her. "You are most kind. Though I think jackets are going a bit out of fashion, don't you?"

"I know just how they feel."

Her lips plump a little as she reaches for his wrist, then his hand.

"You have my address," she announces.

"Certainly."

"And you *will* write, won't you? Every so often. You needn't blather unless you feel violently moved."

"I shall blather indeed."

The taxi draws away and, as Lady Brooke's long gloved fingers extend themselves into a farewell, he is surprised by the emotions that briefly wash over him. Surprised, too, by how familiar they feel. Somebody else is leaving.

3

IT WANTS ONLY a few minutes to midnight, but, rather than hail a cab of his own, Vyvyan finds himself returning to the bench he has lately occupied—sinking into it with no immediate thought of rising again. What explains his inertia? Is it the mere prospect of being greeted by the same house in Chelsea Square, plying the same latchkey to the same door with the same mewling cat on the other side? Something like Nefertiti's cry penetrates even now, and in the next second, he feels the unmistakable static crackle of fur against his shin. Looking down, he finds a hulking, glaucomic orange tabby, wrapping a tail round his ankle.

"Hallo," he murmurs, chucking it under the chin. "Are we lost?"

Vyvyan feels round the neck. No collar, no bell.

"Have we eaten? Are we quite sure?"

"From the looks of him," declares a man's voice, "he's been feasting on every rat in London."

In the next second, like something obeying nothing more than gravity, the voice's owner drops onto the adjoining square of bench. Both Vyvyan and the cat fall silent before the spectacle: a gentleman in evening dress, of no immediately clear age, leaning back and crossing his legs at the ankle. The voice, when it reemerges, is an unguent of late-nineteenth-century vowels, suave and intimate.

"I have never told anyone before," says the gentleman, "but there was a tomcat waiting for me when they brought me to the prison hospital. Yes, he came right up, so desperately proud of the little mousey nestled between his jaws, and so genuinely surprised when I started shrieking. I tell you if I had a shilling for all the people who've assured me that mice don't bite. I *know* they don't bite! That is the least of their offenses! They are guilty merely of being mice. That very night, in my cell, I prayed to Saint Anthony of Padua to shield me from all rodents henceforth. It is the extraordinary fact that I never saw one again."

He speaks in the most serene of monologues, as though he has been sitting here for the past two hours, unspooling his mind's bobbin. The effect is to leave Vyvyan feeling himself the interloper.

"I'm sorry," he says. "Have we met?"

The man's face turns then, like a coin slowly spinning on its milled edge, and the shock is not so much that Lord Alfred Douglas is sitting alongside him as that the universe has suffered it to happen in such a quotidian way. As if he were just a train pulling into a station.

"Where has Margaret got to?" he asks.

"She is . . . she is staying with Lady Cunard. . . ."

"Funny, I have always confused Lady Cunard with Lady Colefax. I wonder if they get themselves mixed up, too. Possibly only their secretaries tell them apart."

Vyvyan stares at the etched profile. The white carnation in the buttonhole. It is hard even to name all the feelings that rise up.

"Have you been following me?" he stammers.

"That has rather the air of a bad serialised thriller, don't you think? I prefer to say I have been ambling in your direction."

The fox is in the grange.

"How did you know I was here?" asks Vyvyan.

"Well, I should add it was entirely *owing* to Margaret's desperately awkward attempts to conceal you. She might as well have reached for a follow spot."

Vyvyan removes his hat. Sets it quietly in his lap and rests his hand lightly on the crown.

"And you recognised me? After all this time?"

"Of course! Surely you would have recognised me, too, if Margaret's granitic back hadn't been blocking the way?"

It's a hard question to answer for Vyvyan can't quite let his gaze linger even now. His eyes, by unspoken command, keep skittering toward the edges: hat, boots, cane.

"What do you want?" he asks in a faint voice.

"Oh, I thought you might wish to catch a nibble somewhere."

"I have already dined."

"That leaves only supper. I know just the place. My car's waiting down the road."

Vyvyan glares as hard as he can at the most neutral surface he can find. Which turns out to be his own knees.

"So I'm to leave with you now, is that it?"

"Well, your precious little rat-killer has already absconded. Fresh woods and vermin new."

So it has.

"That leaves only me," says Lord Alfred.

"And what if I don't want to?"

Lord Alfred gives every sign of considering the question.

"Do you have a cigarette?" he asks.

In a Pavlovian way, Vyvyan reaches in his pocket for the silver case of Turkish Abdullas, silently lights one for each of them.

"Thanks awfully," says Lord Alfred, waggling a pinkie. "Now look here, I'm not asking too very much of you. Have we not known each other a good while?"

"It has been many years since I knew you. As it turns out, I never knew you at all."

"Oh," he answers, unperturbed. "you did. But I *do* think, after all that's happened on every side, it's time we spoke. I expect your father would have liked it." He pauses, conjecturally. "Your mother, too."

"Do not speak of her."

"I understand. You adored her, of course. I persist in adoring mine, too, though she persists in living. Tell me, Vyvyan, aren't you just the slightest bit curious?"

"About what?"

"What happened."

"I know what happened. As much as I ever need to."

"No, you don't."

Lord Alfred rises and begins to make a slow circuit of the bench, gesturing with his cane.

"Hear me now, Vyvyan, I present myself to you, in all humility, as somebody who remembers. Oh, it's true! I remember Oscar playing with you in the dining-room. I remember him mending your wooden fort. I remember him reading to you from *The Jungle Book*. I remember him singing you Irish folk songs, atrociously off-key. I remember you recoiling at the sight of a live fish flapping on the floor-boards of a boat and your father saying, *Dear boy, it's only dancing*. I remember him taking you to a children's play at the Haymarket Theatre. I remember—oh, you must recall this, Vyvyan—the way you used to grab for his Malacca cane whenever he walked through the door. What would he always tell you?"

With a sense of purest fatalism, Vyvyan listens to the words crawl from his own mouth.

"That he would give it me once I'd reached its full height."

"And what did you do? I know you remember."

Here the words fail, but that is only because they are now spilling from Lord Alfred.

"You showed up one day with stacks of books tied to the soles of your shoes! I needn't tell you how enchanted Oscar was. He told me later, *That child was rising up from Literature itself!*"

Lord Alfred tips back his head and laughs in that same bell-like, untrammeled way, and he is young once more, and Vyvyan is, if anything, twice as old.

"I don't know what you want of me," he says.

"An hour of your time. That is all. Then we may go our separate ways forever."

"And what is this place?"

"The Marquis of Granby. In Fitzrovia."

"I'll take a taxi."

"My car's just down the—"

"I would rather not."

Across the fine bones of Lord Alfred's face, incredulity gives way to amusement.

"I'm not a white slaver, you know. Even if I were, I should be kidnapping a rather younger specimen than—"

"I shall meet you there."

4

IN THE END, Vyvyan walks, for the distance is no more than a quarter mile, and the feeling of being his own master deepens into some notional freedom. With no trouble whatever, he might keep walking. Leave behind the second son of the Marquess of Queensbury without another thought, and it is only some hours after, in the chilly light of dawn, that he will wonder why he didn't. Perhaps he was not his own master. Perhaps it was simply the locomotive force of his own feet, in their spatted shoes, striding up Rathbone Place. Or did it come down to this? He was *more* than the slightest bit curious. He had spent the entirety of his youth trying to peer over a privet hedge that had been erected on every side and that, in some cursed fashion, remained intact long after the hedgekeepers had perished. He has always known in some abstract way what waits on the other side: ruin, grief. But there also waits the *view* which has been barred from him just this side of forty years. Eyes wish to see, minds to know, and even if they didn't, the maître d'hotel of the Marquis of Granby is already rushing forth, a jacket sleeve pinned round his missing hand and forearm (*The War*, thinks Vyvyan) and a manner just teasing toward unctuous.

"You are meeting someone, sir? That is happy news. Might I trouble you for a name?"

"Lord Alfred Douglas."

"Ah. His Lordship waits below. Might I check your hat?"

From the cavernlike darkness, a violin scratches out a thread, and just as Vyvyan's feet touch ground, there opens out before him a grotto, entirely absent of windows yet, courtesy of the electric chandeliers, coaxed into squalls of suggestion. He sees two dancing couples in immaculate evening dress . . . a heavy-shouldered gentleman in a monocle . . . most surprisingly, a pair of sailors, gazing out from a café table. Vyvyan has already half-forgotten why he is here until, in the far corner of the room, a slender man rises and waves him over.

"I thought you wouldn't come," says Lord Alfred Douglas.

He is no longer wearing his hat, and in the glare of electrical light, Time vaults forward. The blond nymph whom Vyvyan has been carrying about like a tintype for the past three decades becomes a mousy Tory bureaucrat, with a razor-etched part in a head of drably absconding brown hair. The red rose-leaf mouth has been supplanted by two sere ridges of lip. The aquiline nose, once youth's flower, has become, while the world's back was turned, a pocked and bulbous beak, marbled with veins. Even the lovely blue eyes reveal at their back something bloodshot and malarial. The allusion flashes up at Vyvyan before he knows what to do with it. Dorian Gray's portrait, dragged from the shadows.

"You're a good bit smaller than he was," says Lord Alfred.

Here, then, a new shock. Vyvyan has himself been observed. Tracked like a chicken through the grange of the Princess Theatre, Soho Square, and now the basement of the Marquis of Granby.

"Five feet and nine inches," he says, drawing out a chair.

"But the *eyes*," says Lord Alfred, twitching a pair of freckled hands. "They *resound* of him. As does the ponderous nether lip, so redolent of cretinism in other faces. Oh, there can be no question of *your* paternity. I say, Hassan!" he cries. "Hassan!"

Across the floor a young waiter in a jacket perhaps two sizes too large glides toward them.

"How do you do?" he asks.

"Very well indeed. Look here, my friend and I here desire two bottles of your very best champagne. Pol Roger, or Pommery. We must *not* stint, Hassan, there is much to be celebrated."

"Gin," says Hassan.

"No, not gin this time, old boy. *Champagne.*" Getting no response, he vibrates the ends of his fingers. "Bubbles."

"Bubbles."

"That's right. Off you go. The thing *is*," he says, angling back toward Vyvyan, "Hassan is a deeply intelligent boy but in a way so intuitive that it can sometimes be missed. I say, have you any more cigarettes? I have tried to wean myself off the devils, but on occasions such as this . . ."

Vyvyan stares at him. Slides over his cigarette case and his lighter.

"How kind you are," says Lord Alfred. "Tell me, did you care for tonight's play?"

"It was . . . out of the usual way . . ."

"How do you mean?"

"Different to what one usually sees."

"I still don't know what you mean."

Vyvyan doesn't quite know either. He wonders if this was how those first-night attendees greeted *Earnest*, conscious only that some old template was being bent into a new shape.

"It forces us to engage with how things are," he says at last. "However disagreeable that might be."

"Drags us into the *mire*, you mean. I found in it the same degeneracy that has colonised our culture since the War. Your Mr. Coward feeds at the same trough as your Mr. Joyce and your Mr. Eliot. I shouldn't be surprised to learn that they were *all* of them Jewish, up to and including your precious Mrs. Woolf."

"They are none of them *mine*, exactly, nor—"

"I also disliked how the women in the play exhaled their cigarette smoke through their nostrils. Don't you find that common?"

Vyvyan immediately recalls a radical journalist of close personal acquaintance who expels her smoke in the same way as her opinions.

"Never mind," says Lord Alfred, already losing interest. "It is my peculiar fate to care about things that reasonable people no longer trouble themselves with. I am a museum that nobody shall ever visit. Ah, here is Hassan! Now remember, dear boy, how I taught you to open a champagne cork."

"Cheerio."

"No, that is what *we* say once *you* have consummated your task. Do you . . . do you have it? Yes, that's right, grab it by the throat. No mercy. Ah! Pop goes the weasel. Yes, well, there's a bit of an *effluence*, but we aren't harmed. Come back at your next crossing with a rag, perhaps, and mop it up. *Mop*, yes. No worries! Off you go."

He waits until Hassan has left to reach for his handkerchief.

"Dear me, that *is* a mess. And he neglected to pour, which I *have* reminded him about."

Taking care now to fill both glasses, Vyvyan observes that Hassan seems rather young for this line of work.

"That is a property of his being Moroccan," answers Lord Alfred. "That race of people are extravagantly young until they become, in the space of one third of a second, extravagantly old. Your father and I spent some wonderful weeks in that country. It is where we met *Gide*, if you can believe it, who was, in my experience, insufferably pompous. Sea-green incorruptible until he *wasn't*, if you know what I'm getting at."

Vyvyan can only reply that he once translated a Gide short story.

"Did you?" says Lord Alfred, giving his sodden handkerchief a light squeeze before returning it to his pocket. "Have you ever seen larger hands on a creature his size?"

"Gide?"

"*Hassan*. I am very nearly persuaded that his clumsiness is explained by the fact that his true vocation is amateur boxing. Do you follow the sport, Vyvyan? *C'est dommage*, it is too exquisitely primitive and the best possible rebuke to our effete modern age. I must put you in touch sometime with the Italian Futurists. They are all about being young and strong and daring and deliciously *violent*. You know Italian, don't you?"

"Yes."

"Then you'll understand them better than I, at least on an intellectual level, though I'm not sure intellect is where they *dwell*." A trickle of sweat bleeds up from his temple as he settles back in his chair. "What is that wretched violinist playing? It can't be Strauss, can it?"

"Lehár, I think."

"I perfectly abominate operetta, but I *do* believe your father's life would make for the most marvelous *opera*, don't you? Not in the Wagnerian style, of course—though he did have his *letimotifs*—but I think Offenbach might have been just the ticket. Yes, a fearsomely tall and comical mezzo for Lady Wilde and, of course, a perfectly charming little boy soprano for yourself."

"Thank you," Vyvyan thinks to say.

"How much did they tell you back then?"

"They . . ."

"Your mother and the rest."

"About what?"

"Don't be coy, dear boy, your *father*. His *troubles*. What did they tell you?"

Vyvyan stares once again at his knees. How much harder he finds it to speak to a man than to a woman.

"They only told us that he was in gaol."

"But not why."

"No," he says, shrugging. "My mother kept all newspapers from us. Sent us away to schools where nobody knew us."

"When did you learn the truth?"

"Not till I was eighteen."

"And Cyril?"

"Rather earlier."

I was nine, Viv. I saw the headlines. I read everything.

"Tell me," says Lord Alfred, drawing closer. "How many of your present friends know of your parentage?"

"All of them."

"Bit of an open secret then?"

"I expect so."

"Yet *still* secret. How I envy you. Wherever I go in this world—until God Himself calls me to His blessed kingdom—I shall forever be your father's concubine. Not that there is anything intrinsically *wrong* with the title. Though, as you know, I forfeited it some years ago."

Vyvyan says nothing.

"Tell me," says Lord Alfred. "Do girls ever try to rescue you from Oscar's dire fate?"

He flushes. "On occasion."

"Have they succeeded?"

"Yes."

"Has it been to your liking?"

He flushes more deeply. "Yes."

"My wife saved me, too. And I her. We saved each other until we couldn't. Needless to say, God is the only *true* savior."

The second mention of God. Hedgingly, Vyvyan says:

"You spoke of supper."

"So I did! I'll just ask dear Hassan to wrangle us up some cutlets from the—dash it all, where's he gone to?"

But there is no locating him in the murky confines. A moue of disappointment creases Lord Alfred's face, and he relapses into silence. Then, out of nowhere:

"You had a wife, too."

"Yes."

"I understand that she died quite young."

"Yes."

"My condolences. Might I ask how she—"

"No."

It is the first obstacle he has erected since arriving, but Lord Alfred only reapplies himself.

"Might we speak of Cyril then?"

"I cannot prevent you."

"Such a dear lad, wasn't he? When I heard the news, I wept like Niobe. Sniper's duel, I was told."

"Yes."

"So many of our boys never made it back, such a savage business. I don't suppose Cyril left behind any estate to speak of, poor devil."

Only the bridle, thinks Vyvyan, and the revolver and field glasses and an old Jules Verne volume, all passed along by Cyril's battery commander. Vyvyan still has the book.

"It scarcely needs saying," says Lord Alfred, plucking at his detachable collar, "that *your* service, Vyvyan—in behalf of God and country—well, it is something that *all* of His Majesty's subjects can . . ."

The air goes out of him and, for the first time since coming here, Vyvyan is amused.

"Thank you," he says.

"Do you ever dream of him?"

"Cyril? Sometimes."

"What of your father?"

"Sometimes."

"When Oscar *comes* to you," says Lord Alfred, leaning once more across the table, "how does he behave?"

"Apologetic, I should say."

"My father the same! *Oh, Bosie, won't you forgive me? I was only trying to save you from*—well, what? That is the question the Marquess will not stay to answer. Of course, he was dead certain that Oscar was buggering me."

Vyvyan's mouth swings briefly open, closes.

"But why blame Father?" Lord Alfred sweeps on. "Everybody else thought the same. Pretty little lad, stout older fellow. The entirety of England plied its narrow, frozen, sex-famished, *corporate* mind to our little Sheffield handcar and concluded it could only travel down the one track. But I wish it to be known," he says, forsaking volume for proximity, "*I have never been buggered in my life*. Not by your father nor by any man. You may ask around if you like."

"I don't think I shall."

"Are you sure?" he asks, screwing his left eye into a wink. "No curiosity on that score, either?"

"None."

"Does the subject repulse you?"

"Only your desire to repulse me repulses me."

In that moment, Lord Alfred is a Sheffield handcar that might fly off down any number of tracks. To Vyvyan's surprise, it chooses hilarity.

"By Jove! That is a Wildean paradox if I've ever heard one. Kudos to *you*!"

They touch glasses, glancingly, as the Marquis of Granby carries on around them. How close the air is beginning to feel, thinks Vyvyan, as if they were all exhaling into one another's faces.

"Do you want to know why Oscar and I got on so well?" says Lord Alfred. "It wasn't the sex—that passed rather quickly, though he *would* badger. It was that neither of us was English. Oh, I know he cast off the Irish brogue somewhere in Oxford, but he couldn't cast off the mother-land, could he? Or the *mother*, God help us all. As for me, I am a proud Scotsman," he says, shifting briefly to his native burr. "To make matters worse, I am a poet, and the English hate *all* poets. *Real* poets, I mean, not the ones who recite things in drawing rooms. England *only* gets sentimental about her poets once they are safely dead. It is why she is finally coming round to your father, for all that she hounded him to—"

"I'm sorry," says Vyvyan, lurching to his feet. "I'm not feeling very . . ."

Inclined to stay, he would say, but Lord Alfred is making the quickest of appraisals.

"What is it, belly trouble? Something lower? Lav's that way," he says, jutting his chin toward the far corner.

Rather than dispute the diagnosis, Vyvyan wanders off with a feeling of perfect relief. Travels down a half-lit passage, lined with blunder-busses and coaching prints, and pauses before two doors, neither of them marked. Pushing through the nearest one, he finds a young woman in a beaded fringed dress repairing her lipstick before a mirror.

"I *am* sorry," cries Vyvyan.

"It's all right, love, I'm nearly done."

The voice is deeper than his, but the face, pale and lightly talcumed under golden hair, is as alluring in its way as the drunken scavenger hunter.

"Well, come in already," growls the stranger. "I don't bite, do I?"

Vyvyan closes the door softly behind him. Makes as if to doff his hat, then remembers he doesn't have one.

"You with *him* then?" asks the stranger.

"Him?"

"His lordship."

"Oh." Vyvyan's mind goes casting about. "For an hour," he remembers.

"Mind you keep it to that. Has he ordered the gin already?"

"No, champagne."

"So much the worse! You be bloody well sure he's there when the bill comes. I reckon he's already cadged cigs off you."

"Well . . ."

"Might want to cut that off, too, duckie. He gets to coughing and hacking round two or three in the morning. Dancers don't like it."

"Look here, I'm not . . ."

"Oh, I know, you're a bit older than what he goes in for, but all cats are grey in the dark, aren't they, dearie?"

Eyeing himself narrowly in the glass, the stranger purses his ruby lips for one last pop. Then, turning, gives Vyvyan a light kiss on the cheek.

"Wish me luck. It's a proper ambassador tonight."

The imprint of the lipstick is still there when Vyvyan himself steps up to the glass. He dabs it lightly with his handkerchief, then walks back down the corridor. Before his very eyes, the basement of the Marquis of Granby has become a new place. The monocled, cigar-sucking German field marshal proves himself to be a monocled, cigar-smoking woman. The bartender reveals, as if by sleight of hand, a single mother-of-pearl earring. The two sailors have abandoned their café table for a complicated tango step across the checkerboard floor. The violinist has traded out Lehár for "Oh, Lady Be Good." Vyvyan wanders through in a trance and, upon reaching his seat, finds it blocked by a chuckly, liverish fellow in a Homburg.

"Vyvyan!" cries Lord Alfred. "Permit me to introduce—oh, bother, what's your name again?"

"Barker."

"How euphonious. Dear Vyvyan, Mr. *Barker* here wants to know if you'd like to go fishing in—the Hebrides, I think it was . . ."

"The Tortugas."

"Tortugas, of course."

Vyvyan carefully reclaims his seat, returns his napkin to his lap.

"You are most kind to invite me, Mr. Barker, but I fear that I am rather occupied for the present. I am . . ." *Don't.* ". . . editing a series of translations of eighteenth-century French romances . . ." *Stop.* ". . . two or three of which I am myself translating. . . ."

"Very *warm* in the Tortugas," says Mr. Barker. "You take my meaning."

"I would surmise he *does* take it," says Lord Alfred, "being in full possession of his faculties. But, see here, you mustn't squander your charms on *us*, Mr. Barker, I am very nearly certain that the gentleman in the white kid gloves just now winked in your direction."

The suggestion affects Mr. Barker as wind to a weathervane. He points himself and follows.

"Potty," murmurs Lord Alfred. "Though he must have *packs* of money or they'd have kicked him out eons ago."

Vyvyan drags his index finger up and down the side of his face.

"I am trying to understand why you invited me here."

"Why, for purposes of education. Don't you see this is the very sort of establishment your father and I used to frequent in our Gilded Age? The scene of our crimes, if you like. Oh, I *know*," he says, with a glittering smile, "you believe me a recidivist. Or, worse, a nostalgist. In fact, I am a *missionary*, Vyvyan, and I am here, on God's charge, to show the *misérables* of this haunt of infamy that a man may rise *above*. Indeed, *must* or sink forever. What better example than myself?" he adds, lightly touching his breastbone. "Thirty years ago, no man, excepting your father, was more calumniated, more condemned in all of England. Yet here I am, ready to bear witness to God's mercy."

Don't laugh, thinks Vyvyan. *Don't rage.*

"Like a Methodist?" he thinks to ask.

"Now you really *do* offend. Surely you know that I converted to Roman Catholicism."

"I'd heard something of it."

"God, of course, is most infinite in His patience, but he is indeed the Hound of Heaven! A man can run only so far. Thus I made the—the truly *hallowed* choice, Vyvyan, to stop running. But you know surely of what I speak. Do you not belong to the One True Faith yourself?"

It is like being asked to recall a long-dead maiden aunt who sat in black by the pianoforte, sewing things. And was so distracted by her sewing she neglected to save a boy's mother.

"I was a schoolboy," he says grimly.

"Dear Vyvyan, you know that a lapsed Catholic is the worst of all. Never mind, I forgive you, as I am called to do. But, I must add, it is a great comfort to know that your father was given last rites on his death-bed. Until then, I would conjecture that he engaged with the faith on a purely aesthetic level, and who could blame him? The Catholic liturgy far outstrips its pale and denatured Anglican facsimile. But I daresay that, in his final moments—though I was not invited to partake of them—he was groping toward *transcendence*, Vyvyan. And surely . . ." Lord Alfred shakes out the last few drops from the second bottle into his waiting glass. "*Surely* it is a testament to God's exquisite sense of harmonics that my own father did the same on *his* deathbed. The Marquess of Queensbury, as you probably know, was a most infamous atheist who repented all his manifold sins in the very hour of his parting, and it would have taken at *least* an hour, Vyvyan. When I look round this room . . ." His head executes a periscope pivot. "When I see all these creatures who—I hesitate to use the word *fallen*, but so they *are*—so are we *all*—so were we born to *be*—when I look at them, I repeat, I find only *mission*. I am here, by the fact of my former corruption, to point the way to some less corrupted state. Why, yonder comes Hassan to enact that very principle. *Hassan*, you retrograde Muhammedist."

With that, Lord Alfred unexpectedly coils his arm around the boy's waist and draws him into his lap. Vyvyan will later recall that Hassan assented without protest—indeed, with a look of resignation that suggested this was as much a part of his evening as uncorking champagne.

"Now then, Hassan. *Who is the Creator of everything?*"

"God."

"Very good. *Is God the Blessed Trinity?*"

"Yes."

"To be certain. *One* God in *Three* Persons. And *which* are the Three Persons, Hassan?"

"Oh."

"First is the Father."

"Father."

"Then?"

"Son," suggests Hassan.

"Very good. *And . . .*"

Small white teeth peep through Hassan's rosy lips.

"I don't."

"Oh, you little infidel," says Lord Alfred, giving his cheek a soft pinch. "It is the Holy Spirit, of course."

He cinches his arm more tightly round Hassan's waist, impulsively plants a kiss on the boy's smooth cheek, another on his nose.

"Next time, I shall test you on Man's Dignity, Duty, and Destiny, so you had best study, do you hear? Now off with you." Beaming, he turns back to Vyvyan. "You see? One plank at a time."

Vyvyan pours himself another inch of champagne.

"Hassan's progress would seem to be incremental."

"Oh, I am in no hurry."

And, having made the declaration, Lord Alfred suddenly subsides in his chair. The front of his boiled shirt puffs out like Father Christmas's belly. His carnation droops farther from its buttonhole until it lands entirely intact on the tablecloth below. Mr. Barker wanders over to ask if they would care to dance. ("We've both a touch of the gout," says Lord Alfred.) The maître d'hotel, with an air nearly sorrowful, leaves a check in a leather album.

"There is no rush, your lordship. We only want you to have it in case you are at great pains to leave."

Across the windowless room, the heat piles like layers of peat. The music slows in reply. Vyvyan, with a decisiveness that surprises him, slides back his chair.

"I think it's time I pushed off, don't you?"

Through the cirrus cloud of his cigarette smoke, Lord Alfred's mouth folds itself into a furrow.

"Has my company failed to scintillate?"

"You did say an *hour*."

"I don't think you should go," he grumbles and, in the next second, reaches across the table. "Dear Vyvyan, I hope you will not scorn me, but I believe that God Himself has brought us together. No, I pray you, do not laugh! Who else could fathom that your thoughts about me—in whatever direction they tend—could not be *resolved* until the *object* of those thoughts was present. Thus I proffer myself to you now, entirely undefended. Have at me. Yes, have at me!"

Vyvyan slowly prises his hand free. Studies each liberated finger.

"With all due respect, Lord Alfred, I am not sure that now is the time to *adjudicate* disputes that have been—"

"If not now, then when?"

Vyvyan drags a finger round the crater of his eye.

"You might save us both a quantity of time if you told me what you wanted me to say."

"Well, you might start by owning that—due to entirely misleading accounts of my conduct in bygone days—you now despise and revile me."

"Those words would imply that I have granted you far more tenancy in my mind—my *heart*—than I have ever—"

"Oh, I can hear your brain clicking. You blame me for everything. I know you do."

"Not *exactly* everything. I don't think, for instance, that you single-handedly started the War."

"Of course not," answers Lord Alfred. "That was the Jews."

Vyvyan stares at him.

"Oh," he answers. "You really *are* poison, aren't you? Very well, since you have asked me to speak plainly, I believe that you killed my father. I believe that you killed my mother. Perhaps my brother, too. One way or another, with your abominable selfishness and spite and egoism, you killed us all, and if you want to sue me for that statement, please know that the only things you can claim by way of damages are some furniture and a cat. Who will deliver *mousies* to you until her dying day. You have nothing more to take from me."

He watches now as the older man inspects the carnation that lies on the table and, with some difficulty, inserts it back into his jacket.

"You are in luck," declares Lord Alfred. "I have given up litigation for Lent. And for the rest of time, it appears. What God makes a Scotsman *do*. I say, do you have any more cigs?"

Vyvyan shoves over the last of his supply. Shoves the lighter after it. Lord Alfred puffs for a minute in silence.

"Thing is," he says, in a reasonable tone, "if it hadn't been *me*, it would have been some other fellow."

"Nobody else would have made so many demands of him. Nobody else would have dared masquerade as a family friend."

"Not Robbie? Robbie was his first, you know."

"Oh, do not," says Vyvyan, jutting out his jaw. "Robbie Ross was my father's *ally* and executor. The *lone* figure who kept alive his work, his name . . ."

"Granted . . ."

". . . his *memory* . . ."

"Yes, and at my expense! It isn't every poet's dream to go down in literary history as Judas Iscariot. Nor is it even remotely fair."

"No?" Vyvyan plants his forearms on the table. "Did you not goad my father into a perfectly doomed lawsuit?"

"We didn't *know* it was doomed."

"And then fail even to show up in the courtroom?"

"His lawyers asked me not to."

"Or visit him in gaol?"

"*He* asked me not to."

"You left him behind in France. You left him behind in Italy. . . ."

"You may not even *speak* to me of Italy. We ran out of *money*, thanks to your mother and mine. The only way we could survive was to separate, but it was never meant to be *permanent*, and if you want to know, I was a good sight more faithful to him than he ever was to me. All I remember now is dashing off *letters* and *wires*—a never-ending stream of assurances. *Yours forever. Yours faithfully.* And it was never enough, *never* enough, and I don't know what else I was supposed to *do*. I was a *child*, really."

"So was I," says Vyvyan.

And remembers as he says it the boy in Bogliasco, waiting through days of blazing Italian sun for the *specific* day when a mother and father would be restored and all should be well, and all manner of things should be well.

Lord Alfred reaches for his handkerchief and, finding it still sodden, applies it like a compress to his brow. From out of the gloom, the violinist tosses a chain of notes, fat and Mitteleuropean.

"*Liebesträum*," groans Lord Alfred. "Has it come to that? Hassan, fetch us another bottle!"

"Hassan has gone," says Vyvyan. "And I don't think I particularly want—"

"It's not for *you*. I intend to get good and squiffy before I'm done."

"I would humbly suggest you are."

In a systematic fashion, Lord Alfred makes a study of his regions.

"Not enough," he concludes.

He spreads his handkerchief across the table and slowly folds it back up, one corner at a time.

"You know, when I think back on that time—all that horror—I can't help wishing that the world had simply left us alone."

"By *us*, you mean . . ."

"Oh, I mean *all* of us, Vyvyan! You and Cyril. Oscar and me. Your mother, too, of course. We might have been—oh, I know it sounds ridiculously sentimental to speak of *family*, at least in the orthodox sense of the word . . ." He pauses, temporarily stymied. "What I mean is suppose we'd all found a *place*. Somewhere out in the country or somewhere, away from prying eyes. I think, under those conditions, we might have cobbled together some sort of plan to—to live together. Be *happy*, even, if that's not too profane a wish."

"You and my mother? Happy together?"

"Oh, pish," answers Lord Alfred, with a soft flap of his hand. "We'd have just imported Arthur Clifton every weekend, and she'd have been fine."

Vyvyan's jaw tilts just slightly out of axis.

"Arthur . . ."

"It's funny, the refuge I keep returning to is that charming farmhouse Constance rented down in Norfolk. Do you remember it?"

"I wasn't there."

"Really? Are you sure? I could have sworn. Well, it holds a particular place in my heart, and not just because it's where Oscar and I—oh, very well, *began*—but because it was the nearest thing to a haven that I'd ever encountered. No, it's true," he adds, with a chagrined smile. "The whole time we were there, I don't recall anybody in all of Norfolk spending a particle of energy wondering who we were or what we were up to. Not even that curious photographer who came wandering by. The cheque cleared, that was all they needed to know. I remember thinking: *We might spend the rest of our lives here.* And you and Cyril could have been my little brothers or—*nephews* or something—and Oscar and I . . . well, we would have been free to become what we were meant to be. Yes, I think even God would have approved in the end. For I think, under Oscar's influence, I would have been a more Christian soul. Oh, it's true!" declares Lord Alfred, tugging once more on his starched collar. "Nobody ever loved me as much as *he* did. I don't suppose you ever read that perfectly vengeful letter he wrote me from prison?"

"Bits."

"Do you remember how he signed off? *Love.* Ha ha! *Love, Oscar.* You know, he used to tell me, *Bosie, I don't adore you because you are an angel. I adore you because you are* not *an angel.*"

Lord Alfred's head rocks slowly back into his cradled hands. The stream of his breath siphons straight to the ceiling.

"I think sometimes that's why the grief won't go away. I keep pushing the same rock to the top of the same hill, and Oscar's never there."

He falls silent, and the rest of the Marquis of Granby seems to follow suit, as if everyone were wrapping black bands round their arms. Even the violinist, finally touching bottom after hours of sawing, sets down his bow and reaches for his case. The only sound now is the rattle of glass and silverware on trays, and the barman's singsong voice, calling out at intervals.

"Come along, please. . . . Finish your drinks, please."

Wonderingly, Lord Alfred raises his head, stares out across the tables. To nobody in particular, he says:

"I don't know about you, but I'm going to have a little sleepytime."

His neatly cropped scalp is already descending toward the table, and his eyelids have closed by the time his forehead kisses cloth. The breathing is soon that of a dreamer. Vyvyan rises, reaches into his pocket for a pair of pound notes, drapes them over the leather check-presenter, then picks his way through the remains of tonight's revelers. The sailors are gone, but there in the corner sits the stranger from the lavatory, sleeping as soundly and solitarily as Lord Alfred, no ambassador in view. The maître d'hotel tends him the courtliest of nods, and Vyvyan is nearly to the door when Mr. Barker, like one pierced by a lance, cries out:

"Don't forget the Tortugas!"

5

⟨᧚⟩

No CAR IS waiting outside the Marquis of Granby when Vyvyan emerges. Did Lord Alfred send his away, or was there never any car? By rights, Vyvyan should be catching a cab home, but he wanders with no clear end in mind. Miles, though he doesn't know it. Somewhere around four in the morning, he is in an all-night restaurant in Fleet Street, eating sausage rolls alongside a junior pressman in baggy grey-flannel trousers. The cold seems to have settled into his bones like a lodger, and he must swallow down two more cups of coffee before he can even think of making for Tite Street.

By foot, the journey is a little more than an hour, following the Strand past Covent Garden, threading between Belgravia and Westminster. It is when he reaches the Royal Hospital Gardens that he is sure of where he is, for geography now is memory, and he is no more than six, playing touch-wood and cross-tig in the bushes and being invited in for tea and bread-and-butter by the Chelsea parishioners. One of them was a drummer boy at Waterloo who told of coming home in the same ship as the Duke of Wellington.

In the purpling hours of dawn, Number 16, Tite Street, looms up as though it were newborn. A red-brick terrace with iron railings and bay windows and a tiled porch. Standing on the corner opposite, Vyvyan, in his mind, pushes open the white door with the brass knocker, turns right into Father's study. Sees pale yellow walls, a Beardsley drawing of Mrs. Patrick Campbell, a table that once belonged to Thomas Carlyle. It was the auctioneers and bill-collectors who, in the wake of Father's imprisonment, tacked straight for the Beardsley and Carlyle and the presentation copies from Twain and Ruskin—and then, as Vyvyan was later told, kept tacking, room by room, every toy and treasure and garment that hadn't been claimed. Years later, he still stumbles across them in antiquarian stores.

Belts of fog are drifting now before a damp wind. He plumbs his pockets, finds just twelve shillings left to his name. Enough, perhaps, to hail a taxi. Fifteen minutes later, he is standing before 14 Half Moon, wondering if he is too early or else too late. After some debate, he reaches for the brass lion knocker. Raps once, then twice more, and is about to step away when the door draws open to reveal Arthur Clifton, in a robin's-egg-blue Japanese dressing gown over silk pajamas.

"Vyvyan! What a surprise."

Is he surprised? Pleased? Unhappy? Impossible to say for there is a note of light gloom about him at all times.

"I was out and about. . . ."

"So I see. It must have rained."

Vyvyan feels about his clothes, stares at his boots.

"I suppose it must have."

"And you with no overcoat. Well, you might as well come in," says Arthur, opening the door wider. "And let's take off that dinner jacket, shall we? What do you say we retire to the sitting room? Mrs. Bellingham's off today, but I'm perfectly capable of boiling water. Making a fire, too, why not? It's deuced chilly for May."

Five minutes later, Vyvyan is sitting by the hearth, wrapped in a fringed tartan blanket, his face tingling with coal heat, while Arthur Clifton lays out, with his usual economy of gesture, a pot of tea and two cups on a black lacquered chinoiserie tray.

"There's sugar if you want any, and I've some oatmeal in the cupboard if you're—no? Well, suit yourself."

With just the tiniest grunt, he lowers his long limbs into a burgundy armchair, kicks a slippered foot over the opposing pajamaed leg, and reaches for his pipe, already lit and resting by his elbow. Vyvyan is struck by what a dignified spectacle he still presents. The lids are heavier, it's true, and the skin has loosened along the jaw, but the head is as proud as ever and—the one bohemian touch—he has grown his silver hair long enough to send it sweeping in a loose cascade to his ear.

"When did you last sleep?" he asks Vyvyan.

"Oh. I should think it was . . . twenty-three hours ago. No, twenty-two. It depends on what time it is now. I have just spent the evening with Lord Alfred Douglas."

Arthur stares at the reflection of firelight in the slurry-black pool of his tea.

"And was it pleasant?" he asks.

"I don't know, honestly. I went in with certain cardinal principles about him, and now I'm not sure of any of them." He smiles, tentatively. "What do *you* think of Lord Alfred?"

"Oh, I think of him as little as I can. I am pleased to say that English society concurs."

"But if you had to characterise him . . ."

"A viper," answers Arthur. "No, make that nest of vipers. *No*," he quickly adds, "that isn't very Christian. I will light in the direction of charity and suggest that Bosie Douglas is the most astonishing case of arrested development I have ever had the misfortune of encountering."

"This is charity?"

"In the main. You see, I knew him in those days, Vyvyan. He had great gifts—charm, charisma, a poet's ear—*all* his professors thought so—and it all came to naught because he was stopped. *Frozen*, I mean, right there in the very blood and boil of adolescence, with no path forward or back. It's almost the worst fate I could wish on anybody, even him."

Vyvyan taps a finger against his cup. "What stopped him?"

"Trauma, I expect. Or, if you like, publicity. Even an exhibitionist tires of being exhibited. Yes, I think, absent a scandal, he might have grown into a man of quality instead of the rancorous bigot we now behold." He gives his tea a pair of gentle stirs. "I suppose he spoon-fed you tales of his martyrdom."

"Yes."

"And did you swallow?"

"All I can mount in his defence," says Vyvyan, "is that he never forced Father to do anything. Fall in love. File a lawsuit."

"No, he merely *manoeuvred*, as only a clever adolescent can do, then fled the consequences. Going to gaol was probably the best thing that could have happened to him. I only hope they threw him onto a plank bed as they did your father."

Arthur reaches down toward what at first seems like a comforter and then translates into an ancient golden Labrador, splayed and slumbering.

"How goes the gallery?" Vyvyan thinks to ask.

"On its way out, I shouldn't wonder."

"Oh, I'm sorry. . . ."

"You needn't be. Dealing with artists is a young man's game."

Vyvyan makes a quick survey of the surrounding walls. Augustus John. Walter Sickert. Dora Carrington. Not a bad harvest for an old man.

"I hope your wife is well," he thinks to say.

"She is in Sussex," answers Arthur.

Vyvyan can't help but note the clock, unwound. The antimacassar on Arthur's chair askew. A pair of pince-nez, negligently dropped on the Persian rug. A bachelor lives here. Vyvyan struggles now to recall the wife of record: a redheaded watercolourist who once exhibited in Arthur's gallery. Much easier to call up the *first* Mrs. Clifton—another redhead—quite solicitous of the Wilde boys and deeply sentimental about their mother, which rendered them both insensibly spoony about her. In the deepening quiet, Vyvyan pours himself another cup of tea, squeezes a wedge of lemon into it.

"I don't know if you recall," he says, "but you visited us once in Italy."

"Lord, yes, ages ago. You and Cyril were poppets."

"I believe you came on legal matters. Something to do with Mother's settlement on Father. I've been a bit late, I fear, in appreciating how much her money kept us afloat in those years."

"It was the only thing keeping you afloat," says Arthur, gravely.

Vyvyan worries at his cuticles.

"Was that the last time you saw Mother?"

"Yes, I think it was."

"Did you love her?"

He can only pose the question without looking.

"I was very fond of her," says Arthur Clifton after a pause.

"I don't mean fond. And I only bring it up because—well, she was sad all the time in those days, but I remember her sadness had a different colour when you left."

Only now does he dare to glance up. Something hard is carving itself around Arthur's mouth.

"I didn't leave," he says. "She sent me away."

"So you did love her?"

More silence.

"And she you?" asks Vyvyan.

Silence still.

"Isn't it queer," he says, "the things that grown-ups never tell their children. In my experience, they are precisely what children most want and need to hear. When Father was first getting in trouble with the law, nobody would tell us a blamed thing. By the time he was dragged before the Old Bailey, Cyril and I were being hustled across the Channel in the care of a deeply pious French governess we'd never even met. I believe her chief virtues were that she spoke no English and hadn't the foggiest idea who we were. We were only *cargo* to be delivered to—well, neither of us knew. Or knew if we'd ever see Mother or Father again or have a bed to sleep in, clothes on our backs, food to eat. You see, they got it all wrong, our grown-ups. It was the *not* knowing that was far worse." He folds his hands round his teacup. "I suppose what I'm getting at, Arthur, is that, had we known about you and Mother, I believe that, on the scale of disasters, that would have . . ." He pauses to recalibrate. "I think we might have been glad to know she was loved by *somebody*."

By Arthur's chair, the golden Labrador splutters out of a dream, gives a groggy swing of his head, then subsides once more into sleep. Arthur rises from his chair for the ostensible purpose of prodding the coals in the grate. Hovers there half a minute later, the poker still in his hands.

"Your mother did the best she could," he says. "Under the most trying of circumstances."

"To be sure."

He sets down the poker, draws the collar of his dressing gown round the loosening cords of his neck.

"I do think that she would have been gratified and indeed *proud* of the life you have built for yourself."

"Out of the ruins of hers, you mean?"

For the first and last time that morning, Arthur smiles.

"We *are* being a touch morbid."

"Oh, I only meant to agree with you. But, really, what I want to do is speak of Norfolk."

The smile ebbs.

"You mean you are travelling there?"

"In a way."

Vyvyan rises now, wraps his tartan blanket more tightly round him.

"You all went there on holiday, do you remember? It was the summer of ninety-three. Oh, I didn't go myself—I was told I had a touch of the whooping cough—but Cyril was there, and Mother and Father. *Grandmamma*, how could I forget? Lord knows how they sprung her from London."

"Perhaps London pitched in."

And they both laugh, in a way that doesn't feel ungracious.

"You were there, too, Arthur. You'd just got married. Oh, and Lord Alfred . . ."

At first, the seed seems not to have landed. Then, in a musing voice, Arthur Clifton says, "Yes, that was . . ."

". . . where Lord Alfred and my father became lovers. Is that what you were driving toward? Or were you going to say that was where Mother first learned about them?"

In fact, Arthur says nothing.

"To me," says Vyvyan, "to my flimsy little five-year old soul, Norfolk was the villain in the whole play. Just three months after, we had Christmas at Babbacombe, and nobody was speaking to anybody, and everybody was acting as if nothing had happened, only it *had*, and I came out of it all gulping for air, as if some hand were holding my head under water, and it seemed to me that something beastly must have happened in Norfolk, and I couldn't stop it."

"Vyvyan." Arthur gives his temples two slow kneads. "Why torment yourself over ancient history?"

"Because Lord Alfred remembers it all quite differently. You see, Norfolk was for him the place where things might have turned quite around and we might have—you included, Arthur!—settled down into some little utopian colony."

"Ridiculous."

"So I thought, but you see, earlier tonight, I was walking up Rathbone Place, on the way to meeting Lord Alfred, and the thought struck me that I could very easily shirk my appointment and keep walking and never look back. And now I'm wondering: What if there were a Vyvyan who *kept* walking? Went straight home, fed the cat, read a novel, went to bed. What if we even passed each other? Vyvyan and Other Vyvyan, neither aware of the other's existence. So then I return in my mind to Norfolk, a place I've never been, and I ask myself: Why couldn't *that* have been two things at once? The place where everything went south and the place where everything found its true north."

"Two Norfolks?" Staves fan across Arthur's brow. "I don't understand, is this some sort of thought experiment?"

"That does sound rather better than delusion."

"And what is its purpose?"

"Why," answers Vyvyan with an incredulous smile, "to keep us all together. Don't you see? That's all we ever wanted, Mother and Cyril and I.

Father, too, I know that in my heart. Through all the exile and terror, what kept us alive was the thought of being a family again. Because there was no one else like us Wildes in the entire world—*no one else*—and now they're all gone and—I'm *here*, for reasons I don't always fathom but . . ." The breath catches in his throat. "The only explanation I can come up with is that I was meant to call them back. Even if it's impossible. Especially if it's impossible."

He clamps his hands over his face and spends another minute coughing up the last twenty-two hours. Along with the last thirty-nine years.

"The thing is," he says, between sobs, "for that to happen, you must tell me everything. Everything that happened in Norfolk. Everything you can recall. Please."

Arthur waits with an abiding patience for the wave to subside. Then he gently proffers Vyvyan a handkerchief and pours him another cup of tea and, after a decent interval, says in a voice of calculated levity:

"In compensation for my services, I hereby impose three conditions."

"Yes?"

"That you retire to the spare room yonder."

"Very well."

"That you discard all your sodden fancy dress and drag from the armoire any clothes that reasonably fit you."

"Yes."

"That you then stretch yourself across the already provisioned bed—you can't miss it, it has four posts—and go at once to sleep."

"For how long?"

"Until such time as you awake."

"I've a cat back home."

"The cat will survive."

"And you'll be here?"

The driest of chuckles.

"Well now, the circus left town weeks ago, so there's nowhere else for me to be. I'll have another pot of tea waiting. Or, depending on the hour, whiskies and soda."

ACT FIVE

Wildes in the Country

A rented house at Grove Farm, Norfolk
August 1892

1

~

"STOP!" CRIES CONSTANCE.

The command is as much as a surprise to her as to everyone gathered round her. Pausing now in its afterecho, she beholds herself in a basket chaise: Cyril across from her, Lady Wilde to her right, trunks piled at their feet. Slowly, the coordinates reassemble themselves. The Wilde family has been on a late-summer holiday. In a charming little Norfolk farmhouse. Only the holiday now is over, and she and her seven-year-old son and her mother-in-law of an uncertain age are to be ferried to the railway station, whence they will take the next train to London and their respective domiciles. Nothing has happened in any material sense to warrant a change in the itinerary.

"Oscar," she says, from the depths of her cloud. "Help me down."

"What in all of heaven?" cries Lady Wilde.

"I'm sorry, Madre. I've just a small bit of business to attend to."

"But we shall miss our train. . . ."

"Oh, yes," she says, more breezily than she feels. "But there will be another, I expect. There is always another. . . ."

She stands rather unsteadily in the drive, swinging her gaze from her baffled fellow passengers to Oscar himself.

"Are you unwell?" he asks.

"I must speak with you."

"We *have* spoken."

"Yes, but . . ." She gives her head a fierce shake until the leveed words break loose. "Whatever I said, I want to unsay or else *re*say, only I don't know what I'm supposed to say, and I won't know until I've said it."

Looking at him, she remembers suddenly that she was leaving him in a perfect fury. He had betrayed his family. There could be no forgiving him. She cannot explain how these conclusions, the product of long and tortured thought, could prove so insubstantial as to blow away on the first wind. And how, without fury to guide her, there is only a kind of abject vulnerability. Why, she thinks, it is like revisiting her wedding night.

"Please," she whispers. "Let's go inside."

In the next second, Oscar is calling over his shoulder. "Cyril! Mummy and I have the most urgent of appointments. Will you kindly look after Grandmamma while we're gone?" Leaning toward Constance, he mutters out of the corner of his mouth. "Will we be long?"

"I can't say."

"We shan't be long!" he calls back.

But it is not Cyril's voice that follows after them but Lady Wilde's frosty contralto.

"I do not require looking after! I require people keeping to schedule! If I am held here any longer, I shall send for the police!"

2

꧁☙꧂

REENTERING MRS. BALLS'S farmhouse brings Constance no closer to understanding her true errand. She wanders from room to room, smelling the same compound of wax and dust and heat, reassigning all the old scenes to their proper settings. Here is the dining room where Florence and Arthur Clifton bickered over breakfast. Here, the rear terrace where Lady Wilde dozed off after dinner. The reception room where Oscar discoursed on the ontology of golf. The hallway where he took her into his arms and assured her that all was well.

The stairs leading up to the attic.

No matter where she turns, she finds a haunted house, and when she settles at last on Oscar's bedroom, it is not because it is free of spirits but because he himself spent so little time there.

"I'll need a few minutes," she says, and shuts the door after her.

And sits there, in the bright light of noon. Were she a saint, this would call for a seraphic vision. Were she a poet, a Muse might be feathering down. Being neither, she waits, but for what? Something to build on the suggestion that first seized her in the chaise, that departing upon these terms—enacting the hoary conceit of a wife fleeing her unfaithful husband—was not merely bad practice but bad theatre. A failure of the imagination.

At the very last, it is Mozart who comes for her. She remembers that, in the finale of her favorite opera, *The Marriage of Figaro*, Count Almaviva has been captured in the act of seducing a servant girl. Writhing from shame, he croons to his long-suffering countess: *"Perdono, perdono!"* She hesitates—or so the score has her do—and then pardons him as he would wish, her exquisite melody soaring into an even more exquisite chorus that sounds, in Mozart's hands, like the absolution of God himself. All the more sublime for the lingering suspicion that the Count will find more servant girls and be forgiven each time, and how many arias will it take for the Countess to learn that *she* is the one who must imagine some other way? And free them all? A new world awaits for anyone with ears to hear.

Rising, Constance takes now two or three turns of the room, willing her mind to settle. Gradually, an outline appears before her—traced as if by some provisional hand and growing more substantial the more she interrogates it. *What next? And then?* And when at last the brush strokes have cohered into something like a road, she feels an unexpected pang for the road she is leaving behind. The whole Victorian prescription: wife and husband, hand in hand for life's pilgrimage. Strengthening each other in all labor, resting on each other in all sorrow, wasn't that how it went? Was it not the vision of her own girlhood, though she would have been embarrassed to articulate it? This is the path she must now consign to flames—quite as if it never existed—and she sheds actual tears for it because who will be there at the moment of *her* last parting, sharing silent unspeakable memories? Anyone at all?

At last she wipes her eyes in the mirror and, giving herself one last inspection, opens the door and finds Oscar and Lord Alfred standing side by side in the hall—agonizingly suspended, like schoolboys caught in minor thievery. She cannot say why the sight is pleasing to her.

"Come in!" she snaps in a matron's voice. "Hop to it!"

The only lingering question is where the three of them are to be arranged. Constance reclaims her armchair. Oscar, as if to reenact last night's penance, occupies roughly the same square of bed. It is Lord Alfred who, relatively new to the precincts, walks in tangents, opting at last to drape his forearm in an Oxfordian line over the dresser. Only the soft fidgeting of his right hand suggests he is not at home.

"I hope there won't be any wailing or gnashing of teeth," he says.

"Not from *me*," answers Constance, coolly. "What *you* choose is entirely up to you, but I hope you will not grow hysterical. Now let us start with first principles. Oscar," she says, "do you recall what we agreed upon when we were first married?"

"I believe it was *I do*."

"Well, let's not dwell there, shall we? I mean *after* that part. We were on our honeymoon, do you remember? And one night, we got to talking about how marriage should be not a—not a religious but *renewable* contract between a man and a woman. *Leave God out of it*, you said. *He's got quite enough to do with the Mormons*. Well, I was a young bride then, and I didn't want to be any less free-thinking than my groom, so I suggested that either party should be free to leave at the expiration of one year. And you laughed and said, *Oh, my dear, can't we at least push it to seven?* And here we are," she says, smiling more widely than she would have guessed. "*Eight* years in, my darling, and the contract long since up for renewal, and I can't help but wonder if you wish to opt out."

She has always cherished those moments in their life when she can reduce him to silence, and there is joy even now, watching her words circulate through him while his golden tongue struggles to lift free.

"Is that what *you* want?" he asks at last.

"Well now, to be fair, I did ask first, but I'm happy to rephrase if that will buy you more time. Do you still desire to be married? To *me*, I should probably specify."

"Yes," he says, after a pause.

"Why?"

"Bless me, I wasn't aware that I needed to anatomise my—"

"Don't be emotive, I only want to know if this is on account of your career."

"It is not."

"You are certain?"

"I am."

"Because if that *were* the reason—"

"It is not," he insists. "It is not, it is *not* . . ."

Something inarticulable beetles across his face, something that again gets in the way of fluency. *I like a look of Agony*, she remembers, *because I know it's true.*

"How then should you like to be married going forward?" she asks. "In name only?"

"In everything."

"And what does that mean?"

"It means . . ." Something hedges behind his eyes. "Everything but that."

The euphemism, to her surprise, carries no sting, but then why should it? She has seen that very code play out now for five years: a dreary concourse of separate bedrooms and chaste kisses and passing caresses. Yes, she has long since learned to do without *that*, and perhaps the only part that will change (for epiphanies are still dawning) is her tendency in dark moments to blame herself. If they have done nothing else, Arthur Clifton's attentions have reawakened her to her own desirability—or, at least, to the desirability of *being* desired.

"My next question," she says. "Are you in love with Lord Alfred?"

Here, too, he hedges, and it is only the force of her own concentration that breaks him down.

"I am," he murmurs.

"And *you*," she says, angling her head toward the indolent young man in the corner. "Do you return Oscar's love?"

Lord Alfred plunges his hands in and out of pockets, stares down at his shoes. The answer comes at last as the slightest of nods.

"Does that mean yes?" asks Constance.

He nods again.

She trains her gaze out the open window. Blue cloud-shadows are chasing one another across the grass. Sparrows are rustling in the ivy. A thrush is singing. Why, there is an entire world spinning without any regard for them. From behind her, she hears Oscar say, in an unusually wheedling voice:

"Is it too much—is it too early—to ask for your blessing?"

"Yes," she answers, without looking back. "It is entirely too much, and it is entirely too early. You have lied, you have deceived. And now—because you are men, perhaps—you expect me to draw comfort from the fact that you meant no harm, and you fail to see that intention doesn't enter into it. You have followed your selfish inclinations, and I am now, as a direct consequence, a *wronged wife*, and it is that very cliché for which I cannot entirely forgive you. And besides," she says, turning round, "blessings are God's bailiwick, not mine, and you must make your peace with him at your leisure. All I can aspire to in this moment is some sort of crude earthly wisdom, and it seems to me the better *part* of wisdom to recognise . . ."

What?

". . . the change that has come over things and . . ."

What?

". . . find a way to live with it."

Oscar is utterly still at first. Then his hand reaches straight for her.

"Dear one," he says.

"No," she answers, drawing back. "I decline to be a martyr, for you or anybody. This is a transaction, do you see? And in exchange for my forbearance, I ask three concessions of you."

"Name them," says Oscar.

"You must conduct yourself going forward with absolute discretion."

"Of course."

"There is no *of course*, it is the thing you must do. Next, you must continue to see the boys every day, to the best of your ability."

"Nothing would make me happier."

"Finally, you must grant me my own freedom."

She has the gratification of watching him draw back like a spectator.

"Freedom," he murmurs.

"Yes, to be loved as you are. Or do you think me incapable?"

"Of course not, I am only wondering if you had some particular fellow in mind. . . ."

Arthur, that is her reflexive thought. *Not Arthur*, the second thought. And the lingering thought, for her course becomes plainer the more plainly she considers it. The Cliftons' marriage is doomed. Let her not be Doom's agent, or the root of some other woman's suffering, for there is quite enough suffering as it is.

"Naturally," Oscar speeds on, "whomever you choose would be welcomed in a purely fraternal fashion. . . ."

"Oh, bother your fraternity," she says. "Whomever I choose shall neither be selected nor approved by you. Nor perhaps even known to you. And shall himself be the soul of discretion, you may depend upon it. And now," she says, modulating her voice to a new key, "let us take up the matter of your lodgings."

The two men stare at each other, mirrors of confusion.

"Come," she says. "You can't exactly hopscotch naked through the Royal Hospital Gardens. Think of the poor nannies. Now my first thought was of Paris—they have always loved Oscar there—but the hard fact is that London is where his livelihood resides, and it is where he himself must reside. For now. That being the case," she says, rising, "we must look into finding a flat."

"For whom?" asks Lord Alfred, faintly.

"I *do* wish you'd keep up. For the *both* of you. Somewhere in Soho, I am thinking, with an obliging and credulous landlady. I shall interview her myself to ensure she has not a scintilla of worldliness about her."

"Two gentlemen sharing quarters?" poses Oscar. "Wouldn't that rather draw attention?"

"Has it ever? London is crammed to the rafters with confirmed bachelors, sharing two neutrally appointed bedrooms."

"But Oscar is famous," blurts Lord Alfred.

"So I have gathered. For that reason, we must put out word through the usual organs that you have retained—let us say a studio or an atelier. *Away from the tumult of domesticity*, some such nonsense. Under no circumstances are you to engage a hotel room, do you hear? I don't care how much you bribe the bellboys or how much the management promises to put on account. Your account is now with me. Lord Alfred, how should you care to be billed?"

"Billed . . ."

"Are we to call you Oscar's secretary? Amanuensis? Perhaps *translator* might be the best fit for now. It has at least the faint patina of truth."

"But I am a fellow poet," protests Lord Alfred.

"Exactly the phrase most calculated to raise hackles. You might as well stroll down Pall Mall in Greek tunics. Never mind. Between us, we shall find the right nomenclature."

Something seems to shine out of the younger man's face.

"Might we sleep there, too?" he asks.

"On the whole I should prefer that you do. I regret to inform you that your days of rutting in the attic are over. Besides, I already have designs on Oscar's bedroom."

"My bedroom," says Oscar.

"Well, yes, to the best of my knowledge, a London gentleman needs but the one pillow to lay his head upon."

"Pillows!" sings Lord Alfred. "Down, of course, they *must* be goose-down. And might we have silk sheets? White as white can be?"

"If you can supply them."

"Calling cards?"

"No."

"What if we got Beardsley to design them?"

"More emphatically no."

Lord Alfred pauses to reconsider.

"Might we have friends stop by?"

"It would depend upon what you mean by that vague plural noun."

"I believe he means like-minded personages," suggests Oscar.

"So long as they are gentlemen with every bit as much to lose as you, then yes, welcome them. *With open arms*, I was about to add, but that would be gilding the lily. If they have nothing to lose and are the mean sort who demand payment and who specialise in extortion, I advise you to steer clear. And above all, put nothing in writing! Lord Alfred will recall what happens to gentlemen who leave incriminating letters in their pockets."

"What of public appearances?" asks Oscar.

"In any venue where tongues are liable to wag—a gallery opening, a theatre opening, a dinner party—I shall be at Oscar's side. Lest you think me possessive, Lord Alfred, I am perfectly open to your joining us so long as you have been explicitly invited. In the event of your being there, I shall position myself squarely between you and my husband, smiling equally in both directions."

Oscar gives the back of his head a slow and meditative scratch. "There is bound to be gossip."

"All the more ineffectual for lacking a clear point of attachment. Toward that end, Lord Alfred, you might consider casually flirting with me every so often, if that doesn't strike you as too grotesque."

"I can manage."

"I knew you could. You'll also need to make things right with your father."

The heat rolls straight up the celery stalk of his neck.

"My father is a villain and a reprobate."

"I don't doubt it. That type is well represented in my own family line. They *will* bluster, won't they? *And* boil. Then, with one precisely chosen word, they will settle right down again, like a kettle snatched from the hob. The trick, I have found, is never to treat them with contempt. It is the thing they fear most in life for it is what they feel most deeply about themselves."

Grimacing, Lord Alfred runs a hand through his hair.

"Even if I were to desire a reconciliation, I would scarcely know how to—"

"Before this day is out, I shall draft for you a conciliatory letter. You may adapt it to your own cadences, but I urge you to smooth the way with him as best you can. Even if it means inventing female conquests for his delectation."

"You are asking me to lie, then."

"I am asking you to *hide,* which is quite a different thing and which will become second nature with practice. I say this with some assurance as I am a woman."

"That she is," affirms Oscar, stretching back on the bed now with an air frankly amorous. "Dear Constance, had I known you were harboring within you such skills of generalship . . ."

"Would it have changed things?" she asks, feeling something rise within her, too. "Does it arouse you?"

"Indeed it does. Who would have supposed emasculation to be so erotic?'

He smiles at her now with an undisguised broadness, and she smiles back, and the thought briefly takes hold. They could send Lord Alfred away, shut the door and have one last go, for old vows' sake. She riding on top, as he always preferred, gazing down into his eyes as they cloud over, the springs of the mattress echoing each parry. Then she remembers: *Everything but that.*

"Of course," says Oscar, "what you are proposing is deuced unconventional."

"And would the man I married have given a fig for convention?"

"The man you married is now a thrall of the theatre."

"Which only makes it more imperative that we become our own playwrights."

The same imperative infuses her now as, under some foreign sensibility, she proceeds to draw an invisible curtain.

"Behold. On this side sit the three of us. On the other side: *England,* in all her narrowness and horror and her childish need to be entertained. Yes," she says, "we will *dance* for them. And they will walk away with no understanding of what they have just seen."

From out of Oscar's face, a smile buds forth.

"Why," he says, "it will be just like Mr. Poe's purloined letter. The thing that everybody is looking for is sitting there in plain view."

"Yes, where better to put it? Have you ever known a Victorian to distrust the evidence of his senses? That is his limitation and our escape."

Oscar is silent for a long while. Then, in a heavier voice:

"You would go to all these lengths for us?"

"Oh, do not mistake, I have the boys' interests foremost in mind. Did you not yourself say that we can't let them sink? Don't you see that the only way to accomplish that is to stay buoyant ourselves? To live our real lives where society can't see them and then, in public, give them the lives they would have us lead. We must wait them *out*, my darling. Until they are ready to know us."

His lips part and then slacken, and something like a shudder passes through his giant frame.

"And what if they are never ready?"

"Then, in our dying breath, we will scorn them. And travel to our reward, wherever it is. Until then, we will live our lives as best we can. And come back to Norfolk every summer, why not? For here is freedom of a sort." She bends slowly toward him. "The thing you must understand is that, for all that's happened, I still take pride in calling myself Mrs. Oscar Wilde. It makes me feel a woman of some importance."

His head executes a ponderous nod and keeps nodding until it is resting in his hands. Through the lattice of his fingers, a single convulsive sob claws free. Then, gathering himself, he says:

"You are more than that, you are the ideal wife. And I am a man of the greatest good fortune."

Constance fumbles through his jacket for his handkerchief and, lifting his face toward hers, sets to dabbing the tears from each eye.

"Dear Oscar Fingal O'Flahertie Wills Wilde, do you hereby renew your contract for another year?"

"Oh, my dear," he answers, smiling. "Can't we at least push it to seven?"

From the corner of the room, like a sorrowing ghost, comes Lord Alfred's chastened murmur.

"A thousand apologies, Mrs. Wilde. I sorely underestimated you."

"Oh, that's no matter," she answers, refolding the handkerchief and returning it to her husband's pocket. "I underestimated me, too."

3

⁓

SHE WILL LATER be unable to recall who broke the spell or how they even left the room. All she will remember is Cyril waiting in the hall. Looking more diminutive than ever in his Eton collar and bow tie.

"Darling," she says, "what is it?" For her first thought is that he has overheard them.

"Grandmamma sent me with a message."

"Did she?"

"*So help me Heaven in my last hour, if your mother doesn't come out this very instant . . .*"

Constance can't help but laugh.

"And did it end there?"

"No, it was still going. Did I get it right?"

"Well, I can't be sure, darling, but it sounds lifelike." She softly traces the contour of his cheek. "I'll go see to her, shall I? And while you're waiting, why don't you—oh, Bosie?"

From down the hallway, Lord Alfred starts at the sound of his own name.

"Yes, Mrs. Wilde?"

"Enough of that formality, you'll call me Constance, won't you?"

"Of course."

"I was wondering if you might play a spot of lawn tennis with Cyril."

"I should be delighted."

"You are too kind."

"Mummy," whispers Cyril. "Last time we played, Lord Alfred kept running toward the net. He wouldn't even let the ball bounce."

"Then you be sure to loft the ball right over his head, do you think you can do that?"

"Over," he muses.

"Yes, he isn't nearly as high as Pappa."

Wondering as she says it if size has any gradation for a seven-year-old. Perhaps everybody is big.

"I'll try," says Cyril, setting his mouth in a fierce line.

"I know you will, darling. Oh, but don't wander too far, we might . . ."

Might what? Leaving seems as unlikely now as staying, and it is with some sense of postponing the decision that she returns to the basket chaise. Lady Wilde is just where Constance left her, erect behind a palisade of trunks. Looking, in her black bombazine and lace headdress, like Queen Hecuba in Troy's ruins. With the help of the coachman, Constance clambers up beside her and, for some seconds, the two women sit in silence.

"We have missed our train," says Lady Wilde.

"Yes."

"I hope you will not insult me by insisting there is another on its way. At my age, there is not always another train. This very minute, back in London, I've a sheaf of Celtic myths on my escritoire that I'm to translate for Mr. Yeats's anthology. Oh, I *know*," she adds preemptively. "Writing for money is a very dull thing compared to writing for a revolution, but a woman does what she must." Frowning, Lady Wilde fingers the black brooch that hangs on a pendant round her neck. "I hope at least that your bizarrely importunate mission was successful."

"It is hard to know just yet," says Constance. "I do think that Oscar and I have come to a bit of a *rapprochement*."

"*Rapprochement?*" Lady Wilde's head totters slowly back. "I had no idea things were so bad."

"No, Madre, it's—"

"I confess that I overlooked a great many offenses in Oscar's father, but I let him know in no uncertain terms that, if he ever brought us to the verge of *rapprochement*, he would not see me again until the Day of Wrath, and perhaps not even then."

"Perhaps the better word is arrangement," suggests Constance.

"Oh, my dear, that is a good sight worse! You might as well set your marriage vows on a Viking warship and send it flaming to sea."

Constance closes her eyes, sends a prayer to the midday sky.

"Really," she says, "it is just a matter of logistics, Madre. Oscar has been feeling a touch *confined* in Tite Street. So much commotion."

"He has his library, does he not?"

"Yes, but you know how it is in the theatre . . ."

"I am proud to say I do not."

"Well, the deadlines are so exacting, you see. Mr. Beerbohm Tree needs his pages when he needs them, and Oscar *does* like reading all the parts himself—he says it helps him keep them straight—and, one way or another, it grows a trace awkward."

"For whom? The fire of creation warms all those who sidle its way."

For the servants, Constance thinks to say, before reflecting upon Lady Wilde's servants, who have been sidling away from that same fire for as long as she can remember.

"He just craves a bit more quiet, Madre. Perhaps a charming little flat somewhere."

"You mean to say he will live there?"

"Well, some of the time, yes. For convenience's sake."

"Alone?"

There must be a note of something in Constance's face, for lines of rancor sprout round Lady Wilde's kohl-rimmed eyes.

"Pray do not tell me that my son purposes to share rooms with that Scottish dunderhead."

"If you mean Lord Alfred . . ."

"Whom else?"

". . . I do think it makes perfect sense for him to pop over at intervals. He *is* translating Oscar's play, after all."

"Yes, it is the only time I have ever pitied Salomé. Oh, *cara mia*," she says, impulsively reaching out her hand, "can this be what *you* want?"

"On the whole, I should say yes. I should say decidedly yes. And, of course, we won't be quit of Oscar at all, he'll be coming and going at all hours. You know, he can't bear the thought of being away from the boys."

"Or you."

"Or me," she answers automatically. "But there's only one rub, Madre. With Oscar gone more often, the whole place is bound to feel a bit emptier."

"He *looms*."

"That is *le mot juste*. Over the course of his many absences, I have found that one feels the vacancy most particularly in his bedroom. It being scaled so entirely to him." She listens to her own voice, inspecting it for thinness, for strain. "But, of course, *being* so capacious, the same room might house virtually anybody. Anybody at all."

Even this is not enough, and, with words failing, she gives Lady Wilde's gloved hand the gentlest of squeezes and then watches with relief as something blooms through the other woman's skin. In a voice of nearly childish wonder, Lady Wilde asks:

"You mean you want me to come stay in Tite Street?"

"Oh, dear Madre, it would only be to keep me company. And I wouldn't solicit such a favor of you under normal circumstances, only I *know* what a bother urban living can be—all that nonsense of managing servants and paying tradesmen—when there are so many more pressing things with which you might engage your hours. And if you are worried about your salons," she presses on, "I have experimented with dragging down the shades in the parlor, and the effect is quite as Stygian as in your own home. One can't even see one's own hand. I suspect your guests might not even notice the difference."

Still in a slight trance, Lady Wilde gazes directly outward as the afternoon arches its back over them.

"You must know, Constance, that I have never wished to be a millstone about my boys' necks."

"Of course."

"I have sought always to pattern for them the tenets of self-determination which Ireland herself must embody if she is to be free."

"And in this you have succeeded, but see here, if you came to live with us, you could be just as independent as before, and the boys would have all the profit of imbibing your—your *robust* republican principles. Straight from the fountain, as it were."

Lady Wilde nods. Her large, vigorous hands contract briefly into fists, relax again.

"Isn't it funny?" she says. "When my boys were still young, I harbored so many ambitions for them—every mother does, I am sure—but the thing I most wanted for them was to find good women. And Oscar did."

Constance can no longer trust herself to speak, for she is calling to mind her own mother, not a particularly good woman, nor a maternal one. Even with all the apparatus Lady Wilde drags after her, she remains a bargain.

"Very well," says Constance, nervously tapping her fingers together. "We can sort out all the details later, can't we? And now, at the risk of presuming even further on your goodwill, might I ask one last favor? Might we spend just one more night here?"

"*Gah.*" Lady Wilde casts a beseeching look to the clouds. "An hour ago, you couldn't wait to leave."

"I know, I *know*. I suppose I just want to see how it feels not to run away from something. Mrs. Balls will see to your trunks."

"She may do as she likes. Not that anybody cares, but I am in urgent need of sleep."

"I'll ask her to make up your bed."

"No," says Lady Wilde. "Here will do."

Slumber takes her before another minute has passed. Constance props her parasol just above the older woman's head, then climbs down to earth as gently as she can. She is nearly to the front door when a voice calls after her. Turning now, she finds the chaise driver, exactly where he has been the whole time. He doffs his cap and declares, in a gruff but respectful voice:

"I charge for sleepers, ma'am."

4

THAT NIGHT, OVER dinner, Oscar clinks a knife against his glass.

"Ladies and gentlemen and most distinguished *child*, I should like to call out, for your joint approbation, the distinguished author who has condescended to stay with us tonight. There is no need to enumerate her many titles as that would consume many seconds, even minutes, and tedium, as you know, has ever been my enemy. Suffice it to say that our esteemed guest has, through diligent labors, secured for herself the highest plaudit of all. She is the Author of Our Happiness. Assembled souls, I give you Constance Wilde."

The glasses chime in near-unison—even Mrs. Balls isn't ashamed to hoist a spot of bubbly—and the applause is warm enough that Constance can actually feel it on the underside of her skin. Half of her takes pleasure, the other half slinks from view, and once she is done smiling, she harbors a quiet wish that everyone will go away. To her surprise, they comply. Madre hustles straight for bed. Bosie volunteers to teach Cyril chess, and Oscar, to everybody's surprise, says there's a bit of Act Four that needs working through. Mrs. Balls and her nephew Patrick sweep up all the remaining plates and cigarette butts, and Constance, to her relief, finds herself alone on the rear terrace. The day's events have extracted from her more energy than she realised, and she reclines into her folding chair with two thimbles' worth of champagne. The sea (two fields off) carries on its moaning, and on every side, the flowers have closed except for the evening primrose. She pulls her shawl more tightly around her and watches the twilight melt away.

Our happiness. Is that what she has authored? Or has she just cobbled together a brief stay against doom? So many things could go wrong; so many players might forget their lines. Bosie, with his childish piques and adult sexuality. Oscar, with his egoism and disdain for consequences, his readiness to fly as close to the sun as the sun will allow.

And what of the larger world? She thinks back to the coachman who sat so quietly on his box while she and Lady Wilde spoke. He had only to keep his ears even halfway open to know as much about the Wilde family as anybody living in England, and he becomes now, in her mind, indistinguishable from the supernumeraries who populate Oscar's plays. The butlers and housemaids and footmen and gardeners and grooms and pantry boys who hustle across the rear of the stage on their varied errands. Silent on pain of dismissal but never deaf—indeed, capable at all times of learning whatever scandal is unfolding. *There will always be eyes and ears,* she thinks. *Mouths, too.*

More obliquely, there will always be her own body, exacting new betrayals every day. In just the last half-hour, the chain of pricks along her right leg has resolved into its usual numbness, and there is this newest symptom: a blind spot in her right eye, swelling without warning from a speck into a smudge. The darkness is once more nibbling away at her, and what better proof than this? Cyril, bursting through that same blind spot and materializing with a percussive force in her lap. The shock is almost greater in the part of her that cannot feel it.

"Why, hallo, little man," she says, with a light laugh. "Is the chess lesson over?"

"*Cyril's* the one playing chess."

"Then who are *you*, presumptuous child?"

She bends her face toward his, only to find an entirely different face gazing back. Fairer than Cyril's. Milder eyes and straighter hair. A longer nose, a more appeasing smile. Such a stark change that her own smile freezes and she has just enough air to speak the name.

"Vyvyan . . ."

"Hallo, Mummy. Did you forget I was here?"

"No, darling, I . . ."

In a spell of wonder, she touches his face at all its promontories, just to feel something touching back.

"Your whooping cough," she murmurs.

"Oh, Mummy, I got over that last week."

"But how did you . . ."

Get here? Did she not leave him in Hunstanton? With instructions to her friends to keep him close until she returned, owing to his whooping cough? How could he have traveled such a distance? Why did nobody wire her?

The answers come as a series of doors, each swinging open in sequence and revising what comes after. Vyvyan in Hunstanton, running after her to assure them he was quite well enough to come, too. Oscar prevailing upon her to grant him passage. Vyvyan and Cyril crouched together in the train to Cromer, giggling and plotting, and then, having arrived, sharing a cot specially provisioned by Mrs. Balls. Vyvyan and Cyril taking turns as Oscar's caddy and finding together a rabbit named Blackie and an extraordinary hidden room in the attic. Vyvyan playing croquet and officiating every tennis match and, one night, resting his head on impulse in Lady Wilde's lap, a gesture that moves the old lady to declare he had a soul indeed.

Vyvyan just an hour ago, tasting champagne for the first time and declaring it the vilest stuff a boy ever had to swallow. ("It's still in my nose, Mummy.") Vyvyan, by whatever miracle, *here*, the whole time, and most particularly now.

"Did you forget me?" he asks.

"Oh, no, darling," she says, fighting off tears. "It's just your mother is such an odd duck. Can you bear to forgive her?"

"Only if you quack."

"That's just it, you see. I'm so odd I don't even quack."

He pauses to consider.

"You needn't if you don't want to."

With a hunger that surprises her, she lowers her face to his, the better to breathe in his scent. Cloves and grass and soap and peppermint and is that the barest hint of Norfolk rabbit? For she suddenly remembers that Blackie drew nearer to Vyvyan than to anybody else in the Wilde family, and the thought that he might never have known that honor becomes the deepest of afflictions, until the only words that can emerge from her at last are:

"I'm sorry."

"For what?"

Everything, she would say. All the thousand natural shocks that children and their parents are heir to.

"I only meant I'm sorry I didn't fetch you after dinner. I was rather tired, you see, but then I got to feeling lonely."

"So did I."

"Well, then, there's a pair of us. Lonely no more."

She loops her arm round his waist, and they sit in silence.

"Mummy, Cyril says the house has ghosts in it."

"Oh, I suppose that's possible."

"Then why don't we ever see them? I think it's because there's more of us than them."

"You may be right."

"Do you think I'm fearsome enough to scare away a ghost?"

"I do, I sincerely do."

So emboldened, he tilts his head back and roars straight to the moon.

"My dear!" she says, laughing. "You'll wake Grandmamma."

"Oh, nothing does that. Did I sound a proper lion?"

"You most certainly did. I believe you have frightened off every ghost from here to the other side of the North Sea."

"Yes," he answers, matter-of-factly.

From the evening sky, the stars begin to wink forth, one by one. The harvest moon wells out as if it weren't even waning. The rest is a dome of darkness, and as she gazes upward, she softly traces the part in Vyvyan's hair. At some point, she cannot say exactly when, Cyril materialises by her side. Not at all perturbed to find his little brother occupying her lap but merely planting his chin as gently as possible on her left shoulder.

"I just beat Uncle Bosie at chess," he whispers.

"Aren't you clever?" she whispers back, and thinks:

Uncle Bosie.

The relation in question ambles out a few minutes later. Makes a point of congratulating Cyril for his Falkbeer Countergambit—a name that drops into Cyril's brain as a stone into a pond—then positions himself a couple of yards off, smoking in a more leisurely fashion than usual. Oscar emerges not too long after, still in the grip of the play, coughing out fragments of speech. In most other respects, the terrace of Grove Farm is silent—even the foxes and owls have left the auditorium to the toads— and Constance is so lulled after a time that it comes as a shock to find a hawkmoth resting on her arm. Bearing on its wings, like a cameo painting, the most beautiful make-believe eyes she has ever seen: black pupils with celestial-blue irises. Staring into them, she feels a quick, shuddering chill; in the next moment, she has swum clear of it.

You haven't got us yet.

It is left to Vyvyan, five years of age, to flick the moth from her arm and to say, quite as if he were divining her thoughts:

"All will be well, Mummy."

"Yes," she answers, squeezing his hand and, in the same instant, reaching back for Cyril's. "You may be right."